The Orchids

The Orchids

Thomas H. Cook

396254 (handwritten)

Boston

HOUGHTON MIFFLIN COMPANY

1982

98912

Library of Congress Cataloging in Publication Data
Cook, Thomas H.
The orchids.
I. Title.
PS3553.O554650O7 1982 813'.54 82-9175
ISBN 0-395-32503-x AACR2
Printed in the United States of America

P 10 9 8 7 6 5 4 3 2 1

In particular,
for Susan and Justine.
In general, for all those
who will not be
comforted.

This is a work of fiction,
not of history.
It is not meant to portray
any particular place
or person.

Day's Eden brightness still relieving
The awful Night's intense profound . . .
— Goethe

Part I

Part I

YOU CANNOT LEARN the nature of man from the sunrise at El Caliz. It begins with the merest suggestion of light, then a shimmering incision slices along the ridges of the far mountains, outlining them in a thin, silver band. From this band, a wave of Prussian blue rises slowly, brightening the upper sky and yet allowing it to retain the muted impenetrability of porcelain. The urns of antiquity had this contradictory delicacy, an opaque flatness that was at the same time vivid, almost diaphanous, and as elusive as romance.

When the first wave of heat strikes the earth, it sears the moisture still clinging to the palmetto leaves, and the river receives its cue to run. Throughout the night it has appeared motionless, a mute, dark pool, turbid as spilled blood. Now it seems to awaken, inhaling the first warm air, drawing in its sides, then releasing them, the waters lapping against the mud bank in small waves, rhythmic as a pulse. Mist rises from the water, leaching the darkness from its body and leaving the surface a cool, impenetrable green, smooth as polished marble. For a moment a curious stillness pervades as the mountain, river, and jungle harmonize in the primeval quiet. But this comforting natural camaraderie is all illusion, for by noon the sun will have turned the mountains a smoldering pumice and bleached the sky to the color of living bone.

Gazing to the left from my verandah, I note that my companion, Dr. Ludtz, is again making his way down to the little sepulcher he has built for himself over the years. From the beginning, he has been continually altering its shape. Unsatisfied with the original, solidly medieval structure of gray stone and dark mortar, he has obsessively beautified and adorned it, hacking at the encroaching liana vine or adding some crude architectural refinement. The result of all his labor has been to transform its earlier modesty into a grotesque rococo hideousness, a monument made in the image of its maker. Perhaps Dr. Ludtz would have been better served to dedicate the whole of his life to this monotonous reshaping of inert matter. But as he did not do so, he can now relate with some detail the look of drowsy, childlike vacancy that rises in a man's face after chloroform has been injected directly into his heart.

The heat is building now, smothering El Caliz under a broadloom of sun. Dr. Ludtz moves slowly, ponderously, as though the very air were gelatin. The trees press against the sky, burnished to its surface. Even the river seems tamped down into its bed, and only the little family of capuchin monkeys cavorting mindlessly in the trees across the river appears to be unburdened. Though they live in the limbs, they do not choose to die in them. Instead, as death approaches, they climb down to earth and squat upon their haunches, bony knees hugged under their drooping chins, until they fall forward like toppled statues. We could have used monkeys, but we didn't. There was no need; we had many creatures of our own design.

Dr. Ludtz has reached his altar, where he kneels, his ankles half-buried in the grasses he periodically shovels under. His shirt billows out in a sudden breeze and he looks around fearfully, as if touched on the arm by a stranger. He still believes that someday they will come for him, that the indefatigable Arnstein will finally locate him and dispatch his commandos to take him back for trial.

"They've gotten most of the leaders now," he said to

me frantically one night when he had mistaken the chattering of crickets for the sound of boots creeping through the undergrowth. "They'll get down to people like us soon. They'll never give up." A few days later, he told me that if the commandos did come to El Caliz, he did not intend to use a gun on himself, like the Minister of Light, but cyanide, like the Minister of Air.

My servant, Juan, passes Dr. Ludtz without looking at him. He has come from the mud-floored hovel he calls his home. Many years ago I offered to allow him and his family to take up residence in the main house, particularly during the rainy season. He refused, claiming that the incessant breeze of the ceiling fans inflamed his joints. That was a lie. Juan fears this house as an abode of devils. There is too much strangeness in it, too many eerie odors comprised of the reality of medical potions and the memory of edelweiss.

Juan tips his ragged straw hat as he passes me. He has pulled most of the buttons from his shirt, and it parts loosely over his brown chest. His pants, rolled at the cuff, hang just above his ankles. His shoes are heavy with dried mud.

I rise and grasp the railing of the verandah. "Buenos días, Juan."

Juan stops and turns slowly to face me. "Buenos días, Don Pedro."

Casually, so as not to frighten him, I ask Juan what he intends to do today. He takes his hat from his head and holds it at his side. Flowing behind him, the river seems to pierce Juan's body like an enormous shaft. In Spanish, he tells me that he is going down to the greenhouse to tend my orchids. Some must be trimmed. Some must be repotted. He fears that some evil force has fallen upon them. A dream has warned him of it during the night.

The blight. Juan's evil force. The fungal spores that consume the orchids, choking them in yellow powders. I tell Juan that if any flower has been attacked, then it must be cut and burned. If only the sheaths have been harmed, then they must be treated with sulfur or mercuric chloride.

Juan nods, then says that the the orchids cannot breathe, that they need more air.

I shake my head. "No." Orchids may die of too much ventilation.

Juan looks at me curiously and asks if perhaps they are thirsty.

I tell him that the orchids should not go into the night with moisture on the petals or the sheaths.

Juan stares at me evenly, and though he does not respond, I can hear the tumblers in his mind. He believes that it is all a plot, that I am lying to him, that my intention is to destroy the orchids. He suspects me of being a manifestation of the evil force. His wife has told him so.

I dismiss Juan with a wave of the hand and watch him trudge down the small embankment toward the greenhouse. The orchids have become his passion, his religion. He sees angels in the Bow Bells and Miltonias and finds faith in transfiguration with the regal Dowiana. They are everything to him; and to me, nothing.

When I first came to El Caliz, I tried to find beauty in the jungle's splendor, hoping to discover in its natural majesty something that would whisper of its creator. I looked into the shimmering streams and the damp caverns. I sat on cliffs and dove to river bottoms. But in the end, all I found was mute existence, and one thing became for me no more beautiful than another. And so I decided to become a creator myself. I had Juan build the greenhouse, and for years I nurtured the orchids, massaged and syringed them, trimmed and repotted them, diagnosed their maladies and sat with them through the night, trying to lose myself in the luxury of their perfume. Now I have passed their care to Juan, who prays for their recovery and guards them against my malediction.

In the distance I see Juan enter the greenhouse, glancing suspiciously in my direction. Amid the unquestioning silence and beauty of the orchids, amid the steamy, comforting clouds that enfold them, he is at home in paradise.

I ease myself back into my chair. There is no dew left on the leaves now. I can see the rippling heat rise from the ground, then curl toward the river, sucking at it like a thirsty mouth. I shift slightly and feel the old pain in my legs. I do not want to dwell upon it, so I turn again to the left. Sweat is darkening the back of Dr. Ludtz's shirt as he kneels beside his self-made monument. His hands are folded in prayer, his head bowed, his lips moving slightly. After a moment he rises and crosses himself — an odd thing, since he is not a Catholic. And yet, of late Dr. Ludtz has become a man in love with gestures. The graceful bow, the courteous nod, the sign of the cross — with these things Dr. Ludtz affirms himself as a man of substance and experience, one who has seen misfortune and yet triumphed over it. With a single courtly affectation he has erased his past and rejoined the community of civilized mankind. Through the screen of smoke and blood that has besmirched his life, he sees only aging, crinkled snapshots of his long-lost portly wife.

I turn away from him, then back again. Nothing should be avoided, not even Dr. Ludtz. He rises from his knees and slaps the dust from his trouser legs. When he catches me in his eye, he nods with an exaggerated grace, a gesture that might have found its proper place in some elaborately curtained Viennese ballroom, but which has no meaning here amid the chaotic chatter of the monkeys.

I lift my hand in greeting as Dr. Ludtz makes his way up the narrow trail to the steps of my verandah.

"May I join you?" Dr. Ludtz asks.

"Please do."

Dr. Ludtz moves heavily up the stairs, then drops his body into one of the polished rattan chairs. He breathes with some effort, as if his bulk were pressing down upon his lungs. He smiles, pulls his pince-nez from his nose, and rubs the fog from the lenses. "Dr. Langhof, tell me, have you ever read any of the writings of Meister Eckhart?"

"Yes."

"Extraordinary, don't you think?"

"Ja, aber ich habe viel vergessen."

Dr. Ludtz flinches. He does not wish me to speak in our native tongue. It is a method of identification, a verbal fingerprint, the abiding language of our crime.

"Please, Dr. Langhof," he whispers quickly. "Even here — silly as it seems — I would prefer English."

He has never learned Spanish, considering it a peasant tongue.

"As you wish, Dr. Ludtz," I tell him.

He leans back, relaxing slightly. "Well, to the point. I am much taken with his — Eckhart's — notion of transcendence, of triumphing over our creaturehood."

"Creaturehood?"

"Ourselves," Dr. Ludtz explains, slapping at a mosquito.

I nod. "Yes. Eckhart prefers the God-man."

Dr. Ludtz smiles delightedly. "Ah, you do remember. Yes, precisely. The God-man. What do you make of it?"

"Nothing."

Dr. Ludtz looks disappointed. "Nothing?"

"What is one to make of such a notion?"

Dr. Ludtz blinks quickly and replaces the pince-nez. He has adopted this style of eyeglasses because he thinks it makes him look scholarly. If it were that easy, we would all be wise.

"Well," Dr. Ludtz begins, somewhat taken aback, "it seemed quite interesting to me." He does not wish to argue with me. He fears that I might take offense and refuse him the protection and permission to reside in the Republic I purchase for us both by giving El Presidente a diamond each year.

"Many people find Eckhart's writings interesting, Dr. Ludtz," I tell him. "It is simply that I do not."

"Yes, of course," Dr. Ludtz says. "Quite true." He rises, wrenching his body forward, his belly drooping heavily over his belt.

"Would you do me the honor of joining me for breakfast?" I ask with deliberate formality, an Old World ritual with which I expect Dr. Ludtz to be pleased.

"With great thanks, no," Dr. Ludtz replies. "With your permission, I must be about my chores."

"Of course."

He turns and walks uneasily down the short flight of wooden stairs. The sweat has oozed through his clothing, plastering his pants as tightly against the globes of his buttocks as the lid of an eye. Halfway up the path to his private quarters, he glances right and left over his shoulder, sensing abductors in the brush. He has denuded the area immediately surrounding his cabin of all vegetation, so that it sits forlornly on a great clay embankment, a monument to enforced aridity. I hope the Valkyries will bury him in his weedy sarcophagus, for I do not know if I can. I have so little taste for farce.

Esperanza, Juan's wife, brings out my breakfast and places it on the glass surface of the small oval table in front of me. A large woman whose skin is the color of gingerbread, she wears a bony amulet around her neck. It dangles from a small pouch that smells like red cabbage.

"Buenos días, Don Pedro," she says.

"Buenos días."

"Tengo su desayuno."

"Sí."

She eases the rolls and butter closer to me, pours a cup of thick, pasty coffee, and then, from another pitcher, pours a strange lemon drink of her own design into the glass near my right hand. She claims this drink will drive the devils from my mind. Once, long ago, before I attained even the rudiments of grace, I threw this drink into her face. She stood watching me, not the slightest bit unnerved, as the greenish liquid dripped from her hair. At that moment, I believe, she began to hate me. She did not stop bringing the drink, but now she brings it not to drive evil from my brain, but to keep it there.

"Gracias," I tell her.

"De nada."

Esperanza lumbers back toward the rear of the house. She is the spirit-woman of the small village that bakes alongside the river a few miles below the compound. She is Eckhart's God-woman, to whom dusty peons come, bringing their insurmountable fear and grief. Over the years I have seen them come by the hundreds. They cradle dying children in their arms, or old men drooling papaya juice. For a time, I tried to intervene, to drive Esperanza back into the musty cave of her superstition. But the villagers would not come to me. Perhaps, like Juan, the ceiling fans inflamed their joints.

The morning humidity has already done its work on the rolls, turning them soggy. I push them away and watch the butter liquefy in the hard, white light. Many years ago, on the train to this final home in El Caliz, I was stalled briefly on a rickety railway trestle. An odd, familiar smell wafted through the open window, and for a moment I knew that it reminded me in some strange way of home. I thought of street cafés in the capital, of old men in buckled shoes and lederhosen, of girls in pigtails singing lightly to the accompaniment of twin accordions. I turned to the man sitting next to me, smiled as best I could, and asked what the smell was. "Ugh," he said, grimacing, "it's that slaughterhouse upriver where they burn the animal remains."

It is time for my morning walk. I grasp the banister firmly and ease myself down the stairs. Old men must move slowly or they will hurt themselves.

On the ground, I feel reasonably safe again and make my way down toward the greenhouse, which sits beside the river. Juan is inside, fingering the orchids, following instructions that come to him in dreams, hoping in this way to secure the orchids against the evil blight. The air is sweltering, but the orchids thrive. They have defeated heat. It is their nourishment. Their radiant petals open to it like the mouths of hungry children.

I nod to Juan. "Juan. ¿Qué tal?"

"Bien, Don Pedro."

He does not turn from the flowers. His fingers are half-hidden within the petals of one exquisite bloom.

I compliment his handiwork, tell him the flowers are beautiful.

Juan does not leave his work. "Sí, Don Pedro."

"Hermoso, muy hermoso," I say insistently. Beautiful. "Sí."

Here in El Caliz, they are beautiful. But there are certain worlds where beauty itself may become transmuted into obscenity. I remember that day they lined the vermin up outside the great wall and made them undress under the square, smoking chimney. One of the guards noticed her, a naked woman who had been a famous dancer in her day. He walked over and began to taunt her. "Dance for us," he said. "Dance for us. It's your last chance." She shrank back and tried to dissolve into the line, but he persisted, dragging her out, demanding a performance. Finally, she began to dance. She turned slowly at first, then her movements gradually gained force and momentum. She raised her arms delicately over her head and, rising to her toes, kicked at the gray dust under her feet. She danced more and more powerfully, her legs soaring over her head, her eyes widening in the remembered splendor of her art. Crouched against the wall, the others watched her, and part of her strength seemed to flow invisibly into them. The guards saw that and quickly leveled their guns at the crowd. Then they shouted for the woman to stop dancing. She did not, and they shouted once again. She did not obey but instead kicked a spray of dust in their direction, then turned slowly in a magisterial pirouette. They fired, but in the unreal world of her turning, she had transformed everything, so that the gunfire sounded like an orchestra building to its height, the twitch and stumble of her body as it fell became the final bow of something great and free, the blood bursting from her body nothing more than orchids blooming on a pure white gown.

WHEN RAIN COMES to the Kalahari it turns the desert lush, and seeds that have not sprouted for decades suddenly come alive, turning the desert radiant and bountiful. But here in El Caliz, the jungle foliage is so rich the rains cannot increase it. Here, we are strangled by our luxuriance, so that the rain only serves to make the landscape more torturous and malignant, only serves to accelerate the rot that — after fresh rain — fills the air with the odor of decay.

El Presidente is the undisputed lord of this pullulating kingdom. He is due to visit me soon to collect his annual tribute. His silvery helicopter, festooned with the nation's gaudy red and orange flag, will soar over the far ridges, then dip down toward the compound and hover over the river, whipping the water into a frenzy. It is El Presidente's pride to come with the sound of locust and dive with the force of storm. He will be sitting in the red velvet throne-chair that he has had installed in his craft. The peasants will be swept up in his grandeur, for in his towering opulence and waste he uplifts their lives by permitting them to cast their eyes on something splendid and unrestrained. And after he has collected his diamond, he will rise again in his chariot of the air, the winds ripping through the trees, terrorizing the monkeys; and the peasants will gaze after him, stupefied, their eyes blinking against the harsh light. For El Presidente has a standing order that his craft must always rise toward the sun.

I have seen them come and go, seen them all. I have sat upon my verandah, sipping vodka laced with lime, and watched the long, strutting parade of bejeweled potentates who have marched through the history of the Republic. They are nothing more than dung-crusted scrappings from the monument of him who came before them, the little orphaned paperhanger with the big ideas.

He, the Leader, refused, even in his last hours, to confess. For him, there was no reason for penitence. He had nothing to confess but the weakness and timidity of his race. In the dank, burrowed solitude of his bunker, he issued a call to arms, reiterated the pillars of his certain faith, all those fiery ideas with which he had hoped to transform the world, and then, bowing courteously before the eyes of his adoring secretary, he took his leave.

You may be sure that El Presidente will not leave the world so remarkably unbowed. And even should he wish to dictate some final message to mankind, he would have to do it in a motley, disorganized fashion, for there are no professional secretaries here in the Republic to record his lachrymose pronouncements. Indeed, there is little paperwork at all in the Republic. And although the file cabinets no doubt bulge in the Ministry of Police, those other great engines of government are here reduced to the pieties of the clergy and the rhetoric of the state. Here all is fever, usurpation, and combustible religion. That in the midst of so much richness, presided over by so much squalor, there is no one to be found to scratch one's thoughts across a page as they are dictated presents itself as one of the contradictions of underdevelopment.

And so, those who wish the lineaments of immortality here in the Republic are reduced to the machinery of transcription, a little purring disc spooling up yards of slick brown tape. El Presidente, in his last hours, must rely upon imported gadgetry to deify himself. The Leader, in his relentless stolidity, in his raging appetite for esteem, would have cringed at such indignity.

And yet, it is difficult to know at what point the search for dignity descends into the vulgar. It can be said of my father that he had a certain bearing that was not without dignity. He was a tall, stately man who all his life affected a benign but studiously military carriage. The walls of our small provincial house, the walls inside which I came of age, were adorned with large paintings of heroic and myth-ological events. Suffering Prometheus hung upon his moun-tain fiercely defying black hordes of rapacious birds. Icarus soared above a little globe of earth, his wings melting for-lornly at his sides. My father walked confidently among these icons of tortured heroism, but there were times when his eyes seemed to take on a latent ferocity, a bewildered rebellion against the unremitting mediocrity of bourgeois life. In the arc of his belly and the flaccid droop of his jowls, he sensed the insult of his body. He dreamed of the hard muscularity of his Teutonic gods and in his victim-ized imagination saw himself as a trim, steel cylinder of righteousness and knight-errantry. Once, during a Wag-nerian excess at the opera house, I looked up and saw that he was panting. In this, even the boy I was could sense the grunt of his desire. In his pained and inescapable low-liness, he wished to clothe himself in immortal light, to rise above the petty annoyances and insufferable trivialities of his legal practice, the incessant bickerings of his dis-ordered marriage, the pinched and carping contrivances of the bureaucratic state. He seemed always charged and ready for explosion. In the mute bitterness with which he endured his frustration one could sense the last strivings of his romance. Once released, his volcanic resentfulness could certainly have been channeled into special and ca-thartic action.

"Peter! Peter!" It was my father calling. I could hear him in the little foyer down the hall. I opened the door of my room and saw him standing in the distance, his bald pate slick and shiny under the frosted lampshade that hung above him.

"Yes, Father." I remember my child's voice as weak and thready, a sound that must have grated horribly on my father's robust ear.

He stretched out his hand. "Come."

I walked forward and took his hand. He led me out into the street and down the small alleyway toward the little park near the center of our village. The sky overhead was pewter gray, flat and monotonous as a sheet of smudged paper. Perhaps it might rain, I told my father, perhaps I should get my boots. He tightened his grip on my hand and quickened his pace.

At the park he sat down and positioned me in front of him, standing at attention like a little toy soldier. To my right I could glimpse the brick-and-wrought-iron stand where the military bands played marches in the spring.

"Peter, look at me."

I looked at him. He was a perfect representation of the stolid, provincial burgher, dressed in a suit and white shirt buttoned to the top, his shoes carefully laced and double-knotted. He had a pink, plump face with cheeks so flushed they looked purposefully rouged. His eyes bulged slightly behind his neat, black-framed glasses.

"Peter," he said, "the war is lost."

I was nine years old. What could such a statement mean to me? For children who are not actually devastated by it, war is no more than a merciful interruption of routine. In the schools there had been drives for steel and tin and clothing, each of which added a certain tension to the day, made it pass more quickly than usual.

"Do you understand me?"

What was I to understand? What does a child know of defeat, of humiliation, of devastated pride? We knew that in France since 1914 something mighty had been going on. But what, in the end, did it have to do with us? How could something so far away bring such sorrow to my father's face?

I said nothing. It was getting dark, the trees turning black against the sky.

"We have been defeated," my father said. He shook my shoulders slightly. "Defeated, do you understand?"

"Yes, Father," I said in a low voice.

His face seemed to shrink back as he looked at me. I know now that what he wanted — what he always wanted — was for me to join him in his fantasy, to play Lohengrin in his Parsifal. "Is that all you have to say?" he demanded.

"Defeated," I repeated. I could feel the air of evening turning cool.

My father delicately removed his glasses and wiped his eyes with a folded handkerchief. Even in grief, he was obsessively fastidious. "It's not our fault," he said, replacing his glasses. "You must remember that."

"Not our fault," I said.

"Yes," my father said. He drew a deep, painful breath that seemed to expand his bulk from within, as if something were blowing up inside him. "It's important that you remember that it was not our fault."

"Yes, Father," the little brigadier said.

My father placed both his large hands on my shoulders and pressed down. "I will not have you growing up defeated, do you understand?"

I nodded. A small breeze blew a strand of hair across my forehead. He quickly swept it back.

"We are never to feel defeated," my father said. His voice was restrained, but there was an undiscoverable ferment behind his eyes, a crazed unrest.

"I won't, Father," I said.

He touched the side of his head with his index finger. "We must keep this in our minds."

I imitated his gesture. "In our minds."

"It is important."

"Yes," I said.

My father watched me suspiciously, his lower lip trembling. All his life, he was a creature of unfathomable loneliness.

I stood quietly in front of him and probably would have stood there through the night if he had wanted, but suddenly the smell of sugar cookies surrounded me, lifting my spirits. I smiled.

My father frowned. "What is it?"

I stiffened my back reflexively. "Nothing, Father."

"That smile, what was that for?"

"Nothing."

My father squeezed my shoulders. "Answer me!"

I could not.

My father stood up instantly and stared down at me with intense disapproval. "How can you smile after what I've told you?" he said angrily.

"I was not smiling," I said quickly. The very idea of sugar cookies became nauseating.

My father glared at me, then raised his hand and slapped my face. I could hear the sound of the blow ringing through the park.

"You dishonor me!" he cried.

"No, Father."

"You dishonor me!"

I lowered my head.

He took my chin in his hand and lifted it up. "You are like your mother," he said. His face showed his disgust.

"I'm sorry, Father," I said desperately.

"Like your mother. Stupid. Stupid."

For a moment I saw myself positioned in his sense of the Chain of Being, a vile, crawling thing that sickened him unspeakably.

"I didn't mean to do it," I whined. "I didn't mean to smile. It was the sugar cookies."

My father's face hardened. "Sugar cookies?"

"Yes."

"Sugar cookies? What are you talking about?"

"From the bakery on Telemannstrasse," I explained. "They are making them. They smell sweet."

"How can you think of such things?"

"It was just the smell," I said, trembling. "I didn't mean to smile."

My father dropped to the bench, his shoulders slumping forward. "Sugar cookies," he muttered.

Then I saw defeat. Not in France, but in him. "Father, I'm sorry," I said weakly.

My father's head bent forward. I could almost see my face reflected in the sleek smoothness of his skull.

"I didn't mean to smile, Father," I said again.

He looked at me. "You must learn to care about things, Peter. Do you think the world is sweet? Do you think it is made of sugar cookies?"

"No, Father," I said. "I'm sorry."

My father shook his head. "It doesn't matter," he said wearily. And then, in a low voice, almost to himself, "They will come here. We are at their mercy now."

"Who?"

"The enemy."

In my childishness I could not even be sure exactly who the enemy was.

"It'll be all right, Father," I said.

"I don't know what will happen now," my father said without looking up.

"Nothing will happen. It will be all right," I said. I felt the urge to touch his shoulders, but I was afraid to do it.

"They will come here," my father said. "The enemy."

And then in my imagination I saw them, the enemy. They were not people at all, but great, woolly monsters. In my mind I saw them clawing up the pavement of the Unter den Linden and scratching their matted, filthy behinds on the lofty archway of the Brandenburg Gate.

OLD MEN watch the world from a certain distance. From the heights of my verandah I can see Esperanza as she bends over the river scrubbing my white linen shirts on a large flat stone. There are no modern conveniences in El Caliz. And throughout the Republic there are very few. Of course, in El Presidente's palace the rooms are stacked to the ceiling with every imaginable mechanical contraption. He is a connoisseur of all the little humming trinkets of advanced industrial society. From the great enterprising nations he imports thousands of toasters, televisions, electric pencil sharpeners, and the like. It is said that he has devoted one huge hall to the working of such things. The walls are empty save for row upon row of electrical outlets. These he uses to feed a current through a jungle of extension cords powering hundreds of small machines, infinite in their variety. When he pulls the switch, they clang and hiss and sizzle, and it is said that nothing can be heard above this metallic bedlam except the gleeful laughter of El Presidente.

Esperanza slaps a shirt against a stone. The very monotony of her action makes it clear that part of the tedium of the primitive lies in the incessant passing of day into day until the nature of labor becomes, finally, the nature of life. The lowly character of Esperanza's work reflects the low esteem with which she and all her kind are regarded by El Presidente. And yet Esperanza has triumphed over the debased quality of her circumstances. From within the depths of her impoverishment she has seized a spirit in its flight and prisoned it within the confines of her potions and incantations. She has captured God, and dispenses his indecipherable favors to the villagers who gather nightly in her hut. They come to hear their futures spun out from Esperanza's mouth like the endless string of Fortune's wheel. Will the child be a changeling? Will the sugar cane rise tall in season? Will the bats suck dry the herds? To all these questions Esperanza gives certain answer, and the villagers, in the desperate precariousness of their need, remember when she is right and forget when she is wrong.

In the Camp, there were others such as she, people who claimed special powers of clairvoyance and enchantment. The withered vermin came to them, begging for blessings from their bony fingers. They sat hollow-eyed and shivering while these prophets rolled their eyes toward the sky. They pleaded with a special fervency for news concerning lost family and friends. The prophets listened quietly, then bleated these same questions heavenward, knowing all the time that the ashes of the loved ones were smoldering in the crematoria.

Esperanza bats at a mosquito, then turns back to her work. Loudly, she slaps the shirts onto the rock, then kneads them with her fists. The sky is bleaching overhead. Heat in El Caliz acts as a great sponge, sucking up speculation. The heat is the given, a world unto itself, beyond which nothing is truly imaginable. El Presidente, however, has three huge air conditioners in his gilded throne room. He has attached long multicolored ribbons to the vents so that they blow wildly in the air, filling the room with the sound of their snapping. In the unnatural cool El Presidente may exercise his mind, hatching exotic visions of deflowered maidens and the smooth brown thighs of uninitiated boys. But Esperanza, slowly cooking in the heat, can think only of God and water.

The Archbishop of the Republic also thinks of God, though less of water. He serves as spiritual adviser for El Presidente and acts as personal emissary between His Excellency and God. Often, he sits in the left-hand corner of the throne room, snoozing beneath his vestments. But there are times when he is said to rise and whisper advice into El Presidente's gnarled ear. Citizens are not privy to the Archbishop's recommendations, although it is known that on occasion he has warned against the education of the masses, a suggestion based upon his fear that they have not yet been properly prepared for the burdensome responsibilities of intelligence.

Thus, learning in the Republic remains a matter of seed and prayer. The seed is winnowed from the ripening crops and gathered up in burlap bags. These sacks are held in the Central Warehouses, which are the exclusive possessions of El Presidente. On occasion — and at a whim — he is said to have denied access to these cordoned and garrisoned depositories, and whole villages have disappeared. It is not within the competence of El Presidente to hoard the fruits of prayer.

Esperanza finishes her last shirt and rises, placing the large basket of clothes on her head. She lumbers toward the main house, her feet sinking slightly into the sodden clay along the riverbank. Her determined lurch suggests resolute purpose. She has taken on the intransigence of her task, and each gesture reflects this hard determination. Clothes must be cleaned because I, Don Pedro, have required it. There can be no turning from the task. The spirit world that flutters in her brain must momentarily retire into its own tumid cavern. It cannot be allowed to swirl in the soap and water, cannot be permitted to becloud the priority of labor.

Two separate worlds coexist in the Republic: leisure and labor. Labor does not purchase leisure. It is a dreary coin that can buy nothing but more of itself. Leisure is the prerogative of birth. In the great rubber estates to the east, the children of the aging barons snore quietly under the vaporous whiteness of gently fluttering marquisette. For them, all labor is reduced to tending periodic disturbances of the head and bowels. They are born into a world of latticework and vine, marry under an arboreal arch, betray their spouses in a pool of water lilies, stupefy themselves with vodka imported from the workers' paradise, and wait for their elders to die amid the priestly mummery of Christ. When at last they come into their legacy, there is nothing for them to do but acquire. And so they import vast quantities of luxury goods from the great nations of the developed world. They fill their halls with television sets, stock their kitchens with refrigerators and electric mixers — though often the web of electric wire that crisscrosses the Republic does not extend to their distant haciendas. Hence the tedium is unrelieved, and the local elite merely lounge on French settees or stand blank-faced as the portraits of Fragonard under enormous, tinkling, but unlit chandeliers.

For them, El Presidente — both the real one and that of the outlawed poet Casamira's wild invention — has nothing but contempt. Born from the grimy union of a sheepherder and his toothless wife, he has seen the fire blazing on both sides. In the humid forests to the south, El Presidente came of age among the squalor of his kind. He saw banditti nail his brother to a jute tree and drunkenly throw darts at a crude target carved upon his chest; saw his simple-minded cousin dragged slowly to death by a team of burros through a field of stumps and briar; saw his mother spit a clot of maggots from her mouth three days before she died. Beneath all his lunatic vainglory, El Presidente understands the Republic, understands the craving of the fallen for the holy, understands that nothing less than man transmogrified into God can hold the leprous body still. And no one in the Republic more clearly knows the value of a lie.

In Casamira's *Official History of the Republic*, El Presidente's birth is described thus:

> El Presidente did not come easily to his people. The birth was long and torturous, and his mother, Mary, a gentle woman of the village and beloved by all the inhabitants there, behaved throughout her ordeal with that patience

and self-sacrifice which have become the hallmarks of her firstborn son.

El Presidente's mother was named Juanita. She had already borne seven children, four of whom had died, one of them under suspicious circumstances having to do with a cliff.

But on to the *Official History:*

For three days Mary fought for the life of El Presidente. And it is reported by those present at this momentous occasion that her son was delivered into the world wholly clean of any blood or tissue, so that he emerged from the womb without taint or blemish. It is also reported that the sun broke over the ridge at the precise moment of his birth, coming a full three hours before the accustomed sunrise and bathing the surrounding countryside in a gentle, embracing light.

El Presidente's life is full of trinities. He is three days in the birthing. The sun rises three hours early on the day of his nativity. No special attention is drawn to these facts in the *Official History*. Its subject, after all, is no ordinary vulgarian.

To continue:

The birth of El Presidente was celebrated by all the village. This was not the usual custom in the southern provinces, but from the beginning the native intuition of the peasantry was made manifest. Men who seek only after reason will be dumbfounded by the world. But men who sense its mysteries will be rewarded with understanding.

And so El Presidente was born into a land in which intuition triumphed over inquiry, in which faith shackled sense, in which knowledge was seen as the handmaiden of confusion.

The Leader, when he ascended, drew up millions in his train, driving them into the cloud of his mythology with the power of a great machine, so that they became annealed to him, a part of his fiery workings, enmeshed in the warp and woof of his person and intent. And surely if his origins were less auspicious than those recorded for El

Presidente, the perverse majesty of his end dwarfs all those feeble pretenders who have followed him seeking to emulate, to surpass.

But now let us pass El Presidente's allegorical debut and move toward his divinely ordained development:

> Nurtured among the idyllic surroundings of the southern provinces, El Presidente reveled in the beauties of nature and their profound import. From the start, he seemed possessed by nature. Among the peasants, he was known to be one who could divine the mysteries of wind and water. He could predict the coming of rain and once saved his village from a terrible storm by confronting the rampaging elements with his own body and demanding their retreat.

Thus, in the Republic, nature is both good and evil, an animated spirit that both conserves and debauches. Those "possessed by nature" are good, perhaps divine, but only if they can overcome nature's Manichean aspect, harness its schizophrenic drive toward both redemption and destruction. El Presidente, by piercing into the mystical heart of nature, enslaved it. In the Republic, to know a thing is to conquer it.

And again:

> From earliest youth, then, El Presidente was regarded with awe by the simple people of the village. They came to him with their problems and he endeavored to acquaint them with the facts of their existence. No easy task in the southern provinces.

And what are these facts of existence which it is no easy task to teach in the southern provinces? The *Official History* enumerates them:

> Satan coils under every shrub.

> All things must serve the common good.

> A people who do not believe in their own destiny will not have one.

> Sheep herds should not be kept less than one kilometer from human habitation.

> Darts is a game for fools.

Thus enlightened, the southern provinces flourished. But it was the destiny of El Presidente to depart them. And so he embarked upon that journey which would take him to his own, private destiny. He traversed the southern districts in search of revelation. According to the *Official History*, he was assailed periodically by "blinding lights" and "burning rivers." Once, to test himself, El Presidente fought a lion with his bare hands, finally strangling it to death. Much is made of this in the *Official History*, even though there are no lions in this hemisphere.

Here in the Republic, no witnesses are permitted. Those who appeared pale-faced and withered before the press to tell of El Presidente's mortal combat have since been swallowed up by earthquakes or entombed in landslides. The entire village of El Presidente's birth was mysteriously erased by what the *Official History* calls "a band of wicked and hideous marauders." A picture is presented as proof. Amid the smoking ruin of the village, a single uniformed soldier can be seen standing absently over the body of an eviscerated woman. Under a looking-glass the insignia on the soldier's sleeve is clearly visible, a large red A encircled by a field of blue. Company A was a unit under the exclusive command of El Presidente.

The facts are not significant in the Republic. But there are realities upon which only the satirical can shed light. Thus Casamira, exiled poet of the Republic, writes his sardonic *Official History* with a pen dipped in vitriol. He is made of equal parts, mockery and vituperation. Sometimes I see him in a dream sitting among the imagined ruins of El Presidente's palace. He is clothed in smoke, but with a look of unutterable peace. He leans back on a fallen column, propping himself casually on his elbows. A smile of complete satisfaction plays upon his lips, suggesting the totality of his triumph. He closes his eyes slowly as the wind shakes the banana trees.

THE LEADER believed that history stopped with him. His greatest tactical mistake was his inability to subdue his own cosmic egotism. Because of that, he attempted to accelerate history so that his titanic dreams could be accomplished within the pinched scale of a single human life, his own. This form of individualism is so severe that it is no longer aware of its own dreadful whimsy. Here is an epic compression, Napoleonic in its strenuousness and awesome in its sweep, a juggernaut of self that endeavors to move not with the insufferable lethargy of evolution, but with the girded power of passionate and unalterable human motive. Of all forms of cowardice, the Leader most despised the timidity of time. And the greatest achievement of his delusion lay in convincing us that we could stoke the engines of history with such force and momentum as actually to bring it to its termination while we lived. To see paradise in one's own lifetime, to see the triumph of the species, the final actualization of existence, to sit upon the blazing, uplifted tower of our completedness, to ride for one glittering moment at the pinnacle of that ultimate creation of all man's effort and resource — that was the dream he offered, the apotheosis of romance.

From the rooted dreariness of individual life and the recent humiliations of national history he extracted the necessary substance with which to forge his ideal and himself, and which he then joined together in the musty arenas of our minds. At El Caliz, where the searing light seems to boil the river, it is easy to comprehend the process as it presents itself in the graven image of the superficial. Scholars bending feverishly beneath the green shades that glow within their studies have seen as much and called it explanation. But for those who were actually ingested into the infernal workings of his machine, those for whom memory is either misery or accusation, the judgments of scholarship are as futile and unenlightening as the shards of bat bone Esperanza uses to divine the rain.

And so we must look again and again and again, becoming as we do scholars of monstrosity.

Look again, then, and see the little boy standing in the park, his stomach recoiling from the detestable smell of sugar cookies.

· · ·

My father stood up and grasped my hand limply, as if touching something that defiled him, as if my hand were some pornographic device that repelled him, but to which he was inseparably attached.

"Where are we going?" the little soldier asked.

"Home," my father said.

"So soon?"

"Home," he repeated.

At home we sat in the dining room under the small brass chandelier, which seemed to twinkle irreverently in the gloom. My father made delicate incisions in the wurst and forked the pieces glumly into his mouth. My mother bustled about obliviously, and I suddenly saw her as my father always had — a large, flabby woman who cared nothing at all for great ideas or events and for whom national defeat could be rendered wholly meaningless by a flick of the wrist and a disgruntled groan.

"Dessert?" she asked, and when I did not reply, she plopped a sodden piece of strudel onto my plate. Its smell reminded me of sugar cookies. I pushed it away.

"What's the matter with you?" she asked.

"Nothing."

"You don't want strudel?"

"Not tonight," I said. I dropped my hands into my lap.

"Perhaps he'd like to have a sugar cookie," my father mumbled without looking at me.

I felt a wind blow through me, scattering my insides like bits of soiled tissue paper.

"Are you sick?" my mother asked.

My father looked up from his plate. "Leave him alone and go about your business."

My mother shrugged and began gathering the dishes. When she had finished, she marched silently into the kitchen.

"You want to be like her, Peter?" my father whispered.

"No, Father."

"What, then?"

I shook my head. "I don't know."

"You don't know? What kind of answer is that?"

I turned my eyes downward. Hearing him sit back in his chair, I knew he was still looking at me and that what he saw disgusted him.

My mother strode back into the dining room and pinched my cheek. "Maybe you'd like to go to the cinema tonight," she said cheerfully.

"Cinema?" my father roared. He banged the table with his fist. "You ass, don't you know what has happened today?"

My mother turned toward him, aghast.

My father leaped from his chair. "Get out of my sight!"

My mother stepped back and raised her hands as if protecting her face from blows.

"Get out of this house," my father shouted. "I don't care where you go, but get out of my house!"

"Martin," my mother said helplessly, "are you all right?"

"Get out," my father bawled. His eyes looked like small red bulbs.

My mother glanced at me timidly.

"Get out!" my father screamed. "Get out of here this minute!"

My mother rushed out of the room, hiding her face in her hands. A few moments later I heard her close the front door.

My father bent over the table and raked his bald head with his hand.

I sat frozen in my chair. I had never in my life seen such passion. He raised his head and seemed to gather himself together slowly.

"I will not endure such insults," he said threateningly. "Do you understand?"

"Yes, Father."

"I will not endure it."

I nodded fearfully.

He began to weep softly. He lowered his head to the table again, cradling it in one elbow and gently hitting the surface of the table with his hands. They were soft, muffled blows and each seemed to me like a moan.

I stood up and thrust out my chest. "I will not endure it either," I said loudly.

My father did not look up.

"Father? I will not endure it either."

My father drew his head up slowly.

I assumed the strong, firm-jawed look of the soldiers in the war posters. "I will not endure it," I repeated.

My father stared at me coldly. "You are nothing to me," he said.

I felt my chest cave in.

"Nothing, Peter," my father said evenly, "nothing to me at all."

"Father ... I ..."

"Sugar cookies," my father said bitterly. "Strudel. Cinema."

I could not bear the intense reproach in his eyes. I turned away and watched the wind rustle through the ivy that clung to the sides of the window.

"There is nothing now," I heard my father say grimly. "Nothing."

His chair grated across the floor as he pushed himself away. I wanted to fall at his feet, to beg his forgiveness for whatever crimes I had committed against him. But for some reason I was immobile, and I think now that it was shame that held me in place, that clawed at my ankles, holding my feet against the floor.

For a moment he did not move. Without turning from the window, I knew that he was staring at me, and I wanted to turn to him if for no other reason than to offer my face for his blows. But his agony was like a wall between us.

Finally I heard him turn and leave the room. Sitting in place, I could hear his feet scraping up the carpeted steps to his little law office on the second floor. Then, a few moments later, I heard the pistol shot. It sounded like the cracking of a twig, nothing more. I ran upstairs. He was seated in a dark red wing chair, one leg crossed primly over the other, his head tilted slightly to the side, as if he were simply a tired middle-aged shopkeeper who had fallen asleep by the fire.

I RISE from my chair and walk through the door to my office. In the Camp I had only a monkish cell in which to sleep. But here I have a spacious compound of several buildings and enjoy the luxury of a private office. The office is filled with mementos from my past. Some are on display: a lovely crystal vase, a stethoscope, a commendation from El Presidente, and the little riding crop I used to crack against my boot. Some things are hidden in my desk drawer: a battered tin box and a machine pistol. The aging Casanova of Schnitzler's beautiful invention whiles away the hours remembering the inanity of his conquests and regretting that never in his life had he been loved, or even taken seriously, by a woman of intelligence. As I review my mementos I have but one regret: that there is not a single one among them for which I have any genuine affection.

Dr. Ludtz knocks softly and politely at the door of the office. He has said that he does not think it healthy for me to spend so much time alone. But that is a lie. He fears that I am composing my memoirs and that his own name might find a place within them. Each time he enters my study he casts his eyes about suspiciously, hoping to discover the protruding edge of some unfinished manuscript, even though he cannot imagine a man actually writing the words I would have to write in order to detail my life.

"Come in, Dr. Ludtz."

Dr. Ludtz smiles as he enters. "Ah, you're here then. Why so much time spent in this office, my dear friend?"

"The ventilation is pleasant."

Dr. Ludtz nods, pretending satisfaction with my answer. "The ventilation, yes." He glances at the empty chair in front of my desk. "May I?"

"By all means."

He sits down and looks at the ceiling fan slowly turning above his head. "Excellent for ventilation."

"Yes."

He turns back toward me, his eyes carefully searching over the cluttered bookshelf behind me. "Have you read anything of note recently?"

"It is getting more difficult for me to read now," I tell him. "I think my eyes are dimming slightly."

Dr. Ludtz looks at me sadly. "Perhaps you're overtired. Working so much in this office, that must be quite taxing, don't you think?"

I do not reply.

"And the arthritis?" Dr. Ludtz asks gently. "Is that any better?"

"Arthritis does not cure itself, Dr. Ludtz."

Dr. Ludtz shakes his head. "No. That is true. But it is bearable, I hope."

"Bearable. Yes." I have often wondered what Dr. Ludtz's bedside manner was like before he became a doctor for the Special Section. I expect that it was gentle, kindly, utterly proper. Those large, beefy hands must have stroked the small pink cheeks of thousands of children before they became familiar with electroshock devices. We all have ironic histories, I suppose, but history has made some a good deal more ironic than others.

Dr. Ludtz watches me sadly. "Ah, the natural shocks that flesh is heir to."

I smile indulgently. "You must learn to speak outside quotation from time to time, Dr. Ludtz."

Dr. Ludtz looks slightly scolded. "But with learning one discovers that everything one might say has been said better by someone else, don't you agree?" He turns away and rests his eyes on the river. "It's very calm today. Perhaps we could get Alberto and Tomás to take us rowing on the river. That would be relaxing, don't you think, Dr. Langhof?"

In the Camp he relaxed by lounging on his bunk blowing smoke rings at the ceiling. It became one of his obsessions to blow ten of them in a series, one after the other, like boxcars.

"I'm afraid I cannot join you," I tell him.

"May I ask why, my dear friend?"

"I am in the middle of preparations."

Dr. Ludtz blinks and stares at me worriedly. "Preparations for what?"

"For El Presidente's visit."

Dr. Ludtz looks relieved. "Ah, yes. I see." He smiles contentedly. "I suppose it will be a lavish affair, as usual."

"El Presidente prefers it lavish."

Dr. Ludtz leans forward. "He must be treated with the greatest deference."

"Yes."

Dr. Ludtz smirks. "An esteemed visitor."

"Indeed."

He chuckles gently. "Tell me, Dr. Langhof, have you heard of the visit Hölderlin made to Goethe?"

"In Weimar?"

"Yes, Weimar. But have you heard the story of what passed between them?"

"Tell it, if you like."

"Well, Hölderlin was only a young poet at the time," Dr. Ludtz begins, "and of course Goethe was the old master. As you might imagine, Hölderlin had dreamed of this visit for quite some time. He expected an exalted conversation to pass between them. Such was not the case, however. In fact, the interview was very disappointing. For you see, Hölderlin found that all he could talk about in Goethe's presence was the superiority of the plums he had eaten on the train between Jena and Weimar." He laughs loudly. "The absurdity! Can you imagine?"

"How is your tomb progressing, Dr. Ludtz?" I ask.

"What's that? My tomb? Oh, yes. Very well, of course I don't really think of it as a tomb."

"The liana vines seem determined to obscure it."

Dr. Ludtz does not hear me. He has turned back toward the river. "So calm," he says to himself, "wonderful for rowing."

"Yes, quite wonderful."

He turns to face me. "If I may be excused, Dr. Langhof, I think that I might take advantage of this fine day."

"By all means, Doctor."

"Are you sure you would not wish to join me?"

"Yes, I'm sure. I must make these preparations."

"I understand, believe me," Dr. Ludtz says. "El Presidente must have everything as he likes it."

"If we are to continue to have everything as we like it," I add.

"Yes. Absolutely," Dr. Ludtz says quickly. "Absolutely correct in that."

"Good day, Dr. Ludtz."

Dr. Ludtz rises. "Good day to you. And please, not so much time in this office."

"Thank you for your concern."

He vanishes behind the door of my study, the little bulge of the automatic pistol clearly visible in the large back pocket of his flannel trousers. He sleeps with it on his nightstand, the barrel toward his coiled rosary. In all his life he has spoken one memorable sentence. As we stood watching the smoke billow up from one of the great brick funnels of the Camp, he turned to me and said in a voice of almost wistful repudiation, "One cannot imagine waltzing after this."

He is outside now. I can see him through the window, his body neatly dissected by the blades of a large green fern. He is calling Alberto and Tomás, Juan's teenage sons. For a moment they do not see him, caught up as they often are in a kind of manic play, an endless, banal chase from which no clear victor ever emerges.

He has caught their attention, and I see him motioning toward the small boat that bobs lightly on the river, a length of braided rope holding it to the bank. He is right. The river is very calm, a perfect day for rowing. And I can see him years before, sailing in a sleek white skiff, a blue European river rolling beneath him and crashing up against the sides of the boat, covering his face with spray.

Alberto and Tomás secure the boat. They smile at each other mockingly as they watch Dr. Ludtz lumber toward the boat and then heave himself awkwardly into it, causing it to groan and sway. To them this Teutonic Falstaff is no more than a mound of blubber who by some incomprehensible twist of circumstance employs and therefore commands them. Their bodies are tawny and sleek; his, ruddy and gelatinous. They are the trim young bulls; he, the imprisoned Minotaur. They cavort mindlessly in the humid forest, far beyond history's mortmain; he is history's dilapidated product.

With Dr. Ludtz securely seated, Alberto and Tomás leap agilely into the boat and take up positions fore and aft. Then they paddle slowly from the bank, the boat sliding across the surface of the river as effortlessly as a knife through air. Dr. Ludtz grabs each side of the boat and steadies himself. He does not trust the depths. Though the river is for rowing, it also has the terrible ability to swallow him up entirely. For him, the crocodiles that drift indifferently beneath the boat are wily demons from the underworld. His is the anxiety of the paranoid who has come to fear even his paranoia.

As the boat moves toward the center of the river, a large red bloom drifts slowly toward it. Dr. Ludtz watches as it nears him. When finally it has come close enough, he leans forward to scoop it up but, as he does so, jostles the boat. He quickly renews his grip. Holding to the edge of the boat, he watches the bloom float past him, his face slightly drawn and disappointed, a famished Tantalus from whose grasp all good things recede.

THE YEARS immediately following my father's suicide were difficult but not altogether unpleasant. Scrupulous in all matters, he left my mother and me quite enough to get by without undue hardship. But he also left us with a stigma, one my mother was hardly aware of, but which I used to the utmost. The child of a suicide has about him something of the radiance of celebrity. His peers presume that such a person is in touch with occult circumstances, that he has seen behind the locked door and gained some dreadful knowledge that has so far been denied them. It is a dreary notoriety, not unalloyed to pity, but for such a one as I, it was not an altogether unfavorable condition. As I felt no real love for my father, or even very much respect, his loss was no great matter. I tried to grieve, but the cold solitude of his life, his inability to touch without awkwardness, to speak without formality, so distanced him from me that his absence seemed little different from his presence. As a consequence, I was granted the special privileges of my condition without having to experience the pain. Indeed, the only real sorrow I felt at my father's death was my mother's survival, and that from now on I would be under her authority exclusively.

As the months passed, my mother grew increasingly worthless and embarrassing in my eyes. I continued to

attend school and gained some small acclaim in swimming
and academics. I met Anna. These were happy circumstances, so I cannot really excuse my life by an unhappy
childhood, as so many others habitually do. For whatever
discomfort attended my coming of age, it was discomfort
only, not torture. What discomfort there was originated
almost entirely with my mother. She was much as my father
understood her — altogether beyond reflection on matters
that did not immediately attend to the domestic. Ignorant
of literature or art, heedless of the political turmoil that
increasingly swept around us, beyond concern for any of
the issues that enlivened public debate, utterly at home
within the confines of her own grotesque physicality, and
smelling always of raw fish, my mother came to epitomize
everything I wanted to escape.

To the people of the village she was simply the unfortunate Frau Langhof, whose crazy husband had taken a
pistol to himself. But to me she was a large, dull mop of
a woman, unkempt and frowsy, her oily, matted hair forever licking at her eyes. Perhaps it could be said that it
was her slovenliness that inspired my later commitment to
the study of hygiene. And yet if it were that easy to explain ourselves, we would know a good deal more of what
we are.

I do know this: that beside my mother, Anna, my four-
teen-year-old infatuation, appeared as a creature out of
myth, the very image of perfect maidenhood with her pale
blue eyes and elaborately braided hair. She radiated health
and vigor, while my mother lumbered forth in a cloud of
putrescence. Anna was lithe and agile, a body glinting in
the sun as it sliced through the waters of the public pool.
My mother was squat and unwholesome, with small milky
eyes that stared mindlessly over my proudly squared
shoulders.

"What are you reading there, my dear Peter?"

I was sitting in the half-light of the dining room when
she came in. I shut the book immediately. "Nothing,
Mother."

"In a dull light, it hurts the eyes."

I looked up at her. A thin line of milk glistened over her upper lip. "What do you want?" I asked.

"That you should go to the butcher. For veal."

I could see her gnawing the raw meat like a scavenger. "I'll go tomorrow," I said.

"It's for tonight. For dinner. I want you to go now."

She handed me a piece of folded paper. "And give this note to Kreisler in the butcher shop. Here's some money, too."

I stood up. "All right then," I said, taking the note and wrapping the crumpled bills around it. She stared at the book suspiciously. "Not good to read without light, Peter."

I snatched the book from the table and deposited it on the umbrella stand as I left. From behind the closed door I could hear her calling for me to hurry and get back, not to linger on the corner.

I rushed down the stairs as if her breath were chasing me from the house, filling it with contamination. Some of the village services had fallen off and I could see bits of paper lying in the gutter. In the Camp there was no such litter problem. Any scraps of paper were quickly snatched up by the prisoners and dropped into their watery gray soup to give it bulk.

The butcher, Kreisler, was a large, big-boned man, vain of his huge black handlebar mustache, which curled upward on either side of his mouth. He looked at me from behind the counter. "So, Peter, what for you?"

"Veal," I said, and handed him the note and the money.

He quickly read the note, and I could see a little smile playing on his lips. When he had finished, he placed the note in his apron pouch and retrieved two choice cutlets. He held them up for me to see. "How about these two?"

"Fine."

He wrapped the veal quickly and handed it to me with the change. "Tell me, Peter," he said, "how is your mother?"

"Fine," I said indifferently.

Kreisler gave me a penetrating stare. "Is she seeing anyone?"

I could not believe his words. "Seeing anyone?"

"Is she going out, I mean. That sort of thing. With a man, my boy. Surely you're old enough to understand."

I could not imagine such a thing. "She certainly is not," I said.

Kreisler scratched his face, then rolled one point of his mustache between his thumb and forefinger. "It's been a long time since your father's death," he said. "It's not good for a strong woman to live alone."

So that was it. Kreisler had his eye on my mother. I could imagine them rolling like two pink pigs in the grimy disarray of my mother's bed. And what was that note? Suddenly it took on a hideous aspect. Had I been reduced to the role of go-between for these two creatures? "My mother does not intend to remarry," I announced.

Kreisler grinned. "Who said anything about marriage, Peter?" There was nothing but insult in his eyes.

"Well, then, she does not intend to see anyone," I said haughtily.

Kreisler winked as if he knew better. "Is that so?"

"Yes."

Kreisler's little smile broadened. "We'll see about that, my boy."

In my short life I had never felt such outrage. I snapped the package under my arm and marched toward the door.

"What are you, a little Red?" Kreisler called loudly after me. "You don't believe in marriage?"

So he did have marriage on his mind, marriage to my mother. I spun around to face him, but my tongue seemed to draw back in my mouth. He was big, after all, and the huge mustache gave his face a terrible malevolence. I turned around and stepped out onto the street.

Anna, a fellow student for whom I longed, was standing quietly in front of the confectionary across the way. She wore a dark blue coat with large white buttons, and a long braid of blonde hair hung over each shoulder. A cast on her arm reached from her wrist to just above her elbow. I felt my stomach squeeze together. That such a beautiful girl could be damaged seemed monstrous at that moment. I wanted to heal her miraculously in an instant. Years later Ginzburg sat in his striped suit, glanced at the medical bag on my bunk, and asked if I had ever used the instruments in it to mend a wound.

I walked over to Anna. "What happened to you?"

"I broke my arm," she said. She smiled. "It'll be well soon, though."

"How did it happen?"

Anna glanced down the street. A band was playing marching tunes in the distance.

"How did you hurt your arm?" I asked again.

"In gym class. I was doing a tumble and missed the mat. My arm twisted as I fell. I don't know how it happened exactly." She looked at the cast. "Isn't it silly?"

"I hope it doesn't hurt too much."

Anna waved her other hand dismissingly. "No. Not much at all." She lifted the cast slightly. "It's just a nuisance, that's all."

I lifted my package. "I just came from the butcher." Kreisler's face rose in my mind and I felt something stiffen in my neck.

Anna nodded. "Yes, I saw you in the shop. What did you get?"

"Veal cutlets," I said. I wanted to ask her to come home for dinner, but I knew that to her perfect eyes my mother would appear as a bedraggled old Grendel heaving scorched strudel into her plate.

"We have veal on Thursdays," Anna said, peering down the street again.

"Are you waiting for someone?" I asked. I pictured him tall and powerfully built, her mighty Lohengrin.

"Only the parade," Anna said lightly. She smiled. "Do you like parades?"

"Very much," I said with relief. It was a lie — one of my first. For I did not like parades at all and was even mildly offended by their noisiness and dazzle.

"They have wonderful parades during Oktoberfest," Anna said happily. She tossed one of her braids lightly over her shoulder. "I see as many as I can."

"So do I. You know, I would love to play in a large orchestra someday."

Anna's eyes brightened. "An orchestra! How wonderful. Do you play any instrument?"

"The piano," I said, then felt myself grow horrified at the thought she might ask to hear me play. "Only slightly," I added.

"Do you practice much?"

"As much as I can."

"Do you like to practice?"

"Yes," I said, "Someday I'd like to play the organ in a great cathedral."

Anna raised herself on tiptoe and looked down the street. The band music was growing closer. "I prefer the piano," she said. "The organ is too loud."

"Yes, that's true," I said quickly. The smell of the veal wafted up into my face, churning my stomach. "Well, I'd better get home now."

Anna turned toward me. "Aren't you going to stay for the parade?"

"My mother is waiting," I told her, lifting the package. "For dinner."

"But you must stay, Peter," Anna said excitedly. "It's no fun to watch parades alone."

I felt as though the sun had suddenly broken upon my face. "You really want me to?"

"Oh, yes. Please, Peter. Just stay for the parade. It's almost here!"

I turned and saw the band marching briskly toward us, the drum beating loudly, the horns echoing over the brick street, the flutes filling the air with their happy tones.

"It's a fine band," I said.

"A wonderful band," Anna said. She bobbed lightly on her feet.

I returned my eyes to the street. Several pedestrians had stopped to watch the parade move by. Some of them lifted their arms and held them rigidly at an angle above their heads.

I laughed. "What are they doing?"

"Saluting the flag," Anna said matter-of-factly.

I looked at the banner, which was held high by the booted mascot of the band. It showed a design of broken black lines on a field of red.

"That's not our flag," I said.

"It's my father's flag," Anna said. Her eyes held firmly to the marchers in the street.

"But that's not our national flag," I said.

"My father doesn't salute the national flag any longer," Anna said. "He salutes this one."

The banner bobbed left and right as the mascot thrust his legs stiffly out, coming closer to us with each step.

"Quick," Anna said, "help me salute."

I looked at her. "What?"

"The cast," Anna said, "it's hard for me to hold my arm up. Help me lift it."

For a moment I did not move. The idea of touching Anna was so delicious that it frightened me, but I also hesitated because the gesture itself, the outstretched arm and stiffly pointing fingers, seemed ridiculous.

"Hurry," Anna cried. "Help me, Peter."

I tucked my left hand just beneath Anna's elbow and raised her arm, lifting my right arm along with hers, saluting as she did, and holding both our arms high in the air as the banner joggled past us — comically, it seemed, and yet with an arrogant confidence in its own future.

AH THEN, so that's the fateful nexus: a man may be seduced, may be led to great misfortune by the wiles — innocent though they are — of a little girl. Our young hero, Langhof, lifts his hand in salute because he does not wish to go against his first adolescent love. That is the beginning of all that follows. During the last months in the Camp, when it became clear to everyone that ultimately some answer would have to be made for all the things that had taken place there, during those final days a few men searched their minds for reasons that might serve as excuse, if not precisely justification. These few — for most did nothing — lolled on the steps of the administration building or slogged through the mud and snow muttering questions to themselves: What happened here? How did I get here? How was I led astray?

Their answers, if compiled, would form a pathetic epic of self-pity and self-delusion. Schuster blamed the doctrinaire socialism of his father; Nagel proposed his puny physical stature; Luftmann claimed Catholicism had brought him to his ruin, while Kloppman recalled his readings from Martin Luther. In the end, it all came to the same thing. For denser than the smoke that enveloped the Camp and more powerful than the odors carried within it was our compulsion to dismiss our role as something over which we had no control. Here in the last days crime became mere misfortune, and in the final analysis most of those who even bothered to review their actions during the preceding years came to blame the vermin for their fate: if they had not existed, we would not have had to kill them.

I see Dr. Ludtz's boat sailing back toward shore. It was a short excursion, as they all are. He is afraid to roam very far downriver, suspecting, as he does, commandos skulking in the brush, the thin crosshairs of their rifle sights intersecting on his head. During the great plague of the fourteenth century, the Prince of the Church, Clement VI, secluded himself in a single chamber at Avignon and sat between two huge blazing fires, muttering to an emerald said to have mystic powers. For his talisman Dr. Ludtz depends upon the small automatic pistol that snuggles against his right buttock. He worships the power of technology, particularly the calculus of force, even though against any serious assault his puny weaponry would be of no more use to him than a garland of garlic or a bay leaf dipped in rabbit blood.

I take my pipe from its rack and tamp in a small portion of tobacco. The boat washes up to shore. Alberto and Tomás leap out and steady it for Dr. Ludtz's ponderous disembarkation. His body evinces great disproportion, a gargantuan tuber surmounted by a small, round head filled with the banal ecstasies of Eckhart and inane anecdotes from the literary life.

He moves up toward his unfinished tomb, dismissing Alberto and Tomás with a quick, ungracious flick of his right hand. They nod to him and turn away, free now to cavort with each other like the monkeys across the river, free to discover the rudiments of earth and the energies of youth, free to dream of humid nights with some village Jezebel, their fingers prying at her body, exploring with untutored glee the limits of their empiricism.

Here the body is supreme. It is the temple of all the people's fortune and misery. Here, the heat melts the tortured dualism of Descartes, merging body and mind into one pulsing vessel of succulence or dearth. In temperate climates, men may inhabit some lofty empire of the word, engaging their minds in endless litigations between the spirit and the flesh. But here, amid the swelter that brings the orchids to extravagant command, all is subservient to the tyranny of matter. In the Camp, man and matter became one, fused together in the furnace and the pyre.

Alberto has begun his run. I watch his body twist gracefully through the vines, the great leaves slapping against his bare chest like the spread fans of adoring ladies. Running, he is all speed and muscle, his long black hair fluttering behind him like a stallion's mane. He rushes through the foliage in pursuit of absolutely nothing save the fire and tremor of the run itself.

In the Republic, there is much to be fiery and tremulous about. It is a nation of extremes. What does not reinforce order serves chaos; what does not subdue, enflames. In the cumbersome workings of his brain El Presidente knows at least this much. At the base of all his farcical display lies the remote but obdurate recognition that all that does not uphold the Republic undermines it. And so within the scheme of El Presidente's order the Church rallies the belabored spirit with tales of coming paradise; the schools flounder in a welter of mindless texts and patriotic zeal; the publishers churn out witless and beguiling episodes of upper-class romance; the theaters dapple the night with flickering reels of cowboy vengeance and requited love. And in response, Alberto chases shadows in the bush with a beauty that is innocent and lame.

He reaches the river and plunges in, splitting the surface like a bronze knife. Rising, he waves his arms wildly in the air, as if signaling to something concealed in the jungle. He heaves forward, curling his body downward, and disappears head first into the water, then rises from it again, shaking his head, sending a glittering spray left and right.

Out there, somewhere in the jungle framed by Alberto's uplifted arms, it is said a small contingent of rebels huddle by their fires, picking briars from their mud-caked feet and lice from their matted beards. From time to time, along remote, twisting roads, they make chaotic war on the armed agents of El Presidente's rule. They fire from the brush, which the imported defoliants cannot conquer, and then disappear into the mountain caverns. El Presidente is said to be concerned that their power is growing like a tumor in that body politic which is inseparable from himself. Monday reveals a provincial delegado slumped over the steering wheel of his jeep, a bullet in his brain; Tuesday a remote arsenal is successfully pillaged; Wednesday finds the gowned body of a garroted priest floating face down in the shallow pool of the papal garrison; Thursday the wastrel son of the Minister of Agriculture is thrown from a bridge, bursting the water like a large, flat stone; Friday we are told that a local chief of police was bitten fourteen times by a viper slipped beneath his sheets; Saturday a foreign industrialist is machine-gunned while sipping brandy in a fashionable street café; an army officer is neatly decapitated on Sunday by a thin metal wire strung neck-high across the road. These are the minor but recurring themes in the fugue of the Republic.

Atop this feeble structure, El Presidente sits like a watchful mastodon. Beneath his stolid, immobile figure, all things writhe with impatience or despair. The Church abhors his stable of ravished maids and sodomized young boys. The fledgling intelligentsia cringes at his risible pomp. The lords of moderate but acquisitive estate seethe under the levies he imposes on their greed. The engineers of high technique groan at the clutter of his style. The metropolitan herd withers under the shortages engendered by his squandered wealth, while the rural masses bake in the heat of his indifference. Over all this flammable mass, El Presidente squats, a yellow-eyed Caligula, smothering the fuse.

And in the midst of all of this, Alberto emerges from the water to resume his run. He moves with all the strength at his command, the air beating against him like invisible curtains. He turns suddenly and stops. His head arches back proudly, and he prances in place for a moment, his knees almost touching his chest, his feet thudding forcefully against the ground. Slowly, he brings his head down and turns to face the river. He takes a deep breath, as if gathering all the force of wind into his lungs. Then he explodes forward, his feet ripping at the ground and yet barely touching earth. He runs with all the power of his youth and the speed of his ignorance, runs under the whip of a mindless dynamo through all the engulfing splendor of his years.

Watching him, I sometimes think that if Alberto could be saved, then so might all the world.

D R. LUDTZ is moving up the stairs toward me. His face is almost soothing in its blankness, a pink and hairless mass, featureless as a wad of gum. For years we toiled together in the Camp, effacing our disparity of thought with an identity of act.

At the top of the stairs he taps at my door, then eases himself in. "Still in the office, Doctor?" he says. "It would be good for you to get out once in a while, you know."

A wall of heat enters with the open door. "Perhaps."

"The day is first rate."

"I can see that. Did you enjoy your excursion on the river?"

"It was wonderful. You should have joined me."

"Perhaps next time, Dr. Ludtz."

Dr. Ludtz eyes me suspiciously. "I also noticed — I didn't mention it earlier — but I also noticed that you were up quite late last night."

"Was I?"

"I could see the lights burning here in your office. I was somewhat worried, you know."

I can imagine him sitting by his window, peeping through a slit in the shutters at the lights burning in my office, wondering if at that very moment I might be in the hands of some commando unit Arnstein has sent to snatch us both.

"I don't sleep as well as I once did," I tell him. "Age, I suppose. The arthritis."

"Very uncomfortable, I imagine."

"Yes, sometimes. Would you like for me to have Esperanza prepare something for you?"

"No, thank you, Dr. Langhof," Dr. Ludtz says. He leans back in his chair. It cracks softly under the pressure of his weight. "Tell me, what do you have in mind for El Presidente?"

"In mind?"

"Festivities. What sort of festivities?"

"The usual arrangements."

"Nothing special?"

"Everything will be prepared," I tell him. "You need not concern yourself."

Dr. Ludtz looks slightly rebuked. "Concern myself? No. Entirely your affair, Doctor. I assure you I have no wish to interfere. Just curious, that's all."

"Well, as it stands, there will be a dinner, of course. And I intend to invite the entire village for his visit. As you know, El Presidente enjoys large welcoming crowds for his arrival."

Dr. Ludtz nods enthusiastically. "Yes. Large crowds. A necessity. Anything else?"

"Perhaps some fireworks after the evening meal to light up the sky in celebration. He would no doubt enjoy such a thing."

Dr. Ludtz grins conspiratorially. "He would probably prefer a comet, don't you think?"

"I cannot provide a comet, I'm afraid."

Dr. Ludtz laughs rather stiffly. "No, of course not. More's the pity." He pauses, looking at me cautiously. "Would you mind a suggestion, Dr. Langhof?"

"Not at all."

Dr. Ludtz smiles happily. "Well, in terms of the actual

display, I think it should be done with a concentration upon bright oranges and reds — the national colors."

In the Camp, Dr. Ludtz was nothing if not meticulous. He had a jeweler's eye for the significant detail. Once I saw him carefully measuring the toenails of three sets of twins who had been provided him. They had been shot in the back of the neck so as not to mar any important physical characteristics. They rested on their backs, naked, their faces perfectly serene, while he examined them tirelessly, making measurements and recording his findings in the spattered data book that lay beside the bodies.

"Well, what do you think of my suggestion?" Dr. Ludtz asks.

"Orange and red. Yes, I think that would be best."

"Excellent," Dr. Ludtz says excitedly. He claps his hands.

I turn toward the window and watch a sudden rustling of the leaves. "Do you remember, Dr. Ludtz, how in the last year, spring seemed never to come?"

Dr. Ludtz stares at me quizzically. "Last year?"

"Of the war."

Dr. Ludtz shakes his head nervously. "No, no. I never noticed." His face seems to have curdled.

"Perhaps it was only the gloom that made it seem so," I tell him.

Dr. Ludtz waves his hand dismissively. "Long ago. Best not to recall."

I can see the tension growing in his face. I do not wish to drag him through the squalor of his past. Once, in the Camp, I saw a guard press the face of a young girl into her own feces.

"Perhaps you're right," I say.

"In any event," Dr. Ludtz says quickly, "I do suggest a bright orange and red motif. We do want to make it as pleasant as possible for El Presidente."

"Quite right, yes, Dr. Ludtz. Thank you for the suggestion. I will do what I can."

"Very good," Dr. Ludtz says softly. He watches me

with ill-concealed apprehension. "You really should try to enliven yourself a bit, Doctor," Dr. Ludtz suggests.

I turn to face him. "Enliven?"

"Yes."

"How?"

"I don't know," Dr. Ludtz says worriedly, "but you have become somewhat depressed of late, am I right?"

"Perhaps."

"Do you know why?"

"One grows old."

"I hope that you are not...well..."

"Becoming like my father?"

"Certainly not that, I trust," Dr. Ludtz says.

Not long after I came to El Caliz I related the story of my father's suicide to Dr. Ludtz. I told it very coolly, but I could see pity in his eyes. It disgusted me that I had sunk so low as to initiate his compassion.

"Don't concern yourself about it, Doctor," I tell him. "It's the heat that's bothering me. Very oppressive, don't you think?"

Dr. Ludtz wipes his forehead in a sympathetic gesture. "Yes, the heat. Like you, I have never grown accustomed to it." He glances out the window. "It's cooler on the river. You really should come rowing with me sometime. As I keep saying, it would do you good."

"Perhaps someday I shall. But for now, I'm much too busy."

"I understand, believe me." Dr. Ludtz says. "May I ask another question?"

"Of course."

"Have you decided on the menu?"

"Roast pork, I think. And a fine red wine to go with it."

"Excellent," Dr. Ludtz says. He rises. "Let me know if I may be of assistance to you. You shouldn't tire yourself."

"I won't. Thank you."

He moves out the door and down the stairs. He is a man who must continually give the appearance of being busy. There is nothing whatsoever for him to do in the compound. Everything is provided. Like the sparrow, he need neither sow nor reap. And yet he bustles about in a constant state of unnecessary activity, a gyroscope of obsessive redundancy, producing for neither use nor exchange, his incessant labor nothing more than the broom with which he sweeps clean his mind.

Esperanza opens the glass door that separates my office from the verandah. She asks if I have need of anything.

"Nada. Gracias."

She nods and casts a curious glance in the direction of Dr. Ludtz's retreating figure.

In Spanish, I ask her what she thinks of him.

She grimaces. "El ojo de mal," she mutters, and slinks back onto the verandah.

The evil eye, that is what she says of Dr. Ludtz. Here in the Republic, evil is the great reductive principle. Sickness is evil, so there are few medical schools in the Republic, for evil is not a thing that can be ministered to by science. The mouths of children fill with running sores dropped into them by Satan's fingers. Evil demons infect the bush and putrefy the air. They squat under the morning mist and fly upon the hornet's back. They gurgle under the green sludge of the open sewers and mire themselves within the canker's pus. Here, malevolent animism is the great disease, a spiritus mundi against which the clergy fights feeble and symbolic war, sweeping into dying villages, flinging yellow holy water drawn from contaminated streams. And then they sweep out again, leaving the fevered peasants their catholicon of faith, while, overhead, vultures ebonize the sky.

Here it is deemed man's fate to abide patiently within a geography of hell. For evil is our constant curse. It guides the machete in its flight, inflames the rapist's eye, and squeezes shut the strangler's hand. Evil leers outside the maiden's bedroom window and lurks behind the oddly open door. It is war and pestilence and famine. It is poverty and greed and dissipation and lacy garter belts. It is the black scarf wrapped around our eyes.

But in the Camp, evil was made man and kept in check by wire and bayonet until the world could be cleansed of it by fire and poison gas. There, amid an orgy of purification, the world was to be made new, the black stain of evil bleached white in fields of bone.

I N LATE EVENING I can see Dr. Ludtz meticulously removing the lichens from his tomb, his fingers clawing at them like small paring knives. This is his futile thrust toward immortality, a stone table set in the jungle vastness. Despite the irremediable squalor of his life, Dr. Ludtz does not wish to airbrush himself from history, but rather to erect a monument to his being. Having once been, he seeks always to be. It is part of his lunacy and his crime, but the urge is not exclusively his.

Other men choose different methods to immortalize themselves. In the Camp, they carved their names into rotting boards to prove that they were there. They plunged into gullies of poured cement and sank themselves into the machinery of their own destruction. They grasped the sizzling wire or danced insanely by the dead-line while the guards took aim above, cigarettes dangling casually from their lips. And in the capital, far away, the Leader descended into his tomb and ate strawberries and cream while he regaled his dutiful secretaries with tales of early glory. Ginzburg went out whistling and Rausch with a look of rude surprise.

Here in the Republic, El Presidente contemplates his final resting place. He has considered many alternatives, but as he ages the search becomes more desperate. It is said that in the northern provinces entire mountain ranges have been sheared off in preparation for El Presidente's monument. Some say he will build a great glass tomb beneath the sea so that his soul can watch the sharks and barracuda. Others claim that the desert wastes have already been selected and that a great golden shaft is to be erected there, one so tall that its shadow will pass over the curvature of earth.

To nestle the world within the crook of our arm. That is the age-old and ageless dream in its perversity. And this mania is by no means the special pleasure of underdevelopment. In the great manorial halls of the privileged classes, behind the towering walls of stone and marble there are rooms seldom used but elaborately decorated, with great curtains covering intricacies of inlaid glass, boasting hearths of dark malachite, polished floors of mosaic design, and ponderous carved-mahogany doors whose task it is to enclose this splendor. Within all this, one may divine part of the psychology of pomp. For although the grand, silent, empty rooms entomb something that resists ultimate decortication, there is also something that betrays itself within the context of the splendid. Indeed their very grandeur and stolidity bespeaks the paranoia of the impermanent. They are built to withstand the intrigue of time and the whimsy of taste. By their magnificence they attempt to rise above judgment and dwarf all that might subsequently attempt to mar or defame them. They are the very instrument by which power is made manifest on earth, and those who move easily within them carry some physical notion of the re splendent, the immaculate, and the immortal.

The orphaned sons of petty attorneys, however, must find less lofty devices through which to consecrate themselves. Mine was Anna.

At best our romance was not the stuff from which epics could be made. There was sufficient pubescent melodrama to fashion a lusterless novelette, and if it had flowered into marriage and family, perhaps a neat, bourgeois roman-fleuve. But beyond such mundane possibilities, nothing.

Three years after our encounter across the street from Kreisler's shop, we made groping, unruly love in her small room, while two Bavarian milkmaid dolls watched us from atop an oak armoire. Their lifeless ceramic eyes remain as much a part of my memory of that scene as the first shock of breasts and thigh. But I also remember that I wanted to pull myself into Anna's body, wanted to mold a pallet for myself within her. It is one of our illusions to believe that once we have entertained such feelings we never really lose them. But they are, at the most, transitory, and if they are not allied to some form of riches that lies more deeply within us, then they are no more than passing incidents, as vacant and useless as sheaves of paper upon which nothing has been written.

And yet even this, or the prolongation of it, came abruptly to an end.

"I have bad news," Anna said quietly.

We were sitting in a small park. It was late evening and the park was almost entirely empty.

"Bad news?" I could already feel a lethal fluttering in my stomach. I imagined that she was going to let me go, set me adrift, and then rush off to that handsome lover who was already waiting naked in her bed.

"My father has lost his job," Anna said.

I felt relieved. "I'm sorry. But he'll find another one, I'm sure."

Anna lowered her eyes. "He says there are no jobs to be found here."

"No jobs?" I laughed. "Of course there are jobs. He just has to look for one, that's all."

Anna shook her head. "He says there are no jobs."

I leaned forward attentively. "What are you telling me, Anna?"

She looked up. "I have to move away, Peter. We have to go to another city where my father can find work."

For years I had walked about in complete obliviousness to the deepening crisis. Herds of workers marched through the streets, parading their grievances. Speakers harangued the crowded parks with the details of their scheming. The police fired on demonstrators of the right and left. The universities were set aflame with struggle. The government tottered back and forth from year to year, groping toward

some ill-defined stability. Prices soared, along with unem-
ployment. Production collapsed. The old symbols lost their
power to seduce, and by that means, control. Through all
of this I had walked without the slightest care. But now
the times had finally touched me, blotted out a brilliant romance, snatched blonde Anna from her knight's protection.

"You can't be serious," I said. "What do you mean, move
away?"

"I have no choice."

"You can't move away."

"It's not *me*," Anna said. "It's my father. We have to
move."

"No you don't," I said desperately. "Let him go. You
can stay here. We can get married."

"We can't get married," Anna said softly. She touched
my face. "It's no use."

She took my hand and we began to stroll across the park.
A great stone statue of Frederick the Great loomed ahead
of us. He seemed to watch us mournfully.

"We have to do something, Anna," I said.

"There's nothing we can do. We can't get married. You
don't have a job any more than my father does."

"Jobs!" I said angrily. "We can't let something like that
stop us."

"We have no choice, Peter," Anna said evenly.

I could see her evaporating before me, history erasing
her from my life. There were no jobs in the village. That
was the dictate of history, and because of it, this little love
affair must end. For history was the truly great fire, adolescent romance merely cinerary.

"We cannot let this happen, Anna," I said.

"But it has, Peter."

I despised her resignation. "No," I said loudly, "I won't
allow it."

Anna looked at me. Her eyes were glistening. "I don't
want to go on with this. I can't."

And then she rushed away, with something of me still
dangling in her hand, a little thread made out of my desire, unraveling me as she moved away. I watched her as

she darted across the park, running like some teenage heroine of nineteenth century fiction, her hair swaying left and right as if pushed gently by invisible hands. I stood still and she grew smaller in the distance, like a wisp of paper falling from great height toward — who knows — oblivion.

I have no idea what became of Anna. I have no idea where she is, or if she is alive, or, if alive, how mutated by events. I take a piece of stationery from my desk, and then take up my pen.

Dear Anna ..

The page stares back blankly, my letter stopped in its course. I do not know what to say to Anna. And even if by some miraculous circumstance she were to receive my letter, who would it be who received it? Not the Anna moaning softly under the featureless gaze of the milkmaid dolls. Of that I may be sure. But if not that, then what? Could she have taken the road I took? Could there be pictures of her in some hideous archive, perhaps a grainy photograph in black and white of a woman standing black-booted before a wintry background laced by electric wire, a woman staring haughtily into the camera's lens, posturing with her feet spread wide apart, slapping a leather truncheon at her thigh, guarding the vermin as they pass with enforced, truckling grace toward the fire.

I return to my letter:

Dear Anna:
I have come to love all things that move with stamina
through pain.

I fold the letter carefully, then burn it in the ashtray beside my rack of pipes. Watching the smoke, I recall that moment once again when Anna and I faced each other in the park. Here in the Republic one can grow to hate such banal reminiscences. The aggrieved adolescent stands blank-faced in the park, watching his love abandon him, and feels the first touch of history, a mere chill around his shoulders, and then, that moment past, moves on to greater endeavors involving smoke and poison gas.

Greater things, indeed, for one and all. And yet the little prince, rubbing his eyes under the sculptured gaze of Frederick the Great, can feel nothing of his own loss, nothing but sudden drift, dull and anchorless, as if the world's firm substance had suddenly exploded, scattering fragments of earth and bone throughout the universe, as if the seas were made of star-crossed lovers' tears, as if the rising chorus of *Fidelio* were meant to orchestrate the strife of teenage infatuation. For the true romantic, there is no history or literature or art that does not pertain to him.

I gaze into the enclosing darkness. In the Republic, night is a signal for assault. The owls wait on their secret perches for the dark curtain to fall across the jungle floor, their eyes searching the blackness for the small rodents that must go forth, risking everything for food. Silently, they squeeze the branches with their talons and dream of small hearts beating within their grasp. In the blue, lunar glare of the searchlights Dr. Ludtz has installed about the compound, I see Juan puttering about the greenhouse, muttering prayers against the blight. He believes that darkness is the devil's work, that it shields that unknowable miasma which will drift in to corrupt the orchids. To the left, the lights in Dr. Ludtz's cottage are burning brightly through the barred and shuttered windows. Inside he reads Rilke and glances up periodically at the pistol that rests upon his nightstand next to his crucifix.

I turn and walk into my office. Sitting behind my desk, I pour a small amount of absinthe into my glass. Outside, I can hear the night creatures fill the air with calls of mating or distress. Beyond the rim of light that circles the grounds like a thin white wall, the world descends to elemental needs. Out there, small creatures scurry across the leaves, fleeing the swoop of gigantic birds; the great snakes coil around mounds of eggs orphaned by the owls; the beetles inch their way into the viscera of the dead or tumble over lumps of larger creatures' waste. Here, doom is no more than prologue to further violation. Each night the libretto is the same, and things go forth and are cut down, and all things wait to be relieved.

Part II

Part II

S PLENDID TO SEE you again, Don Pedro," Don Camillo says. He roots himself in his chair. I can see a revolver bulging slightly under each arm of his three-piece suit.

"Good to see you, also," I tell him.

Don Camillo looks off the verandah at the light dancing on the river. "A beautiful morning. Absolutely beautiful."

"Yes."

Don Camillo turns to me. "Well, let me say that El Presidente is very much looking forward to his visit." He smiles expansively. Don Camillo is a man of smiles and expansiveness, both closely related to his personal control of the Republic's stock of copper.

"Please give El Presidente my regards," I tell him.

"You will soon be able to give them to him yourself, Don Pedro."

"Of course."

Don Camillo glances about. "And where, may I ask, is my good friend Dr. Ludtz?"

"In his cottage."

"I hope he is well."

"Quite well. He is reading, I suppose."

"A well-read man. I noticed that right away about Dr. Ludtz," Don Camillo says.

"A product of culture's refinements," I add agreeably.

"Refinements, yes," Don Camillo says, nodding his head thoughtfully. "A man of refinements." He takes a deep breath and exhales with affected weariness. "Men of state, regrettably, have little time for such things, such refinements." He laughs. "But then, I suppose we have our place in the world."

"We?"

"Men of affairs. Like yourself. Like me."

"My kingdom is rather small, Don Camillo," I say.

Don Camillo shakes his head. "No, no. Don't diminish yourself. To run an estate such as this — particularly with the rather backward population of El Caliz — that is no small matter, believe me."

Here in the Republic, no man must be diminished. That would debase the sanctity of individualism upon which the totalitarian state is founded. Here in the Republic each man must be free to grab what he can, be it horse or maid — or copper.

"Speaking of men of affairs, Don Camillo," I say, "how is El Presidente?"

"Very well," Don Camillo replies delightedly. He leans forward, lowering his voice. "Of course, we've had a little trouble in the northern provinces."

As he speaks, I can see the "trouble in the northern provinces" trudging wearily through the jungle, a small, bedraggled army infested with lice and infected with disease. They amputate their gangrenous limbs with penknives and machetes.

"I'm disturbed to hear about the trouble."

"Nothing serious, you understand," Don Camillo hastens to inform me. "Mere irritations, but they plague El Presidente. They keep him from the sleep he deserves, wear down his strength." He slaps at a mosquito near his ear. "Damn pests." He rolls his shoulder, the revolvers eating into his armpits. Here in the Republic, men of state must bear such aggravations.

"Well, perhaps his visit here will relax El Presidente."

"I profoundly hope so, Don Pedro," Don Camillo says

worriedly. "As I say, he's not been sleeping well. Bad dreams, I think. Do you ever have bad dreams?"

"Sometimes I dream that in the end all the innocent blood that has been shed will be gathered in a great pit and those who spilled it will be forced to swim in it forever."

Don Camillo's face pales. "Dios mío. How horrible."

"One cannot help one's dreams."

The light seems to have withdrawn from the two gilded medals that adorn Don Camillo's breast pocket. "Such dreams. Horrible," he says. His eyes are full of imagined terrors.

"Perhaps El Presidente's dreams are better suited to his person," I say comfortingly.

Camillo glances apprehensively toward the river. The guards who stand below, near his limousine, stiffen as he looks toward them, then relax as he returns his gaze to me. "Such a vision. Horrible."

"I am sorry to have disturbed you," I tell him.

The monkeys have begun to screech wildly in the trees across the river. Don Camillo turns to his guards and instructs them to fire a burst into the trees. They do so, and I hear the bullets slapping into the thick foliage. One monkey drops from the tree and splashes belly down into the river.

Don Camillo turns slowly to face me. There is a smile on his face, but something dark behind it. "You seem to have become somewhat morbid of late, Don Pedro," he says. "I hope you will try to be in better spirits when El Presidente visits."

The monkey's arms slowly rise from the surface of the water, then drop, then rise again. "You should kill it," I tell Don Camillo.

Don Camillo's eyes seem to recede into his skull. "What are you talking about?" he asks darkly.

I nod toward the river. "The monkey. It is still alive."

Don Camillo turns toward the river and watches the arms rise and fall. Then he turns back to me. "Sometimes we catch one of those bastards from the northern provinces, those rebels. We tie a rope around his waist and hoist him up in a helicopter. Then we fly very low over the marshes, dragging him just above the water so that the reeds can do their work." His lips curl down. "After a while there's not much left to pull up, so we just cut the rope, you know?" He leans forward and stares at me menacingly. "You know why I am here, do you not, Don Pedro?"

"As always, my friend, you have come to make sure that all the proper arrangements have been made for El Presidente's visit."

Don Camillo traces his thin mustache across his lips with the tip of his index finger. "I must be sure about his safety, Don Pedro."

"Why should he not be safe in El Caliz?" I ask. In the river, the monkey's arms no longer rise and the body begins to drift downstream with the river's lethargic flow.

"We are a free people in the Republic," Don Camillo says. "People may travel as they like. Perhaps they may travel to El Caliz, perhaps enemies come here." He smiles. "Perhaps already there are enemies living in El Caliz."

"There are no enemies here, I assure you, Don Camillo."

Don Camillo sits back in his chair. "The world is full of monkeys. Like the ones in the tree, you know. They chatter constantly. Big talk. Crazy talk. But one has to take it seriously."

"El Presidente has always enjoyed his visits here," I tell Don Camillo.

"Very much. Correct," Don Camillo says. "He very much looks forward to it."

"This will go well, I assure you."

Don Camillo looks relieved. "I hope so." He stares about as if looking for traces of copper. "I suppose you have already made plans for the visit?"

"Yes."

"May I know what they are?"

"A large banquet. The whole village will be invited. I know how much they love El Presidente, and how much he loves them, as well."

Don Camillo smiles happily. "Splendid. That should improve his spirits."

"Such is my intent."

Don Camillo eyes the wall of records inside my office. "There is a particular musician El Presidente admires, Don Pedro. I wonder if you might have any of his recordings."

"What is the name?"

"Chop-pin."

"Chopin," I say gently.

Don Camillo smiles self-consciously. "Oh, is that how it is pronounced? I have only seen the name written on the albums. One does not hear such names pronounced very often here in the Republic."

In the Camp, the orchestra was not permitted to play Chopin, because he was a Pole. "It wouldn't matter if you did," I tell Don Camillo.

"I beg your pardon?"

"It wouldn't matter if you did hear such names pronounced here, Don Camillo. Pronunciations are of no importance."

"Exactly," Don Camillo says. "Although I'm sure El Presidente knows the correct form of speech."

"A man of refinements," I add.

"Profoundly so," Don Camillo says. He slaps his thighs. "Well, I think my work is done here, Don Pedro. I'm happy to see that you have made the proper arrangements for El Presidente's visit."

"Everything will be taken care of, you may depend on it, Don Camillo."

Don Camillo rises, draws a handkerchief from his coat pocket, and mops his brow. "This business in the northern provinces, it has exhausted me."

"I'm sorry to hear it."

"Ah, well, part of the job," Don Camillo says. He replaces the handkerchief. "It's those people up there. They are never satisfied. No matter what El Presidente does for them, they want more."

"Perhaps if they had more copper —"

Don Camillo laughs. "Copper? No, there's no copper to

be had in that region of the Republic. Believe me, it has been investigated."

"Something else then, perhaps."

"No, nothing," Don Camillo says with certainty. "It's their nature, that's all. Mountain people. Uncivilized. Sometimes I think that we will never have peace in the northern provinces until every last one of them has been killed." He looks at me knowingly. "A process, I believe, in which you have some expertise, Doctor."

My machine pistol rests in the top drawer of my desk. It is only a few inches from my hands.

Don Camillo laughs, but his eyes do not. "Perhaps you have a plan for the northern provinces."

It would be a matter of opening the drawer, one quick, deft movement, and he would dance until the clip emptied.

"I would not want to be involved," I tell him.

"Once is enough for anyone, I suppose," Don Camillo says with a malicious wink.

I stand. "Tell El Presidente that I am waiting for him with great eagerness."

Don Camillo wipes the shimmering beads of sweat from his mustache. "And you tell Dr. Ludtz that I regret not seeing him." He offers me his hand. I take it and shake it briskly. "So nice to have seen you, Don Pedro," he says.

"And you, Don Camillo." In the Republic, civility is important.

Don Camillo turns and moves down the stairs. His bodyguards watch me, and two other bodyguards a little ways distant watch them. In the Republic, no one can be trusted.

I raise my hand. "Adiós, Don Camillo."

Don Camillo turns before entering his mud-caked limousine. "Y usted, tambien," he calls to me. Then he steps inside the car, surrounded by his sloe-eyed janissaries in their dark green uniforms. They stare out the window, their eyes cruising the river bank or rising to riffle through the trees searching for blue rifle barrels peeping from the vines like the heads of wary serpents.

Don Camillo's car pulls away quickly, heaving up a trail of swirling orange dust. In the distance, I can see Esperanza

watch the limousine. She is wearing a dark red rebozo that
falls over her shoulders and drops almost to her knees.
Ritually, she claps her hands three times as the car passes.
I do not know if this is a blessing or a curse.

I walk off the verandah and into my office. The cut
crystal goblet sits on top of the large wicker cabinet against
the far wall. The light pouring through the bamboo curtain shatters in the crystal, sending a spray of mottled light
across the room. Retrieving it from its place, I turn it in
my hand and observe the delicacy of the pattern, the exquisite design. It was once the prized possession of my
father, a family heirloom passed down through generations
of uninspired petty officials and weary civil servants who
sat with their noses buried in provincial paper and their
minds in middling bank accounts. Warming their feet at
tidy, bourgeois fires, they passed the crystal goblet down
as something like a grail for the Langhof family. On holi-
days or family gatherings they would remove it from its
sheltered vault and pass it carefully from hand to hand as
if it were the heraldic shield of the Hohenzollern princes.
But here in the Republic, the sense of the holy is reserved
for certain raw materials that, when sold, support the titanic waste over which it is El Presidente's function to
preside.

I walk to my desk and place the goblet in a small cotton
sack. I raise the marble paperweight in the air and bring
it down. There is a small crunch as the glass shatters beneath the blow. I open the mouth of the sack and sprinkle
the bits of crystal across the desk. Even in this fallen state,
they sparkle with a blue and silver light. I select a few of
the pieces and begin to file them down, putting each sculptured gem into a small red velvet pouch. Then I take the
pouch and stuff it in my trousers.

I rise from the desk. Esperanza is staring at me from
the verandah.

"¿Qué pasa?" she asked.

"Nicht . . . nada."

"Oí romper alguna cosa."

"Una copa. No es importante."

She watches me suspiciously. "Sí, Don Pedro."

I wave her from the door, then move down the stairs toward the greenhouse. Juan is inside, relentlessly fighting the demons that have come to destroy the orchids.

"¿Juan?"

He turns toward me.

I pull the pouch from my trousers and lift it toward him.

He looks at me strangely.

I tell him to take the pouch and to bury it under the orchids.

He stares at me, perplexed. "¿Las orquídeas?"

"Sí."

Reluctantly he takes the pouch.

I tell him to bury it now. "Ahora, por favor."

"Sí, Don Pedro," Juan says. He eyes the pouch, feeling the edges of the chiseled glass beneath his fingers.

I attempt to soothe his anxiety. "Para la enfermedad de las flores." For the blight.

Juan nods silently, somewhat relieved, but not entirely so. "Sí, Don Pedro."

"Bien."

I walk out of the greenhouse and look toward the distant range of hills to the south. The pale orange cloud of dust billows up from the trees as Don Camillo's spattered limousine speeds along those ancient trails the Indians once carved. In my mind I can see Don Camillo lounging in the back seat, squeezed in between his sleepless protectors, his mind squirming with visions of copper kingdoms in the provinces to the north.

ACK IN MY OFFICE, I sweep the shards of glass from my desk into the wastebasket at my feet. I sit down and think of the nature of my imagined confession:
Bless me, Father, for I have sinned.
How long has it been since your last confession?
There has never been a last confession.
What have you to confess, my son?
I confess that I have made myself a vessel of the will. I confess that I have taken up the metaphor of stars.

Yes, the metaphor of stars. For if the Leader had depended only upon himself, then his success would have been as limited as his person, and his person was supremely limited. I remember that when I saw him the first time in a small street café, I could not see this stooped, slight form hunched rather piggishly over his stein of lager as emblematic of the future. He had rounded shoulders that drooped pathetically under the weight of his military jacket; slick, black hair that poured across his smooth, undistinguished forehead like spilled ink; strange, Moorish eyes that protruded slightly from their oval sockets; a long broad nose, blunted at the end and set within flat, featureless cheeks that curved downward to form a small, trembling double chin; thin lips that arched neither up nor down but rested upon each other in a straight, severe slit, as if sliced by a straight razor; a close-cropped, squared, Chaplinesque mustache whose oddity seemed to blur the surrounding face.

And so it could not have been the Leader. Not for me. By the millions, others trembled at his voice. By the millions, women wept at the sight of him. But not me, not Langhof, the stalwart boy. For me he was never more than a crude parody of what he thought himself to be, a posturing little hysteric who somehow managed to vitalize the inert mindlessness that surrounded him. Never for a single moment did I think him to be anything but what he was.

For me, it was the stars.

The boy stood in the park, watching his blue-eyed inamorata rush from him with something of himself still dangling in her hand. For a moment he felt the wind blow through him, stirring leaves and ashes. Then he began to gather himself together. He was unwilling to go home, unwilling to eat his mother's charred strudel or smell the raw meat on his recently acquired stepfather's soiled shirt. So he began to walk, and the village that was his neighborhood began to appear to him as the city it really was — a swell of grime and noise, a raw carcinoma growing beside a slow, pestilential river. As he walked, his eyes widened in a detestation so intense he could feel its naked energy in his blood. He conceived a larval hatred for everything that surrounded him: for gaudy lights blinking in hideous pinks and blues as the crackling traffic prowled the streets like huge, iron insects; for the numberless whores with rings of kohl about their eyes flirting with the French foreigners; for the jazz bands hurling strident tones and the colored singers wailing through cigar smoke in darkened cabarets; for the fat, smiling provincials and legless beggars, and the gay blades sporting wrinkled spats; for spike-heeled shoes and lacquered fingernails; for the red-brick burlesque palaces that squatted along the boulevard; for the men who danced with men, and the laughter in that knotted crowd; for the old women snoring in their windows and the drunken soldiers pissing in the alleyways; for the aroma of champagne mixed with sludge; for all the books that fanned the flames of all about him; and for all the politicians who soar above the fumes.

It is difficult to imagine a repulsion more pure than that of our hero as he walked the streets alone. It is difficult to imagine how he came to associate all that he saw with filth and grime.

Ah, so *that's* the meaning of our tale: No one can guess what winds may blow within a devastated boy. Our little teenage hero, bereft of his first love, sees the sordidness of life, as all artists must eventually see it, and from that awareness he quite innocently surmises that a great purification must take place; this, in turn, leads him to accept those deranged notions that fluttered about the Leader's mind. Hence, many years later, the Camp. Ah yes, it's all quite clear now.

But it is not.

For although the realities of man's befuddled life repelled our hero, the eccentricities of the Leader's ideology did not attract him. He stood between a broken world and the maniacal schemes that claimed authority and competence to rebuild it. He could not accept the one any more than he could the other. And at that moment — at least figuratively — he looked up, and saw the stars.

• • •

"Was that Don Camillo?"

I look up from my desk. It is Dr. Ludtz who, in his anxiety, failed to knock at my door.

"Yes, it was."

"What did he want?"

"The usual. He always comes before one of El Presidente's visits. You know that, Dr. Ludtz. He merely wants to make sure that proper arrangements have been made."

The tension in Dr. Ludtz's face dissolves. "And was he satisfied?"

"Quite satisfied."

"Did you tell him about the red and orange motif?"

"I'm sorry, no. He inquired about you."

"Inquired? What do you mean, inquired?"

"As to your health."

"What about my health?"

I smile. "Really, Dr. Ludtz, everything is quite at ease. You don't need to disturb yourself."

"All right," Dr. Ludtz stammers breathlessly. "If you say so."

"Everything is quite all right."

"Good, good," Dr. Ludtz says. He does not move. For a moment he seems in a trance.

"Are you all right, Dr. Ludtz?"

Dr. Ludtz shakes his head. "No. No, I'm not. I think I have a slight fever. It seems to have come upon me rather suddenly."

"Have you checked it?"

Dr. Ludtz looks slightly embarrassed. "I tried. But — I don't know how it happened — I broke the thermometer. I dropped it. I'm a little shaky, I suppose."

He is sweating more profusely than usual. His shirt looks as if it has been dipped in drool. "Let me check it," I tell him.

Dr. Ludtz steps over to me. I take a thermometer from the black bag that sits beside my desk. "Here, put it in your mouth."

He takes the thermometer and places it under his tongue. In the Camp, I once saw him holding the brain of a three-year-old boy in his hands, lifting it toward the light. On the table, the boy's eyes had plopped into the hollow of his skull like egg yolks.

I take the thermometer from Dr. Ludtz's mouth and look at it. "You have a slight fever, Doctor."

"Do I?" Dr. Ludtz says worriedly. "I thought so."

"Very slight, that's all."

"But why? What do you suppose it is?"

"Perhaps a virus," I say casually. "I wouldn't be overly concerned."

Dr. Ludtz glances apprehensively at his prickly monument. The grasses are gnawing at its base.

"Really, Doctor," I tell him, "there is no cause to be

alarmed. You know how these things come and go." I smile. "Perhaps it's the season. Even the orchids are unwell."

Dr. Ludtz turns to me. "The orchids?"

"A blight has afflicted them."

"Frankly, it's not the orchids that concern me, Doctor," Dr. Ludtz says. He is slightly irritated. "Men are not flowers, you know."

"True."

Dr. Ludtz wipes his brow anxiously. "I wouldn't want to be ill during El Presidente's visit. He might take it as a slight. You know how he is about things like that. He might become rather offended."

"If you are ill, I will explain it to him."

Dr. Ludtz laughs. "He is not a man for explanations, Doctor. He could easily get the wrong idea. He could take it as . . . I don't know . . . as an insult, a personal insult."

"And do what?"

Dr. Ludtz looks at me knowingly. "You know what. I don't have to tell you."

"He will not send you home, Dr. Ludtz."

"How do you know?"

"Because he wants the diamonds."

"But it's you who have the diamonds, not me."

"I would not give him any if he did any harm to you."

Dr. Ludtz gazes at me beatifically. "Would you do that for me? Would you really?"

"Yes. Absolutely."

Dr. Ludtz grabs my hand and squeezes it gratefully. "Much thanks, Dr. Langhof. I can't tell you what that means to me."

I ease my hand from his grasp. "Go to bed, Dr. Ludtz. Take care of yourself. What would I do in this place without you?"

Dr. Ludtz stares at me, transfixed. "Dr. Langhof, I had no idea that . . . that . . ." He is practically in tears.

"Go now. Get some sleep."

"Yes, of course," Dr. Ludtz says. He starts to move toward the door.

"I will be up to check on you this evening," I tell him.

"Oh, that would be fine, Dr. Langhof. Thank you so very much."

I watch as Dr. Ludtz walks away. He moves heavily, something infinitely curious washed up out of time like a bone from the sludge-pit, strange in shape and texture, belonging to no known creature, a small particle of mystery floating in a galaxy of crime.

FEAR IS a great constrictor. In his terror of the fever and what it might portend, Dr. Ludtz mires his mind in the rudiments of the physical. It is in the nature of illness to reduce the parameters of one's world to a tight little knot of injury. Nothing contracts the self into a small, aching center of restricted consciousness more than a sudden assault upon the integrity of health. The I that is not in pain, the I that is not afraid may follow the ballerina in her flight, may feel the swell of symphonies, may soar along the glimmering rim of verse. But once under assault, once in the grip of terror, the I draws in upon itself in a horrible deflation of sense and understanding. I know this to be true because I am a doctor, and my becoming one had to do with stars.

After his dismal march through the workings of the city, the boy found himself in the park once again. Though weary, he still resisted the idea of going home. He sat down on a bench, stretched his legs before him, and looked up at the sky. And there they were, the stars. Above all else, they seemed to him immensely clean. In his tortured brain he tried to think of something in his earthbound existence that might bear some relationship to this shining cleanliness, this perfect radiance. Nothing appeared. He waited. The stars were silent overhead, as, of course, he fully expected them to be. And so, in the end, he left the park with no grand vision. But that does not mean that he left it with nothing at all. For somewhere during those moments as he sat mournfully watching the sky, the process began that ultimately fused two ideas in his mind: one concerning the workings of the physical universe and the other concerning the workings of man. The thought was simple enough: that man only approached the beauty and clarity of the physical order when he himself studied that order; that is, in the practice of scientific investigation. Later he would find the nature of man's disorder in the metaphor of disease, and that would lead him to what he fully expected to be his life's work: hygienic research. His dream was to discover the secret formula of health, to comprehend the very roots of malady, to touch the darkest pits of sickness, and then to cauterize them until they blazed visible before him.

. . .

"And so you want to be a doctor, Herr Langhof?" Dr. Trottman asked.

Langhof sat in the book-lined office of the powerful and decisive Dr. Trottman, his hands turning waxy in his lap. "Yes, Dr. Trottman," he said.

"You don't need to be nervous, Herr Langhof," Dr. Trottman said softly. "This little interview is not an inquisition."

"Thank you, sir."

Dr. Trottman stared at the curriculum vitae of our hero as if it were a mysterious specimen from the tropics. "Quite an impressive record."

"Thank you, sir."

"You must have applied yourself with great vigor to achieve such distinction in the gymnasium."

"I am a dedicated student," Langhof said, hoping he did not sound haughty or self-serving.

"Yes, I can see that," Dr. Trottman said. He looked up from his desk, his small eyes twinkling energetically through the lenses of his glasses. "Tell me, then — why this determination to be a doctor?"

"I have been pursuing this goal for quite some time."

"That's obvious. But why?"

"I am . . . simply . . . it is simply my greatest interest."

Dr. Trottman squinted. "And what area of medicine interests you most, Herr Langhof?"

"Hygiene, sir."

Dr. Trottman looked surprised. "Hygiene? May I ask why?"

Langhof cleared his throat. "Well, as you know, Dr. Trottman, the history of medicine suggests that more improvement has been brought about by hygienic changes than through all the artifice of medical science."

"Artifice?"

"I meant no disrespect in using that word, I assure you, Doctor."

"Then am I to infer from your remarks, Herr Langhof, that you are more interested in pursuing medical research than in private practice?"

"I would like a private practice as well, of course, Dr. Trottman. But, yes, research is very important to me."

Dr. Trottman studied the young man carefully. "What is your . . . background, Herr Langhof?"

"Background?"

"Background," Dr. Trottman repeated without elaboration.

"Well, my father was a lawyer. My mother was . . . well . . . my mother did nothing."

"No doctors or scientists in your family history, then?"

"I'm afraid not, Dr. Trottman."

"How about government service?"

"Nothing above the rank of civil servant," Langhof said. He had never so pointedly felt the poverty of his history.

Dr. Trottman nodded and glanced again at the papers on his desk. "You have no acquaintance with a large university, I take it?"

"I'm afraid not."

Dr. Trottman continued to peruse the papers on his desk.

"If I may say so, Dr. Trottman," Langhof said, "it is precisely such an acquaintanceship that I am seeking here."

Dr. Trottman looked up and smiled. "Very good, then, Herr Langhof. I shall recommend you for admission. Your record demonstrates great ability. I trust you will never allow yourself to be swayed from your purposes."

And so the stiff little knight who had stared at the stars in the lonely park had found that particular star to which he wished to attach himself. Science, the study of which was allied in his mind to a vision of perfection — a sense that once all things had been made clear, they would also be made clean.

After years have passed, after the stench that rose above the Camp has been blown into the stratosphere, after the trees rooted in the corpses have come to full flower, after a thousand rains have washed the caked ash from the grasses, there will come singers to tell us what it was. They will say that only those who yearn for the extravagantly good can commit the extravagantly evil. With such illogic, romance shall build its symphony again, shading the lines between act and intent, hovering over the stacked corpses that weighed the lorries down, presiding over the paradise of hell with angel's wings, sifting it through the prism of their verse, sniffing in the noxious breezes that befouled the Camp some hint of misdirected good, for poetry is not a scalpel, but a veil.

I turn to the side and catch Juan in my eye. He is opening the door of the greenhouse where the orchids languish. During the day he will massage the petals gently between thumb and forefinger, stroking the stems and moistening the leaves with his saliva. He resides on the outer rim of inquiry, vaguely praying to niggling gods or practicing occult arts. Childlike, with a child's faith and dread, he pursues the orchid's blight with chants and oblations, a science that denies science, a magician's tautology. He believes in his art as he believes in the evil force that stretches its rubbery wings around the globe. His is the intoxicated goodness of the supremely misinformed.

In the medical school I became informed. I learned the colors of liver, pancreas, lung. I learned to chart the brain and extract the spleen. I palpated heart, bowels, kidneys. I twirled meters of intestines in my fingers, scrutinized liters of blood, scraped bones and muscles, severed tendons, cauterized moles, threaded together acres of broken skin. And still later I learned to let frostbite and malnutrition and dysentery go. I learned that green triangles indicate criminal patients and red triangles political ones. I learned the peace of phenol and the sleep of chloroform.

But that was yet to come. For now, the nervous applicant bowed with exaggerated formality to Dr. Trottman.

"Thank you, sir. I am honored," Langhof said.

Dr. Trottman rose. "Herr Langhof, a final inquiry, if you don't mind."

"Of course."

"Have you allied yourself to the Party?"

"To be truthful, Dr. Trottman, I'm not terribly interested in politics."

Dr. Trottman smiled indulgently. "Scientists soar above political strife, is that it?"

"No, sir. It's just that my personal interests are not very political."

Dr. Trottman did not seem disturbed. "I understand, Herr Langhof, believe me. But whether you like it or not, these are intensely political times, as you must recognize yourself."

"Yes, sir."

"My point here is not necessarily a political one, however."

"I'm afraid I don't understand, Doctor."

"Simply this. Think of your career. That is my point. The research you intend to pursue in the future will almost certainly reside within the auspices of the state. I'm not suggesting that it is absolutely necessary, but those who have already made connections with the new regime will, I think it's fair to say, be given precedence in terms of appointment. This sort of thing is unavoidable, I'm afraid. Simply one of the realities of the world, Herr Langhof. I'm merely being realistic. Do you understand my concern?"

"Yes, Dr. Trottman," Langhof said, "I appreciate your concern."

"Think about it, then," Dr. Trottman said. "I assure you that your current attitude will not affect your admission into the medical school. It's later on, after graduation, that concerns me and, I think, should concern you."

"Yes, I see. Thank you, sir."

Dr. Trottman offered his hand. "Well, in any case, welcome to the university community."

"Thank you, Dr. Trottman."

Langhof walked out of Dr. Trottman's office. Evening had fallen. The city lights were alive and winking. A small, grainy snow had begun to fall, like pellets, bluish white, into the city's web of neon light.

IF YOU HAD BEEN there you would know the historical dimensions of the I. You would know that teleology begins with satisfaction and crumbles as it crumbles, that it is built upon the swollen hump of a full stomach and that need sucks it down like a collapsing bellows. You would know that the tailor will not forsake his shop, nor the actor his role; that the dentist will not give up his practice, nor the teacher his classes, nor the architect his plans, nor the writer his latest work of art; that the farmer will not avoid his fields, nor the painter his canvas; that the musician will not unstring his violin, the policeman forget his keys, or the shopkeeper lay waste his goods; that these and millions of others will not skip a beat in the maintenance of their quotidian affairs merely because the world is going up in smoke.

This is the catastrophe of the I, that through it we are rooted in place, nailed to professions and careers. Imprisoned in the I, we clothe ourselves in the robes of predictability, cling to our routine like insects on a floating leaf, hold with battered claws to whatever is familiar, and, above all, refuse to see the world even for one moment through a wall of flame.

And so it was the I, the ambitious medical student bent upon the road of science — anxious for his laboratory and his appointment, made whole by a thousand acquisitions, and immersed in the glories of hygiene — who pondered the generous words of the illustrious Dr. Trottman.

In the world beyond his little room a million torches flickered in parade, while drums and bugles swelled in the chorus of the Coming Order. All was to be made clean. All was to be made pure. This was the voice of the future. And yet, the anxious hygienist remained curiously impervious to the rhetoric that roared around him. Having gained some sense of the bestial from his mother's mutterings and his stepfather's oily fingers, the fervent student held back from final commitment. Although he listened carefully to the speeches of the Minister of Light and even felt a little tingle of nationalist pride from time to time, still the raging voice and hysterical gesticulation of the Minister struck our hero as insufferably melodramatic. Even worse were the ravings of the Minister of Biology, with his ridiculous, medieval calculations of the width of vermin noses. This was not science. This was politics. And it was between these two huge stones that the ambitious student felt himself to be inescapably wedged. Without politics there could be no opportunity for science. In order to hold forth the pure light of inquiry, he would have to pass through the net of political conformity.

And so our hero stood by the window and watched the world go by. He saw the fat little burghers strap on sleek black pistols and march out into the storm. He saw the red-robed judges bend to the new dimensions of the law. He saw writers reorient their words and poets transform their songs. He saw bakers make cakes in the shape of the Leader's twisted symbol, and painters regenerate their canvases with flags. In this arena, the little gladiator made his choice.

"Please come in, Herr Langhof," Dr. Trottman said.

"Thank you, sir."

"Sit down, won't you?"

The first-year medical student sat down and crossed his legs primly.

"What can I do for you?" Dr. Trottman asked.

"I've been thinking about things for the past few months."

"Really? What things?"

"Our first conversation. The one we had before I was admitted. I've been thinking quite a lot about that."

Dr. Trottman nodded. "Yes, I remember. And have you come to some decision?"

"I think that you were right, Dr. Trottman," Langhof said. "One cannot divorce himself from the great things happening around him."

Dr. Trottman smiled amiably. "Quite true, Herr Langhof."

Langhof shifted slightly in his seat. "My point, Dr. Trottman, is that now I would like to ally myself more closely to Nation and People." He cleared his throat. "Of course, I don't agree with every aspect of the new regime."

"No one does, of course."

"Yes. Quite right."

"How would you like this alliance to be made, Herr Langhof?"

"I think my best position would be in the Special Section," Langhof said boldly.

Dr. Trottman's eyes widened. "Special Section? That is somewhat more than mere alliance."

"I am aware of that."

"The Special Section is a very elite organization, Herr Langhof. Are you aware of that?"

"Yes, sir."

"I don't doubt the seriousness of your commitment. Believe me, I don't doubt it. But you see, Herr Langhof, you were never in the Youth Group, isn't that right?"

"Yes, sir."

"Well, in most cases only former members of the Youth Group can be considered for the Special Section."

"I had hoped that you might recommend me, Dr. Trottman. I realize that I have been somewhat negligent in the past. I admit that politics up until now has played only a peripheral part in my life. But now I wish to correct that lapse."

"I see."

"Do you think it possible for me to find a place in the Special Section?"

Dr. Trottman stared thoughtfully over the upper rim of his glasses. "Perhaps."

"That is all I can ask."

"It is quite a lot," Dr. Trottman said curtly.

"I don't mean to be arrogant in my request, Doctor. It's simply that I am anxious to perform what I now see clearly to be my duty."

"I'm not offended by your arrogance," Dr. Trottman said. He smiled. "You are a man of great ability. And you know it. You also know that small matters should not stand in the way of your advancement. That is not arrogance, my dear Langhof, that is virtue."

"Thank you, sir."

Dr. Trottman stood up. "Be assured that I will do what I can for you."

The man of great ability rose quickly to his feet. "I am greatly in your debt, Dr. Trottman."

Dr. Trottman shook his head resolutely. "You are in no one's debt, Herr Langhof," he said. "The world is changing. There is no place for false modesty, for slave moralities. Most certainly, you will learn this in the Special Section."

"I look forward to it."

"The eyes of the world are upon us," Dr. Trottman said stentoriously. "But our eyes are on the stars."

"You will never have cause to regret doing this for me," Langhof said.

"I never expect to, Herr Langhof," Dr. Trottman said. He rose from behind his desk, stepped back slightly, and raised his arm rigidly in salute.

Langhof stood transfixed, not with wonder or admiration, but with astonishment. For the gesture, so melodramatic, so ridiculously perfervid, so quintessentially burlesque, was made with such complete seriousness by Dr. Trottman that it was all the ambitious student could do to keep from laughing.

But Dr. Trottman stood completely still, his eyes staring hotly at Langhof. Finally our hero grasped what was expected of him. He brought himself to his full height, clicked his heels together and, as he had seen the others do, raised his arm. They stood for a moment facing each other, the tips of their fingers stretched out to make a triumphal arch over Dr. Trottman's littered desk.

"You will be hearing from me, Herr Langhof," Dr. Trottman said as he let his arm fall slowly to his side. "I trust the news, when it comes, will be favorable."

"Thank you, sir."

"Good day."

"Good day, sir."

And then Langhof, our hero, turned smartly toward the door and marched out, closing it behind him. In the hallway he did not tremble as he had that evening in the park when Anna fled away. Nor did he hear music, martial or otherwise. He did not see a vision of perfect order or fall upon his knees, a stricken, sweating Saul of Tarsus. He did not goose-step down the hall, but merely turned slowly, strolling past the darkened professorial offices with a little smile playing on his lips. And if any thought came to him at all, it was of the laughable gullibility of people, even quite intelligent people like Dr. Trottman. How easy it seemed to charm and beguile them, to use the insufferable silliness of the times and yet rise above it all, trip lightly over it — even as he now tripped down the hall with perfect insouciance.

HERE IN THE REPUBLIC there is much insouciance. In the village square the men and women leap in a furious guaracha, kicking yellow dust into each other's eyes. In the bars, the old men lean toward the candles and drink mescal down to the worm while the young ones nod drowsily outside the brothel door. And in the capital, the ermine-coated and bejeweled wives of the ministers of state sit in steamy halls and watch endless fashion shows with strained and calculating faces.

And yet, from my verandah I can see the foothills of the mountainous northern provinces, a place where, it is said, humor still exists in the form of low-minded jokes about El Presidente. Huddled around their dying fires, the insurrectionists talk of El Presidente's teeth. It is said that they are made of gold and that he has inserted a small homing device to assure their quick recovery, should anyone be fool enough to steal them. In the northern provinces, every part of El Presidente's body comes in for ridicule. There is much talk of a silver rectum that makes the sound of a cash register when El Presidente makes his toilet. It is said that his urine is tested by a chemical refinery built exclusively for that purpose and that the four-word motto of the Republic has been inscribed on the lead plate in his head. Just beneath the stitched scalp, it

reads in elegant script: FREEDOM OBEDIENCE COUNTRY VUL-
GARITY.

In the far hills of the northern provinces they laugh like
jackals in the blinding heat. They laugh as they flip the
sticky pages of Casamira's *Official History*. They laugh
at the mosquitoes drowning in their coffee. They laugh
at fever, vomiting, and infection. They laugh because it is
absurd to laugh, and find their laughter strange as orchids
growing on the moon.

In the Camp, they laughed at the milky soup and rotten
bread. They laughed at the striped uniforms and the blue
tattoos. They laughed at prayer and mourning. They
laughed at the ridiculousness of their ever being born. They
laughed, while they had strength to laugh, at the slough
of their despair.

And in the small amphitheater that the Special Section
used for scientific displays, they laughed.

The dedicated hygienist could barely keep from smiling
himself at the pitiful figure in the loose-fitting gray smock
who stood before the two officers while the doctor poked
at his ears and nose and legs with a thin wooden pointer.

"One has only to observe a member of the vermin race
in order to understand their inferiority," the doctor said
matter-of-factly. He turned the cringing figure before him
slowly around, then told the two officers to remove the
smock. They stepped forward and pulled it over the vermin's head so that he stood naked except for a wrinkled
loincloth.

"There, now," the doctor said. He looked up at the rows
of silent, uniformed Special Section initiates. "All of you,
observe for a moment."

They observed the figure as the doctor had commanded.
Some of them scratched short entries into their notebooks.
Others grinned humorously and whispered into each other's
ears.

Rudolf Schoen leaned toward Langhof. "What do you
make of that?" he asked lightly.

Langhof pretended to nod thoughtfully. "Interesting,"
he said.

Below them, the interesting specimen of the vermin race made a weak attempt to wrap his arms around himself, but the doctor slapped at him lightly and the arms returned to their positions at his sides.

"Now," the doctor said, "let me make a few observations of my own." He raised the pointer slowly up from the vermin's foot to his waist. "Note the shortness of the legs and their spindly construction."

A few of the students nodded appreciatively and scratched their chins.

"Observe the length of the legs as compared to the trunk," the doctor went on. "As you can see, they are short in comparison. Thus, whereas the waist should be the approximate midpoint between the top of the skull and the bottom of the foot, here we have a definite and unmistakable disproportion."

Langhof suppressed a smile. This was not science. This was aesthetics.

"Now," the doctor continued, "we must concern ourselves, always concern ourselves, with the question of proportion. Proportion is the key, gentlemen. Arms that are too long appear to us as apeish. It is the same with legs, such as these, that are too short." He watched the students. "What are we to gather from this?"

Schoen reluctantly raised his hand.

"Yes?" the doctor asked.

"This disproportion is a sign of degeneracy," Schoen said.

The doctor shook his head. "No. Not at all. Degeneracy would suggest that people characterized by such disproportion once occupied a higher position in the hagiology of race, a position from which they somehow degenerated. No, gentlemen, this is not a case of degeneracy, but a case of . . . arrested development."

The vermin stared straight ahead, his eyes avoiding the gaze of the students.

Schoen leaned toward Langhof's ear. "This is an excellent way to present the facts," he whispered.

Below, the human orrery bent his knees, raised his arms, flared his nostrils on command as the doctor moved through the cosmology of race.

"It is so clear!" Schoen said enthusiastically. "I never thought it could be demonstrated so clearly."

Langhof's head snapped around. "Be quiet, Schoen," he hissed.

Sitting here now on my verandah, as I watch the river take its course, I wonder if it was cruel to speak so curtly to the imbecile Schoen. Here in the Republic — except of course in the northern provinces and certain chambers within the district prisons — no one speaks cruelly to anyone. The people are numbed by constant allusions to their greatness, their nobility, their destiny. El Presidente infuses the nation with grandeur while, on a lesser scale, Esperanza brings the consciousness of God to bear on the villagers' running sores. Harmless illusions. Comforting illusions. In the Camp we made a factory of such ideas and piped our delusions up four square chimneys.

Schoen, rebuked, turned quickly away and held his eyes firmly on the scientific proof coming to a close at the front of the amphitheater.

"Well, gentlemen," the doctor said, "I hope this presentation has been of help to you. It is important that these matters be kept in mind." He paused, watching the students. "Are there any questions?"

The room was silent.

"Very well, then," the doctor said. He took his notes from the lectern and tucked them snugly under his arm. Then he turned, his eyes catching those of the vermin who stood motionlessly before him. And at that moment, something of the past, something of a nobler and kinder world rose quite accidentally within him, odd and out of place, astonishing as an open book on a hangman's scaffold. It was a simple gesture: he bowed quickly to the vermin, in the same courtly way with which he might have excused himself from a men's club. "Thank you," he said.

The vermin stared at him, his eyes taking on a certain incomprehensible light, as if with a mere clapping of his hands he might suddenly change all of this, as if the amphitheater, the grinning, black-booted students, the contrived biology were as frail as papier-mâché, a stage set for some outlandish farce upon which, for some perverse reason, the curtain refused to fall.

In the Royal Chapel that rests within the shadow of the Tower of London, the lords and ladies of the realm came to pray before they were executed. Victims of court intrigue, ensnared by their ambition, they yet retained a certain reverence for style. And so they came to this small, elegant chapel, dressed in their finest attire, looking like the splendid lords and ladies of the court. And here, in the Royal Chapel, they bowed their heads in futile prayer. The block stood outside the chapel door, and beside it, the executioner in his black hood. He must have heard their mutterings, must have heard the soft crinkle of the great, broad skirts as the ladies bowed, then rose, must have heard the muffled pad of their stockinged feet as they moved toward the door, then opened it to face him. At that moment he must have seen their eyes widen, then contract, as they watched his hooded head or stared at the broadaxe nestled in his arms. Did he nod to them? Did he bow? Did he perhaps say, from beneath the anonymity of the hood, "Thank you, my lady, for not detaining me too long"?

The vermin nodded politely to the doctor and stared at him, hollow-eyed. Then two officers stepped forward briskly, each taking one of the vermin's arms, and escorted him from the room.

"Please forgive my rudeness," Schoen said to Langhof in that groveling manner of his.

Langhof watched the vermin disappear behind the door at the front of the room. The doctor remained near his lectern, his eyes perusing a large chart upon which the human skeleton was displayed.

Doubtless, there are certain moments in certain human lives when the intelligence, formerly scattered and disconnected, suddenly forms itself into a thin, firm blade and begins the process of ripping into all the vagaries and seductions that surround it. Proust bites into a madeleine or stumbles on uneven paving stones, and the world shifts into focus. A man is walking with his child, the child lurches from the curb in front of a passing automobile, and suddenly the man sees each person's isolation, each person's helplessness, sees the mechanics of faith and the structure of purpose dissolve before his eyes. There was nothing to seize the child or swerve the car. Nothing. Only the impact of matter against matter, a child's head against a headlight; only metal moving at a certain velocity toward the delicate tissue of brain and bone. At such a moment, even the least lonely feels utterly alone. What is left is only the sullen recognition and an overwhelming sadness.

But was it this emasculating sadness that Langhof felt as he stood among his fellows and watched the vermin disappear behind the great oak door of the amphitheater?

No. Not sadness. Not pity. Only the terror that comes with the first, awesome comprehension of our infinite capacity for contradictions: the hard, irreducible fact that a man could humiliate another man with a wooden pointer and yet retain the sense of high civility that decrees a polite bow and a crisp "Thank you" at the end of the display. It seemed to Langhof that a creature capable of such ideological gymnastics was truly fearful. For if the Special Section doctor was capable of such ambidexterousness, who else might be capable of it? Schoen? Of course. Trottman? Yes. But what about Goethe? Beethoven? The scientist in our hero affirmed the undeniable, that it is a universal capacity. Nor was it only a question of ignorance. Schoen might be overwhelmed by the imbecilic biology of the regime, but no one, it seemed to Langhof, could claim immunity from this greater lunacy.

Given this new recognition, what was our frightened philosopher to do? Perhaps he could announce his discovery — run about in the streets, grab astonished pedestrians by their shirt collars, shake them, shout in their faces,

"Can't you see? It's not safe to be in this world! It's not safe to live among us! Men are not only stupid, they are inconsistent!" How trite an observation, how comic. How horrible its implications.

What, then, did our hero of the intellect do with this frightening new intelligence?

Nothing. Except to pursue the science of hygiene and carefully brush the twin lightning bolts on his uniform lapel.

FATHER MARTÍNEZ lightly brushes the shoulder of his cassock as he creaks up the stairs of my verandah. At the top he leans on a briar cane that he hopes will someday be an archbishop's crosier. He smiles. "These stairs are becoming more difficult for me, it seems."

I point to the chair opposite me. "Rest yourself, Father."

Father Martínez struggles over to the chair and eases himself into it. A rim of dust coats his upper lip like a faint, brown mustache. "I hope I find you well, Don Pedro," he says.

"Yes."

"Good, good," Father Martínez says. He nods slowly, rhythmically, like the tolling of a bell. He watches me for a moment but says nothing. What he wishes to know he will never ask: How did you end up in the Camp? What did you see? Dear God, what did you do?

The silence grows awkward and he breaks it. "How is Dr. Ludtz? I haven't had the pleasure of seeing him in quite some time."

"He has a slight fever, I'm afraid."

"Fever, yes," Father Martínez says. "It's going around the whole province." He takes his shovel hat and places it on his lap. There is only a hint of gray in his hair, for he is not an old man, though he would like to be one. For him, the idea of the aging, kindly priest serves as the perfect symbol of holiness. He wishes to age into saintliness, to grow ancient in the jungle, so that his long years of selflessness and humility might be noticed by his papal superiors.

"You are well, Father?" I ask.

"Me? Yes, of course."

"I'm glad to hear it."

"Of course, the fever is rampant in the village. We've even had some problems with hallucinations. The fever causes them, I suppose."

"Nothing that can't be handled, I hope."

Father Martínez shakes his head. "No, nothing we can't handle. A few women claimed they saw curious visions. Devils, that sort of thing. But nothing serious, Don Pedro."

"Would you like some refreshment, Father?"

"No, thank you, Don Pedro. I don't have long to stay." He watches me again, the silence lengthening. "Actually, I've come on a mission of sorts," he says after a moment.

"A mission?"

"Yes," Father Martínez says. "And a successful one, I hope."

"What sort of mission, Father?"

He looks at me worriedly. "Well, it has to do with the orphanage, Don Pedro."

"I see."

"You know, the one in the village," Father Martínez explains unnecessarily. He smiles. "You've seen it. Your generous gifts helped to build it, if you recall."

"Is something wrong?"

"I'm afraid so, Don Pedro," Father Martínez says sadly. "And, as always, it has to do with money. The fact is, we've run out of money to buy medicine."

"I understand," I tell him. He comes to me often with his requests, believing that I cannot turn him down because my life is steeped in crime. And so I must give in a spirit of atonement, must give money like a palmer's withered leaves.

"The situation has become quite serious, Don Pedro," Father Martínez adds.

"I'm sorry to hear it."

"I knew you would be."

"How much do you need, Father?"

Father Martínez almost flinches at the directness of my question. For people to offer so readily diminishes the laboriousness of his labor, and therefore the glory of his martyrdom.

"Well..." he stammers, "the exact figure .I don't know."

"An approximation, then."

He gives me a paltry estimate. He could ask for many times more, but that would make his periodic trips unnecessary. Although he wants the money I can give him, he wants my confession more, and he believes that ultimately, on one of his little sorties against the obstinacy of my soul, I will break down and give it to him.

I offer three times the figure he has named. "I hope this will keep you in medicine for quite some time, Father," I tell him.

Father Martínez's eyes widen. "So much, Don Pedro! So generous! Please, I could not accept such a large amount."

"I am an old man, Father, what do I need it for?"

Father Martínez looks at me sorrowfully. If I should die, he would be denied the only really noteworthy conversion in El Caliz. "Really, it is too much, Don Pedro."

"Take it with my blessing, Father."

"With great thanks, Don Pedro," Father Martínez says finally, and with great disappointment.

"I hope it will be of help, Father."

"Much help, thank you, Don Pedro."

"Good."

Father Martínez does not move. He looks as if something has been skillfully stolen from him.

"Is there something else you wanted, Father?"

Father Martínez looks at me. His hands move nervously in his lap, like fish flopping about. "Don Pedro," he begins cautiously, "I wonder if you would ever consider coming to the parish church?"

I feel something unspeakably cold skating in my blood. "For what purpose, Father?"

Father Martínez blinks rapidly. "Purpose, Don Pedro?"

"For what purpose should I come?"

"Well, I ... for your own ..."

"What?"

"Betterment, Don Pedro."

"It is a long trip for an old man, Father," I tell him. For years they have swarmed over the bloated carcass of the Republic in their black soutanes and dusty hats. I have seen them come and go, come and go. And some have done much goodness while they watched the jungle roll in its immemorial butchery. But all have died within the immense, consuming fog of their faith's mystification.

"The journey to the village is not so bad, Don Pedro," Father Martínez says lightly. "I make it quite often, as you must know."

"You are not old, Father."

Father Martínez looks at me as if I have insulted him. "True," he says, reluctantly giving in to the distance between himself and the grace of age. He takes a deep breath. "Well, it was only a suggestion."

"One that I appreciate, Father," I tell him.

Father Martínez's face brightens: "I'm told that you are a friend of the Archbishop."

"You are misinformed, I'm afraid."

Father Martínez's smile collapses. "Really? Misinformed? I'm sorry. I had heard that you and His Eminence were quite close."

"Nothing to be sorry about, Father," I tell him. "There are many false stories about me in El Caliz."

Father Martínez watches me curiously, trying to determine which of the many stories he must have heard about me are true. "Well," he says, "since you are the only European in El Caliz, I suppose that ..."

"Yes. That must explain the stories, Father."

Father Martínez smiles weakly. "I'm sure it does, Don Pedro."

"I'll send Juan with my offering tomorrow, Father," I tell him.

"The children will be most grateful, Don Pedro," Father Martínez says. "Perhaps we could give you something as an act of appreciation."

"That is unnecessary, Father."

"But only as a gesture, Don Pedro."

"Let them run and play, Father. Let them be healthy. That will be their gift to me."

"But perhaps I could have them make something for you," Father Martínez insists.

If they made something for me, then he would be required to bring it to me. This is what he wants. "No, Father," I tell him firmly, "I will not accept any gifts from the children."

"Then from me, Don Pedro?"

"No."

He looks at me as if I have slipped a blade between his ribs. "As you wish, Don Pedro," he says softly, lowering his eyes. He is a master of the aggrieved gesture.

"If you require anything else, Father, please let me know."

Father Martínez raises his eyes. "Thank you, Don Pedro." He pauses, watching me. "And if you ever require anything from me — any of my services — I hope that you will also let me know."

I smile. "I will, Father."

Father Martínez glances at the ridges in the distance. "The sun will be setting soon."

"Yes."

"I'd better get back to the village before dark."

"I understand."

Father Martínez rises from his chair. "The night is comforting, don't you think?"

"No."

Father Martínez looks at me with a mildly fearful expression, as if I were some relic from a torture chamber. "But at least there's sleep," he says.

I rise and offer my hand. "Let me know if I can be of any assistance to you, Father. As you can see, I have much to share."

"Thank you, Don Pedro," Father Martínez says. He turns toward the stairs.

"I hope you have a safe journey," I tell him.

Father Martínez glances over his shoulder quickly, as if a threat is hidden in my remark. "Safe? Oh, yes. Well, I'm sure I'll be fine."

"Good evening, Father."

"Good evening, Don Pedro."

He makes his way down the stairs, stooping slightly over his cane, assuming the bent attitude of the holy old man. At the bottom of the stairs he turns toward me. "Thank you so very much, Don Pedro," he says.

"De nada."

He offers me a telling look that he hopes will somehow sear my soul, somehow raise it to life again.

"It will be evening soon, Father," I tell him. "Your children are waiting for you."

The pointed look recoils into his face and something like muted resentment takes its place. "Yes, I must go," he says. "Give my best to Dr. Ludtz."

"I will, Father."

He turns quickly and walks away, a small wind slightly lifting the hem of his skirt.

There was a time when I was tempted to make my way down to the little mud cathedral over which Father Martínez now presides. I was tempted, so very tempted, to lay prone before the altar, my arms outstretched in an attitude of crucifixion. There was a time when it would have been so very easy to split myself open and bathe my soul in the healing light of faith. But what would have come from so self-serving a conversation? Only the acceptance of an illusion that went no farther than myself, that animated nothing, bestowed nothing, taught nothing but the endless repetition of itself. I would have become no more than the vessel of a catechismal chant, a disembodied voice calling some great, imagined tongue down to lick my wounds. But I have come to know that mine are not the wounds that matter, and that even if they were, they are long past mending by priestly ministration delivered in a sacerdotal haze. For in the acceptance of that delusional comfort I would find my soul's repose, and in such repose the seed of yet another crime.

A T THE END of day here in the Republic, the sun drops slowly through a cloud of heat like a ruby through a tube of oil. Across the river, the wind begins its ghost waltz with the trees, pressing against them like a proud but subtle lover. There is never snow here, except, they say, in the northern provinces, where it comes only at the most telling moment, when lovers part or old men die by the window. At such times, it is said to come in huge flakes, drifting as languorously as goose down and remaining, unmeltable, until the symbol has run its course. But in El Caliz, heat is the only metaphor we have.

Juan passes below me, stooped, weary. For him, all metaphorical embellishment is reduced to the thick, dark humus of his impregnable superstitiousness. He lives utterly without benefit of subtlety, responding only to gods and demons who are wholly visible to him. They drown the fields, bake the stream beds, humiliate the orchids. They dispense blessings or maliciously withhold them. Walking through the jungle toward his home, Juan seems to merge with the engulfing brush, a perfect natural man, Rousseau's boyish dream, a simple, humble peasant who could only be accused of crime in some distant, dreamed-of world where men are expected to despise all manner of delusion.

In the Special Section, they taught us to sink all of our petty, personal illusions in the smudgy, boiling cauldron of a great one.

"Allow me to extend my personal congratulations," Dr. Trottman said. He smiled heartily. "A very distinguished record, Herr Langhof. But wait. I suppose I must address you as Dr. Langhof from now on."

The distinguished graduate allowed himself a moment of harmless banter. "That would be appropriate, I think," he said with mock haughtiness.

Dr. Trottman seized Langhof's hand and shook it vigorously. "You will bring great credit to yourself, Doctor," he said, his speech still retaining the arch formality of the professorial classes.

"That is my hope, Dr. Trottman," our hero said.

And so Peter Langhof became a doctor. Langhof, the little boy who watched impassively as the blood trickled from his father's temple, who could not stand his mother's strudel, who spoke harshly to the butcher who later became his stepfather. Langhof, who found Anna and then lost her, who stood in the park and felt the first blessing of the stars, who wished to clean himself in the study of hygiene, who loved science and distinguished himself in gymnasium, university, and medical school. Our hero Langhof, who came to manhood in the Special Section, who was given an appointment at the Institute of Hygiene and then later reassigned to a place he calls the Camp. He, the catastrophic I, who later escaped as the cannons neared, who found his way to Switzerland and then to the southern provinces of the Republic by way of boat and burro and a battered little box of diamonds. He, Langhof, our beneficent Don Pedro, who sits white-haired in the sunset of El Caliz and who speaks with admirable detachment of the unspeakable.

He, Langhof, I, who on a certain day at his new job in the Institute of Hygiene found something curious as he stared at the medical journal on his desk.

"Dietrich," he said, looking up from the open book, "come here for a moment. I want you to look at this."

The lab assistant stepped over.

Langhof pointed to a line he had underscored. "Read that."

Dietrich read the line aloud. "The livers of eighty women who had died suddenly were extracted and examined within ten minutes of their deaths. Findings may be somewhat impugned, since items were in a state of intense excitement at the moment of their deaths."

Langhof watched Dietrich's eyes. "What do you make of this?" he asked.

Dietrich looked at Langhof emptily. "What do you mean, Dr. Langhof?"

"My dear Dietrich, how do eighty women die suddenly?"

Dietrich shrugged. "How do I know? We are at war. People die suddenly. Lots of people."

"Yes. But eighty women?"

"It could happen."

"All right," Langhof said, "perhaps it could. But how is it that their livers were extracted within such a short time after their deaths?"

Dietrich shook his head. "I don't know."

"Think, Dietrich. One can hardly imagine eighty women dying suddenly in a state of intense excitement directly outside the doors of a medical laboratory."

Dietrich laughed lightly. "True, Dr. Langhof."

"Well, what would you gather from this, then?"

"That they were executed, of course," Dietrich said casually. "It's no secret that executions are taking place. My God, we're at war, after all!"

"But this is an odd thing to crop up in the medical literature, don't you think?"

"No," Dietrich said. "I'd be surprised if such studies were not being made. It's nothing new, as you know, Doctor. Medicine has always used certain circumstances to carry on research that would be impossible in peacetime."

"I suppose so," Langhof said. He motioned for Dietrich to go on about his business and then sunk his head again into the open journal.

What was he thinking? Could it have been the unthinkable? Emphatically, no. And when such references began to be sprinkled throughout the medical literature, and when the heads began to arrive upstairs at the museum, each in its own little hermetically sealed tin can, what then? Perhaps for a moment a question entered the intrepid scientist's inquiring mind. But it was not one that could be easily framed. Nor was it one that could be answered under a surgical lamp.

If you had been there, you would know that there are certain things that can only be approached indirectly, through flippancy. And so, confronted by the growing evidence of impropriety in the medical community, Langhof developed that characteristic which had so far eluded him: a sense of humor. He became the master of the quip. Seeing Dr. Friedheim marching up the hall one afternoon with one of those ubiquitous tin cans held securely under his arm, Langhof smiled. "What do you have there, Doctor," he said airily, "a new head for your totem pole?" Dr. Friedheim rushed by, aghast. On another occasion, he met Dr. Ludtz in the lavatory. He folded his arm over Ludtz's shoulder. "They say human blood cannot be washed from the skin," he whispered conspiratorially, "but I have found a lye compound that will do it." Dr. Ludtz stared at Langhof for a moment, not knowing what to say. Then he simply smiled and walked away.

For a time, as you might imagine, Langhof's sardonic remarks were regarded with great concern by the other doctors in the Institute. There was talk of his name being mentioned to those authorities whose task it was to handle such matters. But the smile on Langhof's face, the jaunty carriage of his body, and the wink that invariably accompanied his remarks assured the nervous staff that he was quite a good fellow, an excellent fellow, in fact; one who had a far better attitude about the situation than certain other colleagues who seemed to carry themselves in a perpetual crouch. God only knew what was on *their* minds. But Langhof was sufficiently assured of the value of his work to dismiss its less pleasant aspects with a wink and a laugh.

And so the catastrophic I moved through the Institute of Hygiene as if at one with all that surrounded him — with the vials of acid, the skeleton displays, the books and journals, the shelves of chemicals, the reams of paper, the stacks of tin cans smelling vaguely acrid that seemed to pile up by the hundreds in the rear alleyway. At one, humorously at one, with all of this, the good doctor joked and japed, learning the rhythm of his routine like a standup comic in some cheap nightclub: "It's cold. How cold is it? Cold enough for a freezing experiment." "It's hot. How hot is it? Hot enough to incinerate — what?" A socialist, a gypsy, a Jew, a homosexual, a communist, or any of a million other designated vermin. For the rhythm of the line, for the best laugh, what would be the funniest reply?

By this process, Langhof held to his moorings. He wrapped himself in the armor of ridicule, his old staple, but which was given added charm now by what passed in those sullen corridors for wit.

And yet, there were times when he felt a sudden, awesome dread, the sense of being propelled into the volcano's mouth on a wave of gasoline. And there were moments, later, when he wondered what might have happened to him if he had pursued these dark intimations rather than dismissing them with a mocking smile. Long after those first weeks in the Institute, Langhof walked with Ginzburg as they made their way from the main camp to the factory works. Ginzburg was chewing on a sliver of rubber band and his almost jaunty step made Langhof remember his own days at the Institute. For a moment he stopped, gently turned Ginzburg toward him, and asked: "Would it be better, do you think, if we — I mean as a species — if we had never evolved the capacity to laugh?"

HERE IN THE REPUBLIC, night falls like the collapsing of a tunnel. From my verandah I can see lights in Dr. Ludtz's cottage. It is time for my visit. I rise and as I make my way down the stairs, I can feel the bones in my joints grind against each other, sticks of dried wood making fire. At the bottom of the stairs, I hear the night birds in their revelry and I feel — I can still feel — the richness of the natural world, its miraculous abundance. In the Camp — I am coming to the Camp — this plenitude passed through a terrible crucible: greenery reduced to mud and shit; animal to louse and rat and man. And it will always seem odd to the benevolent spirit that while the smoke tumbled from the chimneytops in that near world, here in El Caliz the parrots sang above the flowers, the great kingfishers sliced the water, and the night birds flew in a world carved out of moonlight.

I tap lightly at Dr. Ludtz's door. I hear the sound of the bedsprings beneath him.

"Come in, please."

I open the door slowly. Dr. Ludtz is sitting on the bed, propped up by three pillows. His hands are under the covers.

"Good evening, Dr. Ludtz."

Dr. Ludtz smiles faintly, then takes the pistol from beneath the covers. He lays it on the nightstand. "Sorry," he says, slightly embarrassed.

"How are you? Feeling better, I hope."

Dr. Ludtz shakes his head. A ring of sweat glistens on his bald pate. "The fever has worsened, I'm afraid," he says softly.

I pull a chair over beside the bed and sit down. "Are you taking antibiotics?"

"Yes."

"Liquids?"

"Of course."

"Well, I'm sure the fever will break shortly."

Dr. Ludtz stares at me mournfully.

"Really, Doctor, I don't think there's anything to be alarmed about."

He folds his hands over the covers and squeezes them together rhythmically. "When is El Presidente due to visit us?"

"In a few days."

Dr. Ludtz glances worriedly at the ceiling. His lips tremble slightly. "I'm sure I'll be ill when he comes," he says.

"There is nothing wrong with being ill, Dr. Ludtz."

"But what if he should be offended?"

"You have nothing to fear, Doctor. You must believe me."

He does not believe me. He has lived in an atmosphere of betrayal too long to believe in anything but God and pistols.

I glance toward the windows, but they are tightly shuttered. He never allows them to be opened. "You should take a look outside," I say. "It's a lovely night."

Dr. Ludtz turns his eyes from mine. "Do you believe in hell, Dr. Langhof?"

"No. Nor heaven, either."

Dr. Ludtz looks at me with astonishment. "Really? You mean, you believe that after death there's nothing. Just oblivion?"

I smile. "Dr. Ludtz, why so morbid? Why these ridiculous questions? Surely you haven't got it into your mind that you're dying?"

"One never knows. I'm not a young man."

"You have a slight fever. Father Martínez says this same fever is spread all over the province. It is nothing to worry about. It will pass."

"I wish I had your confidence," Dr. Ludtz says. Fear is in his face. I can see it like a gray web over his features, spiders crawling in his eyes.

"You're going to be fine, Dr. Ludtz. You need rest, that's all."

"Forgive me, Doctor. Forgive my morbidity. But may I ask another favor?"

"Of course."

"I do not want to be cremated."

I try to smile. "Dr. Ludtz, really, this is unnecessary. You are upsetting yourself."

He stares at me imploringly. "Please, Dr. Langhof, promise me."

"All right. You will not be cremated."

Dr. Ludtz nods toward the closed door. "I have built a little structure, as you know. Out there. I wish to be buried near it."

"As you wish, Dr. Ludtz. But the likelihood is that you will bury me first."

"Still, at my age it pays to make plans."

"All right. I will do as you wish."

Dr. Ludtz smiles. "I suppose I'm a poor patient, Dr. Langhof. They say doctors always are."

"It's understandable."

"I'm sorry to trouble you."

"It's no trouble, Dr. Ludtz. I only wish that you would not alarm yourself."

Dr. Ludtz waves his hand wearily. "Even without the fever, there would be things to worry about." He looks at me sadly. "I suppose you've heard how things are going in the northern provinces."

"Things?"

"The rebels, Doctor."

"What about them?"

Dr. Ludtz straightens himself in the bed. "What if El Presidente should be overthrown?"

"That is most unlikely."

"But this rebellion, the one in the northern provinces. It is said to be gaining strength."

"The northern provinces are far away, Dr. Ludtz. And even if the rebels were to control them wholly, it would not interfere with El Presidente's dominion in the south."

Dr. Ludtz swabs his brow with a large cloth. "How can you be so sure?"

"Such places as the northern provinces are always weak," I tell him confidently.

"But they are sometimes successful, are they not?"

"Rarely. They rely too much on courage, Dr. Ludtz."

Dr. Ludtz's body trembles slightly. "A chill," he says fearfully. "I've been getting these periodic chills."

"It may be anxiety, Dr. Ludtz. Would you like a sedative?"

"No," Dr. Ludtz says quickly, flatly. "I don't take sedatives."

"Very well."

He appears relieved that I do not press the matter. Perhaps he thought for a moment that it was my intent to kill him. Here in the Republic, one cannot be too careful.

"Thank you for the offer," Dr. Ludtz says, regaining his calm.

I push my chair back slightly and rise. "Well, have a good night's sleep. I will look in on you in the morning."

"Yes, thank you, Dr. Langhof."

I turn, walk to the door, and open it.

"Dr. Langhof?" Dr. Ludtz calls from behind me.

I turn to face him. "Yes?"

"Do you really believe that it's just oblivion?"

"Yes."

I walk out, closing the door behind me. The night is black as a dream of death. In oblivion there will be no

color, not even blackness. But if there were a world beyond
this world, perhaps we would be reborn into it not as our
physical selves, but as the simple, irreducible essences of
what we were. The killer would be born again, not as a
man or woman, but as some perfect engine of destruction
— a pistol or an ice pick. The comedian would return only
as a laugh, the victim only as a scream. In such a world
Ludtz might be reborn as a crusty little tomb, and Langhof
as a maggot imprisoned in a tear.

I T WAS on a morning brilliant as this one that I arrived at El Caliz. The sun was rising over the ridge like a burning eye. But more than anything else, I remember the burro. I remember the way it staggered forward under my weight, its ears pinned back with the strain. It was very hot, hotter than people in temperate climates can imagine, a heat that sank into the body like a boiling liquid poured through bread. The burro must have felt this heat as I did, but it was not deterred. I had paid for it with a diamond that glinted exotically in the merchant's hand. He, the merchant, was round-faced with oily black hair and skin the color of scorched wood. He looked at the diamond and asked me what it was. When I told him, he laughed. I assured him that it was real, but he only grinned at me and said that it was pretty anyway, no matter what it really was, and that perhaps his wife might be charmed by it. And so he sold me a wheezing old burro for a jewel he thought counterfeit. The burro was gray with spots of black around the neck and down the legs. It had the face of a sad old man.

I took the reins, which dropped from the bit in the burro's mouth, and walked away. I had a small, tattered map to lead me to the property I had purchased in the capital from the dissolute and debt-ridden son of a dead patron. I had paid for it with diamonds. Diamonds and stars, the twin themes of my romance.

Not long after I arrived at El Caliz, the burro fell into decline. It coughed and wheezed, spitting up large gobs of yellow mucus. I gave it various injections, but it was hopeless. The burro was rotting from within. And so late one afternoon I lifted my pistol to its head and shot it between the eyes. It shuddered as if the world had moved beneath it, then the front legs collapsed and it dropped to the ground, blood streaming from its black nostrils. I told Juan and a few other servants to throw it into the river. They dragged it to the river bank and hoisted it into the water. I stood and watched it float away. The head and hindquarters were covered by water, so that all I could see was one swollen side bobbing slightly like a hairy gray ball. I started to turn away, but suddenly the body began to jerk and tremble. Waves of blood spread out from around the carcass, and I could see water splashing with thousands of piranha. For the one and only time in my life, I utterly lost control. I ran after the burro, ran into the water after it, firing wildly and sending up sprays of tiny, glistening fish. Waist deep in the river, I continued to fire, emptying clip after clip. The surface of the river was split by sprays of bullets, but the piranha continued at their work until the burro turned over, slowly like a sleeping man, revealing the white bones of its stripped side. My hand jerked up and I could feel the barrel of the pistol cool against my temple. At that moment, Juan leaped into the river after me and grabbed my wrist in a tight, unflinching grip. His voice seemed to come to me from down a long tunnel. "No, Don Pedro. No."

Of all our words, perhaps the most beautiful, and difficult, is *no*.

"Surely you cannot say no" was what Dr. Ludtz said to me that September day in my laboratory at the Institute of Hygiene. He looked oddly handsome in his uniform, its sleek cut concealing the somewhat portly body beneath.

Langhof did not look up from his desk. "Why not?"

"It isn't done."

"I have no wish to be reassigned, Dr. Ludtz," Langhof said. "I'm busy here. How do I know what kind of laboratory or staff I can expect somewhere else?"

"Forgive me, Dr. Langhof," Ludtz said, "but I don't think it's exclusively a matter of what you want. These are orders, don't forget."

Langhof smiled and looked up at him. "Orders? When the Leader speaks, that is perhaps an order. But when some low-level functionary speaks, that is a request."

Dr. Ludtz shook his head. "I don't understand you, Doctor. These reassignments are necessary. You should be honored to receive one. It means you have been singled out for some special mission. Besides — and one should not forget this — reassignments always mean promotion."

"I've had my fill of promotions. All I want is to do my work and be left alone."

Dr. Ludtz looked mildly offended. "In times like these, more is expected of us than that."

"Save your speeches for Special Section rallies, Dr. Ludtz. They have no effect on me."

Dr. Ludtz stood rigidly in place, staring down at Langhof.

"Please, Doctor," Langhof said, "I'm busy. Don't you have a new shipment of heads to deal with?"

Dr. Ludtz stiffened. "These jokes are beginning to wear thin, Dr. Langhof."

Langhof stood up. "I have been in the Institute of Hygiene for three years, and I have yet to be given a piece of significant research. Instead, I get this racial mumbo jumbo or some absurd form of skeletal cataloging."

Dr. Ludtz glanced fearfully over his shoulder. "Please, Dr. Langhof. Watch yourself."

"Forgive me. It's just that I am less interested in this sort of research. It may be very important. I don't know. But for me, it's the wrong thing."

"Then all the more reason to take a new assignment, Dr. Langhof. Don't you see that?"

Langhof sighed like a teenager weary of life's complexity. "Perhaps."

"No matter what the new assignment is, it couldn't be worse than this. At least, not for you. Don't you see my point? It would be a chance to start over in a new location with a new laboratory and staff, everything new."

And so the ambitious scientist — who at this time knew nothing of tropical heat or the infirmities of burros — slumped over his desk and considered the possibilities. He sat at his desk, sat quietly at his desk, while Ludtz stood over him, waiting for an answer. He could feel the dread coming upon him, like a pool of black, contaminated water sloshing over his ankles. What might it be, this new assignment? He knew — he would never deny that he knew — of certain improprieties in the east. But he did not know their precise nature. And yet there was this undeniable sense of dread, which was itself a kind of knowledge.

"What do you say, Langhof?" Dr. Ludtz asked. "Will you accept this reassignment? Surely you would be happier in another post."

Langhof thought for a moment and then allowed his desire to overwhelm his suspicion. Could anything be more dreadful, he thought, than this ridiculous Institute, this parody of science?

"Well?" Ludtz asked.

"All right. All right," Langhof said. And thus, another step, taken anxiously and with some trepidation. Another step on the route that would lead him through the trails of night, the ruins of snow, and then, later, to that place where an old burro rolled in a pool of swirling blood.

ALL JOURNEYS are not the same. I watch Alberto and Tomás as they make their way down the trail to the village of El Caliz. Theirs is a journey into the simplest form of manhood. They will find their street of dimly lighted bars and adobe brothels. They will find the small brown girl with full lips reclining upon her chaos of rumpled sheets. They will place a few sticky bills or perhaps a little change on the scarred bureau with its wobbly, cracked mirror. She will smile, nod, then move her finger over the thin black strap of her brassiere. This is what they are looking for, satisfaction. It is not hard to find.

Juan, however, seems in search of rarer game. His journey is toward the devils who gnaw the orchids, nibbling the leaves rapaciously with their little pointed teeth. Because they do not exist, he will find them in every place he looks.

Still other journeys require more patience, are full of effort, and have no known termination.

Langhof took his reassignment, and began his journey by train. It moved through a polar whiteness that not even night could dull. Ludtz snoozed beside him as the train rumbled past miles and miles of unblemished snow, and it seemed to Langhof, as he stared sleeplessly out the window, that the ancient symbolists had been right in choosing whiteness as the emblem of absolute purity. He turned from the window from time to time, for purity is terribly monotonous, and glanced at the medical bag resting near his feet. Inside were the tools of his art, themselves made perfect by hundreds of years of inquiry — made perfect, as all things finally are, by doubt tirelessly applied to certainty.

Something moved in him again. Not a mystical intimation, but a feeling of grandeur shared between himself and his science, a feeling of connection between himself and the first stirrings of human thought. He had not felt it in years, this sense of being moored to something truly noble, and it was a great joy to recapture an essence he thought had utterly abandoned him. He remembered how, long ago, he had sat in the park after Anna had left him. He remembered how the stars had seemed to single him out for some special purpose. And although the boy he was at that time could not possibly have articulated the message of the stars, the man now riding through the snow, his medical bag at his feet, could. The message was for him always to seek the mystery behind the stars, to apply his considerable intelligence like a probing needle into the panoply of the physical world. Metaphorically, his task was to snatch the stars and twirl them between his fingers, to place them on a slide and inquire into their density and structure. Now, as the train rumbled toward its eastern destination, Langhof could feel his mission rising in him once again. For him, there would be no more Institute of Hygiene, with its obsequious debasers of the empirical; no more prattling nonsense from the political professors who traded thought for rhetoric; no more cringing subalterns with their conspiratorial whispers. Ludtz had been right, Langhof thought; anything would be better than that.

And so the train moved forward like a black snake over a pool of frozen milk, while Langhof grew more and more relaxed as the distance widened between himself and the hated Institute. He saw the last years as an intolerable waste, as bleached of any importance as the bundles of bones that arrived almost daily at the doors of the Institute. It seemed he had been given a second chance — that the stars, though no doubt disappointed in him thus far, had withheld final judgment and had offered him one last chance to prove himself worthy of them. Here in this new climate, where the snow changed everything, where the winds were fierce and clean, where the voice of the Institute could not be heard, where the idiocies of the capital could not reach him, where spineless superiors could not besmudge the clean lines of inquiry — here, in a land made brilliant by star-light shining over snow, Langhof might find the natural habitat that the excesses of the times had denied him, a place where, at last, his work could make him free.

It was late in the afternoon when the train finally arrived at its destination. Langhof and Ludtz quickly disembarked.

"It was a tiring journey," Ludtz said.

Langhof did not feel tired. He felt exhilarated. "Not too tiring, Dr. Ludtz," he said. "Rather a pleasant ride, I think."

A tall Special Section officer stood a few feet from them. "Excuse me, gentlemen," he said, "but you are Drs. Ludtz and Langhof?"

"Yes, we are," Langhof said.

The officer stepped forward. "Allow me to present myself," he said. "My name is Rausch. I have been assigned to direct you to the Camp."

"Excellent," Ludtz said.

"I hope you had a pleasant journey," Rausch said.

Langhof inhaled the cool, crisp air. "Very refreshing to be in the countryside again."

Rausch looked at him quizzically. "Yes," he said. "You are Langhof?"

"That's right."

Rausch held up two folders in his right hand. "Your picture is in your dossier."

"Thank you for meeting us," Langhof said.

"The Camp is a few miles from the village," Rausch said. "I have a car waiting."

"Excellent," Ludtz said.

Rausch watched him, unsmiling. "Yes," he said dully. "Well, we'd better be on our way."

Rausch escorted them to the car and joined them in the back seat. "To the Camp," he said to the driver.

The car pulled away from the train station, then made its way out of the village. Drifts of snow were piled high along the shoulders of the road. In the distance, Langhof saw two peasants struggling with a mule. They looked like small ink stains on the landscape.

"Is the weather always this brisk?" Langhof asked, feeling talkative.

Rausch kept his eyes on the road, only occasionally glancing over the driver's shoulder to judge the distance traveled. "It is not the best climate," he said. "Certainly not as pleasant as you have in the capital."

"Have you been in the capital recently?" Langhof asked amiably.

"Not for years." Rausch offered no elaboration.

"The capital is full of activity," Ludtz said.

Rausch said nothing. He kept his gloved hands clenched in his lap.

The car bumped slightly, and Rausch stared about nervously. "There is always the possibility of ambush," he said.

"Ambush?" Ludtz said with fear.

"Yes," Rausch replied. "Only a few days ago a major and two lieutenants were killed outside the village." He looked at Langhof. "One cannot be too careful. Stay near the Camp. That's the safest place."

It was at this point that Langhof realized, fully rather than simply intellectually, that he was now in a war zone. The snow suddenly appeared menacing, a place where partisans lurked in wait for men dressed like himself.

"But we are so far from the front," Ludtz protested.

Rausch did not look at him. "The whole world is at war,

Doctor. Everything is a war. It is no longer a matter of fronts."

Ludtz glanced fearfully at Langhof. "I hadn't counted on this."

"Don't worry," Langhof said. "We'll be safe once we're in the Camp." He turned to Rausch. "How far are we from the front lines, may I ask?"

Rausch seemed to sneer. "What difference does it make?"

"I was only asking."

"Did you think you could spend the whole war in a nice warm office, Doctor?"

"We volunteered for this position," Ludtz said quickly.

Rausch stared at Ludtz without pity. "Never lie to me, Doctor," he said. "You were assigned here."

"Yes, but — " Ludtz stammered.

"What exactly will our duties be?" Langhof asked.

"To take orders. From your superiors," Rausch replied. He uttered the word *superiors* as if using such a term was a mere convention of language, a way of referring to people of higher rank but lower esteem.

"But surely you have some definite plans for us," Langhof said.

"Plans?"

"Assignments. Research."

"Oh, yes," Rausch said. "We do."

Langhof attempted to break through Rausch's reserve. "Look, this is all very new to us — to Ludtz and myself. Perhaps you could give us some advice for getting along well in the Camp."

Rausch turned to Langhof, his face expressionless. "Always keep your pistol close by. Then, if something tragic happens, you can use it to blow your head off."

As the car moved forward through the brilliantly white fields, Langhof — despite Rausch's dark eccentricities — felt another surge of anticipation. Beside him, Ludtz sat nervously, clearly alarmed. But Langhof could only remember the aridity of the Institute, and compared to that, anything that gave the slightest sign of intellectual fecundity was cause for jubilation. He could sense again the dispensation of the stars.

Farther on, Rausch ordered the driver to pull the car over beside a large wooden ramp. A train puffed and smoked beside the ramp, and Langhof could hear people shouting inside the cattle cars.

"This is how your patients arrive, Doctors," Rausch said.

Armed soldiers were scurrying back and forth about the train like ants over a carcass. At the far end of the ramp a band was playing a sprightly melody.

Ludtz, who only now seemed to have noticed that the car had stopped, leaned forward. "What's that?" he asked.

"A piece from *The Magic Flute*, I believe," Rausch replied.

"No," Ludtz said. "I mean these people in the train."

"Prisoners," Rausch said casually. He took a cigarette from his overcoat pocket and lit it.

Langhof sat rigidly in place, watching.

The soldiers had now assembled themselves in a kind of rough order. Some stood, legs spread apart, on top of the train, their machine guns pointing down toward the locked doors. Others had formed a cordon around the train. Some held their guns rigidly forward, others let the barrels droop slightly toward the ground.

"So many prisoners?" Langhof asked.

"Yes," Rausch said. "Many prisoners."

At a signal several soldiers stepped forward and began unlocking the doors of the train. The people seemed to explode onto the ground as if vomited from the cars.

"Many prisoners," Rausch whispered.

As the prisoners dropped from the cars, the soldiers began shouting at them: "Line up by fives! By fives! Quick now! Warm meals are waiting!"

The people continued pouring out of the cars: old men in suits, women with their heads covered by thick shawls, a group of children all dressed in their school uniforms of little red berets and short blue jackets, a man hobbling forward on a crutch. The air filled with the bustle of their disembarkation, their cries and moans and indiscriminate yells. Some scurried about looking for lost relatives, lovers, friends. Others merely stood with their arms folded, staring into the blinding white light.

All around them the soldiers continued their shouts: "By fives! Line up by fives!"

Some of the people began to assemble themselves as the soldiers instructed. But the general confusion seemed to paralyze the rest. Then the soldiers fell upon them, marching into the stunned crowd, beating them with truncheons. Some fell to the ground. Others merely staggered to the side. Some began to shout frantic questions at the assaulting guards. Others instantly fell to the ground and began to weave and wail. An old rabbi dropped to his knees and began digging a hole with his hands. Above him, a guard stood laughing. A woman spread a large quilt on the snow, laid her baby on it, and began to diaper the child. A soldier rushed forward and pulled her to her feet. "No time for that now!" he shouted. Then he pushed her into the moving crowd. The baby continued to lie on its back, watching the dark figures pass above it. It seemed amused, and for a moment it smiled.

Langhof turned to Rausch. "Who are these people?"

Rausch peered at the smoke rising from his cigarette. "A little of this. A little of that."

Langhof turned his eyes back toward the crowd. Some of the people were still straggling out of the cars, stunned by the harsh light, rubbing their eyes. The dead were pushed out a little way from the tracks and stacked in piles, like cords of wood. From the top of one of the cars a guard shouted: "Quick now! There's warm soup waiting! Don't delay! It'll get cold!"

In fives the people began to file past a man who watched them closely and signaled left and right with a conductor's baton. From the caduceus on his cap, Langhof could tell that he was a doctor. He watched as the people moved under the doctor's gaze, following the signal of his baton, one column moving to the left, one to the right, as he directed.

Langhof could feel his eyes pulling the whole scene nearer to him. And after a moment the people seemed to march through a dark tunnel, the pupil of his eye. Marching, their heads bent forward, they seemed to move through him, staring downward at the stars.

HERE IN THE REPUBLIC it is difficult to be wise. For the face of the Republic is like the face of El Presidente in Casamira's portrayal — Goyaesque, with bloated cheeks, bulbous nose, bulging eyes set out from the cheeks like marbles on a board of Chinese checkers. This is the paradise of Dorian Gray, a perfect landscape of green shade where orchids spread their petals in the crystal air. And underneath, far underneath, below those upper layers of black soil where the worms seek cool and moisture, below the tarantula's crusty mortuary and the rocky shades of the iguana, below this is the pit dug for our madness. If it were not bottomless, we might sound it. If it were not a labyrinth, we might trace its pattern. But ours is a feeble labor against the relentless mystery of crime.

Dr. Ludtz, as he watched the vermin descend from the train, suppressed a little yawn. It had, after all, been a long journey. Langhof, on the other hand, sensed that his journey was just beginning.

"Is something amiss, Dr. Langhof?" Rausch asked.

Langhof shook his head quickly.

"Your face. It's pale."

Langhof leaned back in the automobile seat and tried to adjust his body to its irregular contours.

"Are you sure you're all right, Doctor?" Rausch persisted.
"Yes."

Rausch removed his cigarette and exhaled into the frigid air. Watching him, Langhof could not tell where the smoke ended and where his breath began.

"What were you told at the Institute?" Rausch asked.

"Very little," Ludtz replied, although the question had not been directed at him.

"Is that so?" Rausch asked softly. He looked at Ludtz for a moment. "Well?" he said, turning his eyes toward Langhof. "Do you have any questions?"

Langhof folded his arms over his chest and said nothing.

"I have a question," Ludtz said.

Rausch did not turn his eyes from Langhof. "No questions, Dr. Langhof?" he said.

Langhof did not move. He shifted slightly, then turned his lips inward, as if sealing a compartment.

Rausch smiled and turned to face Ludtz. "What is your question, Doctor?"

"Where will we be staying?" Ludtz asked.

"In the medical compound," Rausch replied dully.

"I see."

"Do you have any objection, Dr. Ludtz?"

"No."

"It's really quite adequate. Certainly not as comfortable as an apartment in the capital, but adequate. More than adequate, actually. Considering the surroundings."

Langhof turned and watched the last of the prisoners as they moved away from the train in two ragged columns.

Rausch stretched his arm across Ludtz's chest and touched Langhof's shoulder. "How did you happen to be assigned here, Doctor?" he asked.

"I don't know," Langhof said.

Rausch smiled pointedly. "Curious, isn't it?" He turned to the driver. "Enter the Camp, Corporal," he said.

The corporal bent forward and started the engine.

"Drive carefully," Rausch said, his eyes returning to Langhof. "The roads are treacherous here."

The automobile moved forward. Langhof raised his hand and pulled his cap down lower upon his head. The shadow of the bill fell across his eyes.

"To some extent, you will be treating the prisoners," Rausch said. "But only partly. You will mainly be doing medical research."

Ludtz smiled brightly and jabbed Langhof softly. "Good, that's what we wanted," he said.

Rausch's voice held to the same bleak monotone. "The research is varied. And you should be aware that the facilities for it are rather primitive. This is not the Institute, after all. And of course, there's this little business of the war. We can't expect the government to spend enormous amounts on laboratories and supplies. And even those supplies we requisition often never get to us. Sabotage. There's a good deal of that."

Langhof glanced at Rausch, and for a moment lost himself in studying the terrible correctness of his face. It was somewhat pale and very smooth, with a proper, angular nose and deep-set eyes — a face not at all like the vulpine exemplars of the New Order who strutted about the capital.

"Where are you from, Rausch?" Langhof asked cautiously.

"Where am I from?"

"Yes. Are you from the capital?"

"No."

"Where, then?"

Rausch looked at Langhof sternly. "I am from here. No-where else."

The car suddenly skidded on the ice, the rear end sliding to the left. The corporal frantically struggled to right it.

"Careful, now," Rausch said to him.

The corporal glanced around and Langhof could see a blush rising in his face. Rausch saw it too and tried to ease the boy. "Just be careful, Corporal. No harm done."

"Sorry, sir," the corporal sputtered helplessly.

"No harm done at all," Rausch replied gently. He turned to Langhof. "We try to make things run smoothly here," he said.

F WE KNEW where things began, we would know where to end them. Now, from my verandah, I can see the jungle in all its misery and splendor. I have, during these long years, learned the many cries of the monkey and can distinguish panic from ecstasy. But it has not always been so.

Langhof, rubbing his gloved hands together as the Camp approached slowly like Birnam Wood, knew nothing of how he had come to this moment in his life. And perhaps such moments are themselves nothing more than those points in our lives that we most deeply misperceive. Surely Langhof, as he watched the Camp loom in the distance, wooden barracks enclosed by rusty stretches of barbed wire, felt nothing of the climactic, but only dread rising in him once again. For he was no more than a ball set rolling on an uneven tabletop, dipping this way and that with the contours of circumstance. In his state of profound consternation, he could find the will to ask only one trifling question.

"Have you a handkerchief, Dr. Ludtz?"

Ludtz, ever accommodating, fumbled through his overcoat pockets. "Yes, here."

Langhof took the handkerchief and quietly blew his nose into it. Then he lifted his collar against the wind.

Beside him, the oblivious Dr. Ludtz turned to Rausch

with a look of dismay. "Are we actually going to be *living* in the Camp?" he asked.

"Yes," Rausch said. "You seem surprised by that fact."

"But aren't staff quarters usually outside the prison?"

"Prison? This is not a prison. This is a different matter altogether, Doctor. And you will be living inside the Camp."

The car pulled up to the gate. Two guards stood before it, holding machine guns loosely in their hands.

"Open the gate," Rausch said.

The guards did as they were commanded. The iron gate opened and Langhof passed through it. As he did so, a light snow began to fall. The snow was wholly without symbolic importance, but not to a romantic; for it is part of the blindness of romance to see life, and finally history, as a series of telling moments properly adorned by the imagery of fall or redemption, and to neglect all that lies in between, all that generates, debases, or inspires.

And so the car passed through the gate, the corporal guiding it carefully. A little farther along, he turned the car to the left toward a group of prisoners huddled in the mud. He honked the horn. "Get out of the way, you shit!" he screamed and glanced back at Rausch for approval.

"Just keep a steady pace," Rausch said.

The car proceeded through the Camp and finally stopped in front of a freshly painted building.

"These are your quarters," Rausch said. He stepped out of the car. "Come."

Langhof and Ludtz got out of the car and followed Rausch up a short flight of stairs that led to the entrance.

"This is where you will be living from now on," Rausch said. "You will each have your own room." He opened the door and paused, allowing Langhof and Ludtz to pass in front of him.

"It's like a barracks," Ludtz said.

"More or less," Rausch said. "Are you disappointed, my dear doctor?"

"Oh, no," Ludtz said quickly. "Not in the least, I assure

you. One cannot expect luxurious accommodations in a war zone."

"Precisely," Rausch said evenly. He nodded toward the hallway. "Down there."

Langhof and Ludtz walked down the hall until Rausch stopped them at a particular door. "This is your room, Dr. Ludtz," he said.

"Excellent," Ludtz said.

"You haven't seen it yet," Rausch said.

"I'm sure it will be fine."

Rausch swung the door open and Ludtz looked inside. It was a small, tidy room with a single metal-framed bed with a drooping mattress covered with military blankets. "Very nice," Ludtz said. "Warm."

"Your bags will be brought to you shortly," Rausch said.

Ludtz stepped into the room. "Thank you. Yes, very nice. Very nice, indeed '

Rausch closed the door and turned to Langhof. "Your room is farther down the hall," he said.

Langhof followed Rausch a few paces, then stopped when Rausch did.

"This is it," Rausch said. He opened the door onto a room almost identical to that of Dr. Ludtz. "Not exactly the capital, is it?"

"It is satisfactory," Langhof said. He stepped into the room, looked around, glanced at the window, started to move toward it, then suddenly stopped himself.

"You may look out the window," Rausch said with a little, mocking laugh.

Langhof spun around. "What is your function here, Rausch?"

"I'm in charge of discipline," Rausch replied coolly. "You might say I am a student of control."

"I have no wish to be one of your subjects," Langhof said sharply.

Rausch smiled. "Subject? What an odd idea."

Langhof turned away. "Please, leave me alone."

"Subject?" Rausch said. "What do you think this is,

Doctor? Let me assure you that we are very serious here. You cannot begin to know just how serious."

"I've heard rumors," Langhof said. He was still staring at the bed.

"They're all true," Rausch said. He paused a moment, studying Langhof's figure as it was silhouetted by the window. "You are an interesting man, Doctor. The vermin — I know all I need to know about the vermin. But you — now that's a different matter."

Langhof turned toward Rausch. "How so?"

"You must be filled with questions at this moment," Rausch said. "And yet you stand there and say nothing."

"All right," Langhof said, "I'll ask a question. Those people coming off the train, what becomes of them?"

"They are all killed. Most of them right away. The others die sooner or later."

Langhof shook his head. "That does not seem possible."

"The trick, of course, is not to think of them as people," Rausch said. He smiled. "You must take a lesson from the priests, Doctor. You must learn the value of abstraction."

"Ridiculous," Langhof said.

Rausch shrugged. "They really aren't people, you know. They are simply physical material that history is working on." He smiled. "Besides, you will have very little to do with that. You are a scientist, after all."

"This is not science," Langhof said hotly. "This is politics, nothing but politics."

"Look out the window, Langhof," Rausch said lightly. "Surely you cannot call this politics."

"Then what is it?"

"A great experiment," Rausch said with a wink. "We are investigating great philosophical questions here."

"Nonsense."

"All those little philosophical tidbits we used to debate over our beer in university taverns, they are all part of our situation here. Why, the question of freedom versus determinism alone is undergoing a monumental reexamination."

"Discuss such things with Ludtz," Langhof said. "I have no stomach for them."

"Ludtz is an idiot," Rausch said. "A fool."

He paused and then smiled with what seemed to be genuine good nature. "Oh, come now, Langhof. Let's discuss it a bit, shall we? Tell me, my good doctor, did you freely choose to end up in this little room, or was it preordained from all eternity?"

Langhof stiffened. "Get out."

"Not a very philosophical attitude, Doctor," Rausch said. Langhof shook his head wearily. "Just leave me alone."

"If you think you are above this, Langhof," Rausch said sternly, "you are mistaken." And with that, Rausch turned very quickly, at a military clip, and left the room.

And so Langhof was left alone in his room. He slumped onto the bed and ran his fingers through his hair. At that moment, he saw himself as a figure out of classical drama, the noble spirit fatally and undeservedly ensnared in evil. But he was in fact a figure out of melodrama, mired in self-pity and self-justification, the handmaidens of weakness and crime.

And what was the nature of this illusion that turned Langhof's tragic mien into a shoddy harlequin?

It was this — if now, amid the swelter of my compound, I can know it rightly: that he, Langhof, had been sinned against, victimized, betrayed, stabbed in the back. He believed that now he saw the outside forces that had brought him to his current condition, and saw them clearly. He saw the monumental ones: war, inflation, politics. He saw the lesser ones: his father's suicide, Anna's flight, the velvet-gloved coercion of Dr. Trottman. But in fact, he saw nothing, because he did not see himself. There is no limit to our capacity for self-deceit. And perhaps our greatest craft lies in our manifold rejection of that knowledge which, if we embraced it, would make life almost impossible.

And so Langhof, as he lay down on his bed and closed his eyes, began to believe that he had at last seen all the invisible whips that had driven him to the Camp. And he slept, not knowing he was still a fool, still a shadow, still a riddle wrapped in sable.

Part III

I STAND in the hot mist of the nursery and watch the orchids droop. In some, the petals draw slowly in upon the pistil like Caesar's robed assassins. A soft rot has overtaken the Erwinia, wrinkling the leaves as the internal tissue collapses. The buds of the Phalaenopsis are rotting, brown spots spreading across the knotted petals. Fungi devour the rhizome of the Epidendrum and the Vandas. The nursery has become the slaughterhouse of orchids. Their languishing is critical to Juan, trivial to me. Still, he will not follow my instructions. He has closed the greenhouse, which will suffocate the orchids. He has filled the pots with water, soaking the osmunda fiber, and syringed the buds and leaves, spreading the infection with the flowing water, drowning the orchids in their own disease.

For Juan, I am no longer the protector of the orchids. For him, I am the young Don Pedro in a yellow, wrinkled skin, a strange, white-haired presence who totters about the compound or sits for endless hours in the baking heat of the verandah or strolls into the jungle night, alone.

It does not matter what Juan thinks. Least of all, should I be subject for his thought. For the orchids — and the demon spirits that assail them — are his only concerns. His mind is cast in the mold of a healthy, thriving flower, and his interests do not extend beyond the kissing of its petals. In an otherwise blameless life, this is his awful crime.

I turn, and he is standing in the doorway of the nursery, framed by it like some romantic's portrait of the noble peasant. He nods. "Don Pedro," he says humbly.

"Sí."

In Spanish, he asks me if anything is wrong.

"No, Juan."

He does not move. He is guarding the orchids against my lunacy. He suspects that those devils that plague the orchids somehow reside in me.

I tell him that the orchids do not look well.

He nods sadly, a vassal of the flowers, a last centurion of the princely orchids.

I touch the petals of one of the Lymbidiums and tell him that even in decline, they are beautiful.

"Sí, bellísima," Juan replies. Standing quietly in the doorway, he is the perfect representation of the terrible and inert slumber of the pastoral.

I release the petals. Watching Juan, I know that he will not leave the nursery until I do. I walk past him. "Buenos noches, Juan."

"Buenos noches, Don Pedro."

I make my way up toward the house, then pause and glance back at Juan. He is standing where I stood, staring down at the orchids, assuring himself as best he can that I have not brought them harm. Standing amid the flowers in a hazy square of light, Juan looks like some cheap lithograph of Christ in the Garden. It is the same melancholy face and outstretched arms offering perfect solace, the same head bowed slightly toward the penitent and the wounded that I have seen in a thousand store windows. It is in the nature of religion to take everything into itself, draw everything within its circle, especially the wounded heart. And one day, perhaps, there will be a certain Saint Juan, patron saint of orchids, canonized in the year three thousand because of miracles wrought in the desolate stretches of the Republic, miracles of rebirth and redemption, of half-eaten burros rising from bloody waters to drink from the hand of Christ. And then further miracles of rejuvenated orchids, of crops flourishing in drought, of seeds dropped from a bountiful heaven. Saint Juan who cures the orchids with prayer and air and water. Saint Juan, steadfast in his faith, who in his great simplicity refused the devil's wiles and did not treat the ravaged blooms with Ceresan or amputation, but only caressed the withered parts with his dusty peasant hands and made them whole. There is no limit to miraculous possibilities once the first miracle has been accepted.

It is said to be different in the northern provinces. All insurrectionary ballads attest to the stony pragmatism of the revolutionary mind. In the northern provinces clouds are clouds, not beds upon which angels lounge. And water is water, fire is fire, earth is earth; all the medieval humors are stripped of their ancient prerogatives of mystery and power.

And to the south, El Presidente, snoozing on his satin pillows while the flies grow drunk with wine, must dream from time to time a dream of fallen power, of Ozymandias as desert solitary, a dream suffused with every lachrymose cliché of besotted rule. We are the things that make us weep, and El Presidente shakes with tears at the possibility of ruin. And to the north, the rebels' tears fall into their tin plates, salting the fetid guacamole, their grief fanned to revolutionary fire by their hatred of El Presidente and his torpid, bejeweled entourage. Undeserved suffering and undeserved privilege: this is the dialectic of the Republic.

Here in El Caliz, it is easy to look north and south and in that act discover the nature of our distress. Here the contending forces wave banners announcing what they are and from where they come, and no amount of deceptive plumage can mask the essential line upon which the case is drawn. This is the clarity of underdevelopment, that nothing lives between the uplifted and the debased, that the dust from Don Camillo's limousine can fall only into the eyes of those who live beneath its wheels. Each element of the Republic must adhere to one side or the other; whether it be the Church or the fledgling middle class or the baking peasantry, each must fall or rise to its own density within the heavy liquid of the Republic.

But the forces that created the Camp were of a confused and baffling density, a compound made of thousands of separate elements with no defining structure. Each man had his own valence, and although each also rolled about within the same engulfing stream, still there was the singular unity of each individual person, a unique chemical structure called upon to react in relationship to the greatest catalyst of our time.

But what was this complex dialectic? Of all the people Langhof met in the Camp, only Rausch believed he knew. Opening Langhof's door the day after his arrival, he stood in his black uniform, the naked bulb of Langhof's room shining on his polished boots. "This is the implosion of history," he said with a wholly self-conscious portentousness.

Langhof raised himself obliviously on his bunk. "What time is it?" he asked.

"Time to begin your work," Rausch said. He slapped his riding crop against his boot. "We rise early in the Camp. From now on you'll have to get up on your own. I'm much too busy to be a bunkmaster."

Langhof rubbed his eyes, feeling dread wash over him but dismissing it. He opened his eyes and looked at Rausch standing in the door, his legs spread wide apart, the harsh light before him shading his features.

"I told you to get up," Rausch said.

"Did you wake Ludtz yet?" Langhof asked.

"Your friend is already fully dressed," Rausch said. "I should call him eager." His eyes seemed to squeeze together. "I let you sleep somewhat later. You will have more to endure, I think."

Langhof rose from his bed and took a towel from the rack on the wall.

"No time for showers this morning," Rausch said quickly. "We must hurry."

"But I —"

Rausch smiled. "The whole camp stinks, my dear Langhof. Your particular contribution will not be noticed, believe me. Now, let's go."

Langhof, refusing to be rushed, dressed slowly, then followed Rausch down the hall, outside the building, and into another, almost identical structure. Guards and prisoners were moving all about. Somewhere in the distance a band was playing *Eine Kleine Nachtmusik.*

"You'll be working with Dr. Kessler," Rausch said. He led Langhof farther down the hallway, then opened the door. Inside, Langhof could see Ludtz and another doctor, both in white coats, standing idly before a large metal table.

Rausch made the introductions. "Dr. Kessler, allow me to present Dr. Langhof."

Kessler put out his hand, and Langhof took it. "Happy to have you with us, Doctor," Kessler said brightly. "We're terribly overworked here in the Camp."

"Thank you, sir," Langhof said. He glanced toward one side of the room and saw what looked to be twenty or thirty female bodies stacked neatly, heads pointed toward the wall. They were all pregnant, and some of the fetuses had already crowned, the tops of their heads drooping from the vaginas. Langhof felt his stomach coil... *the livers of some eighty women who had died suddenly* ...

"Don't be alarmed, Dr. Langhof," Kessler said gently.

Langhof stared palely at Kessler but said nothing.

"You no doubt find this somewhat unusual," Kessler went on quietly, "perhaps even a bit macabre."

Langhof tried to speak, but couldn't.

"We don't have very sophisticated facilities here," Kessler continued, "and that sometimes makes for a certain amount of unpleasantness."

"Of course," Ludtz said quickly. He watched Langhof with worry.

Kessler smiled. "As I was explaining to Dr. Ludtz, in this ward we are examining various methods of sterilization. But first — as regards females — we must inquire into the whole process of gestation."

Langhof summoned enough strength to nod politely.

Toward what was he nodding? What was it that he saw? The perversion of science? Of course, but what else? His own pitiful helplessness? Absolutely. Anything else? His own moral and intellectual superiority? Doubtless that, and he even felt a little undeserved shiver of decency, not to say humanity, pass over him. But beyond these things — and the stacked bodies — what?

Nothing.

For Langhof had not yet begun to absorb the Camp. He had not passed into its bloodstream. He still persisted in the belief that it was not his crime, even though at this point, he was — admittedly — an accessory to it. But still, he could not see it as *his* crime, so he could not objectify his experience and then place himself within it. At this point, he could only feel his own, personal distance from the things around him. He could only look down upon them, as if dangling from some lofty aerie.

"We begin by taking females in various stages of pregnancy," Kessler explained. He stopped, dipped into his coat, pulled out a cigar, and lit it. "After that — oh, forgive me, would you like a cigar?"

"No, thank you," Langhof said.

"I don't smoke either," Ludtz said.

Kessler laughed. "Oh, yes. Hygienists. I forgot." He took another puff. "In any event, we extract the fetus — as I said, in various stages of development — and we observe it."

"Observe it?" Langhof asked cautiously.

"Yes."

"How?"

"How what?"

"How do you observe it?"

Kessler shrugged. "We simply look at it, Dr. Langhof. We make whatever notations seem fitting. You must understand that this is *original* research. We have to begin at the beginning ... almost as the ancient physicians did."

"Yes, I see," Ludtz said.

"But that should not be discouraging," Kessler said, his eyes fixed on Langhof. "And imagine the rewards to mankind if we are successful! By controlling the nature of the human population, by eliminating inferior strains, we can project the race toward a magnificent future at an undreamed-of speed." He glanced at the bodies piled on the other side of the room. "The fact is, because of misguided sentimentalism, our forefathers allowed degenerate peoples to overbreed. In a limited world, this can no longer be tolerated. Surely you understand this, Dr. Langhof."

"Yes," Langhof said weakly.

"Good," Kessler said happily, "then let's begin." He turned and called two prisoners into the room. "Quick, now," he said to them, "I want you to place one specimen on each of the three tables here in the room. Be quick, we've already a late start this morning."

The two prisoners set to work. One grabbed the hands, one the feet of a single body. Then they dragged it to one of the tables and hoisted it on top.

"Turn them face up," Kessler said.

The prisoners struggled to turn the bodies. "Shit," one of them blurted as one of the corpses slid to the floor.

"Come on, come on!" Kessler cried. "For Christ's sake, watch what you're doing."

When they had finished, the two prisoners walked to one side of the room and stood waiting for their next orders.

Kessler glanced at Ludtz and Langhof. "Shall we begin? You each have one specimen. What we have to do is remove the fetus. As you know, this can be accomplished with a simple incision, at least in most cases. If the fetus has crowned, however — as I see yours has, Dr. Langhof — you must make the incision considerably lower." He pointed his scalpel. "Here. Make it at this point to ensure that it will not be damaged." He glanced at the cadaver on Ludtz's table. "Yours will be a good deal simpler," he said. "Yours, a bit messy, Dr. Langhof, but nothing you're not used to." He smiled gently. "All right, let's begin."

Langhof stood at his table, staring at the naked body that rested on it. He could hear Kessler's voice like a steady drumbeat in the background. He placed the scalpel at the point Kessler had indicated, tucked it through the black, curly pubic hair, and then pressed down gently into the rubbery flesh at the apex of the mound of Venus.

Picture El Presidente standing on one of the majestic turrets that rise above the palace. Picture him peering out into the night as his soul fills with that peculiar afflatus which comes when one identifies himself with the creative forces of history. If he does not look to the north — which he never does, because he cannot bear melancholy — he will see the lights twinkling in his impoverished suburbs. Out there, in the comforting distance, his subjects carry on the twin responsibilities of good citizenship: to work and to adore.

But what is the nature of the night he sees? Because he is a simpleton, he cannot be moved by its symbolism. Because he is a wastrel, he cannot see it as a time for rest. Because he is a debaucher, he does not need its darkness to inspire his loins. What is left, then, for El Presidente in regard to night? Nothing. Neither peace nor mystery, but only dread of the sleep it inevitably brings, that brief loss of consciousness which El Presidente abhors. Night ends each day with a terrible intimation of oblivion, suggesting, as it must to all great egotists, that nature is forever out of tune with their desire.

After the first day of work in the Camp, Langhof longed for sleep. For him the loss of consciousness became something wholly to be desired, a treasure beyond price. He lay on his bed, twisting, turning, his eyes clamped shut. But the little engine of his mind refused to close down. He tried to read, but the book seemed to dissolve before his eyes. He paced, tramping back and forth across the narrow room, the naked bulb swinging above his head like a pendulum.

"I heard you walking about," Rausch said as he opened the door.

Langhof spun around. "Don't you ever knock?"

Rausch smiled. "Don't you need your sleep, Doctor?"

Langhof noticed that even at this late hour, Rausch remained in his immaculate black uniform. "I might ask you the same question," he said.

Rausch walked past Langhof and stood by the window watching the distant pillar of smoke rise from the orange glow of chimneys. "What did you learn about creation today, Doctor?" he asked.

Langhof turned toward Rausch. "This attitude of yours — this —"

Rausch slowly eased himself back from the window. "What attitude is that, Doctor?"

"This scoffing," Langhof said, "it could get you into a lot of trouble one day."

Rausch smiled. "Trouble? Could it indeed get me into trouble, do you think?" he asked softly. Illuminated by the bulb, his face seemed almost to glow. "What kind of trouble?"

"You know what I'm talking about," Langhof said. "What's to keep me from reporting you?"

Rausch laughed lightly and turned back toward the window. "A lovely light, this corona that edges the chimney-tops. Almost a halo."

Langhof sat down on the bunk. "What's to keep me from turning you in, Rausch?"

Rausch did not turn from the window. "For what? I do my duty, as do you." He shifted to face Langhof. "How many women did you slice up today, Doctor? Five?"

Langhof turned away from Rausch's gaze.

"Ten? More than that? Twenty?"

Langhof stepped to the door, his back to Rausch.

Rausch allowed his eyes to drift back toward the window. "Well, the numbers are unimportant in any case," he said. "The facts are the same. You stood at a table and sliced up a few women. Then you took their babies out of their wombs. You examined these unfortunate children. You scrutinized them under the light. You probably even jotted down a few inane and useless notes just to be on the safe side. Am I right, Doctor?"

Langhof whirled around angrily. "And what did you do, Rausch?"

Rausch's eyes did not leave the window. "I killed perhaps a thousand people," he said casually, "then incinerated them like so much rubbish. That smoke, the smoke here in the room, that's them."

Langhof shook his head. "Unbelievable that this could be happening."

"Not in the least," Rausch said quietly.

Langhof stepped over to him. "Why do you keep looking out that window?" he asked.

Rausch turned to face Langhof. "Do you know what happens when a star collapses, Doctor? It implodes. Everything falls into the pit of itself. That is what we are doing, imploding. This is the whole journey of civilization at the moment when it passes through its own rectum."

"Ridiculous," Langhof said. "This place has nothing to do with civilization."

"We went as far as we could, and now we are racing back," Rausch said. "This is the bottom, the suicide of culture."

Langhof stepped back and sat down on his bunk. "This is just the Camp," he said. "It is not the whole world."

Rausch smiled. "Really? Do you think so? Do you think this is just some vile spot on Europe? Do you think that we are isolated in what we do here, that we are alone?"

Langhof stared evenly at Rausch. He could feel his hands clench the army blanket beneath him. "Yes, I do."

Rausch laughed. "I'm afraid you are quite wrong, Doctor." He paused, glanced toward the window, then back to Langhof. "The people, the vermin, how do you think they get here? Do you think they simply show up with their baggage at the Camp gate?" He shook his head. "They come by train, my dear doctor, and there are lots of little men who run the trains. They know what's on them, but they make them run anyway. They give the proper railway signals. Then there are those who mend the tracks. And others who build the platforms."

Langhof could feel his fingers eating into the blanket. "Perhaps, but..."

Rausch touched the collar of his uniform. "Very nice, isn't it? Sleek. A beautiful attire. It was made by someone else who knew — at least partly — what it stood for. They may have agreed, they may not have. In the end, you see, it didn't matter." He walked over to the bunk and stood over Langhof. "Then there are the people who make the flags and the bugles and the boots. The people who carry the mails and make the mail pouches. The people who make rubber and steel, who censor the books and dismiss the intransigent faculty members." He sat down slowly beside Langhof, took his cap from his head, and dropped it into his lap. His hair shimmered in the light. "All the little people who do the million tasks that allow the New Order to reproduce itself each day. They are here with us. Not soldiers. Certainly not Special Section. And yet they are out there, doing their work, drawing their pay, swilling down their beer in the rathskellers, fornicating in their tiny rooms, breeding the next generation of themselves." Rausch looked at Langhof. A small, bitter smile played on his lips. "Civilization. No, Langhof, the Camp is not a cancer that can be surgically removed. It is the center of a spider's web and its strands stretch everywhere, to everyone."

Langhof stood up and walked to the window without looking out. Then he turned to face Rausch. "And what about you, Rausch?" he said. "You're different. You're not like the rest."

"Different? Oh yes. Haven't you noticed? We all are. None of us is like 'the rest.' But we do the same things, don't we? You and Kessler and Ludtz. All of you did precisely the same thing today."

Langhof lowered his head.

"We are at the bottom," Rausch said, "and we have to see it through. We have to touch the very bottom this time, so that we will always know where the bottom is." He paused, watching Langhof. "Do you understand?"

Langhof said nothing.

Rausch stood up and watched Langhof sternly. "Do you know how you got here?"

"I was reassigned."

Rausch laughed. "Reassigned? All right, we'll start there if you want. Why were you reassigned?"

"I don't know."

"I do."

Langhof raised his head and faced Rausch. "Why then? Why was I reassigned?"

"Because you were noticed at the Institute. A jokester, that's what they said, a person who could be counted on to make light of things. Just the right attitude for a place like this."

"Ridiculous."

"You were reassigned because you had such a wonderful sense of humor."

Langhof's eyes narrowed. "I'm goddamn tired of being mocked by you," he said.

"It's true."

"Ridiculous."

"Never underestimate the power of good humor, Doctor," Rausch said coldly. He stared at Langhof for a moment, then put on his cap and carefully straightened it. "I despise you, Langhof," he said softly. "You are nothing but a stage I passed through long ago. This self-righteousness of yours, this despicable pose of wounded humanity. It makes the air stink more than the smoke from the pits."

"Get out of here," Langhof said.

Rausch did not move. "We have to carry it through this time, Doctor. We have to reach the bottom. It is our mission, the great task of our age."

"Get out," Langhof repeated.

Rausch smiled, but his eyes remained fixed brutally on Langhof's face. "When I was a little boy, I watched my grandfather kill a litter of puppies by swinging their heads against a wall. What effect do you suppose that had on me?"

"I could not care less," Langhof said grimly.

"I remember the effect," Rausch said. "My grandfather was a wizened old man. He looked like God with that white hair and beard. He swung the puppies by their tails, bashed them once, then threw them into the river." Rausch's eyes seemed to sparkle. "It was a thrilling sight."

"I don't want you ever to come in here again," Langhof said.

"You are like the rest. You prefer sentimental tales of loyal dogs pulling drowning children from the raging current. Is that right, Doctor?"

Langhof stepped to the door and opened it. "Go," he said.

"The real story is quite different from what you imagine, Langhof," Rausch said.

Watching the gleaming buttons on Rausch's uniform, Langhof felt an almost physical revulsion. "I prefer my mind to yours," he said.

Rausch laughed mockingly. "Do you? Well, let me tell you something, my friend. If we do not complete the task this time while we have the will to do so, and the machinery, then it will simply start again fifty, a hundred, two hundred years from now, with all the accompanying agony. We must clean the cesspool entirely this time. We must let it all collapse totally. Only then can the reconstruction begin."

Langhof felt as if all his energy had been drained from him. "No more, Rausch," he said.

Rausch stepped into the door, then turned back. "You are an interesting man, Langhof," he said, "but weak, pitifully weak." He stepped into the hallway and closed the door gently behind him.

Langhof turned from the door, walked to the window, and looked out.

Staring out into the thick, humid night of El Caliz, it is easy to understand what Langhof felt at that moment in his history. It was harder then, because he was in the midst of the swirl. The great gift of the survivor is his capacity to rethink horror from the vantage point of distance. Langhof, as he stared toward the raging furnace, watching flames shoot fifteen feet from the mouth of the chimney, could not imagine either himself or his circumstance. If come wily partisan had put a bullet through his head as he stood at the window, his life would have been better than it became, but his mind would have died, and his capacity to tumble through time, back and forth through time, like an eel caught in an eternal undertow, would have been lost.

Even this obvious fact, however, was far too elusive for our hero to grasp. Standing by the window, he could not even imagine a future for himself. No doubt certain escapes offered themselves. He could consult a religious text or write a poem or take morphine or blame his parents. He could perhaps in the future marry a pretty girl who understood him. But Langhof, by his very nature, was immune from these seductions. He did not have the final option of perfect blindness. And so he took the only option he actually had. He fell in love with nothingness. Nullity became his only pleasure. He applied an airbrush to his senses, and although he could not avoid the hideous data they brought to him through nose and ear and eye and hand, still he could elude the feelings that might otherwise have overwhelmed him. But in this he could not be selective. He had to avoid all feeling. He had to reduce the herds to a roiling, featureless mass. Because he could not bear one scream, he must shut out them all. In doing this, in allowing himself to be encased in a glass booth that separated him from both joy and suffering and that gave all life and history the lifeless quality of a photograph, he lost some of his illusions. He never again believed that timidity could suddenly be made courage or intent be made act. But at the same time, he embraced a larger and more debased illusion. He took upon himself the revery of the void, the romance of nihilism and absolute estrangement. And so, in the rapture of oblivion, Langhof acted his part within the Camp, held, as he was, within the grasp of his greatest illusion: that while we are, we can cease to be.

Part IV

G OOD TO SEE you again, Don Pedro."
I had seen the tail of dust wind down the mountainside, soiling the morning air, as Don Camillo's limousine moved toward my compound.

"I was not expecting another visit," I tell him.

Don Camillo smiles. "No, I suppose not."

"Would you care for refreshment?"

"No, not for me."

I glance at the two bodyguards who stand beside his chair. They shake their heads. No refreshment, then.

"I hope nothing is wrong, Don Camillo."

"Nothing serious," Don Camillo says. He roots himself deeply into the chair. "So, I suppose you are wondering what brings me here so quickly after my last visit."

"Yes."

Don Camillo glances off the verandah toward the large tent that is spread across the ground. "Very nice, the national colors."

"Dr. Ludtz's idea, Don Camillo," I tell him.

"Very apt. You Europeans are always so conscious of just the right touch."

"We have planned fireworks..."

"No, no," Don Camillo says quickly. "No fireworks, Don Pedro. It is too distracting for the guards."

I nod. "As you wish."

Don Camillo takes a gold cigarette case from the pocket of his white linen suit. "Cigarette, Don Pedro?"

"I don't smoke."

He takes a cigarette from the case. "I do." He lights the cigarette, takes a deep inhalation, and blows a column of tumbling smoke toward my face. Just the right touch for mild intimidation.

"You were about to tell me the purpose of your visit, Don Camillo," I remind him.

Don Camillo's face hardens with mock seriousness. "You know, of course, about this trouble we've been having in the northern provinces."

"We have spoken of it before," I tell him. "I was not aware that it was very serious."

"Serious? Well, no. But it's growing, I'm afraid, Don Pedro, steadily growing."

"I see."

"It appears that two of the northern provinces have fallen completely to the rebels. Most distressful, as you can imagine."

"Yes."

"Most unfortunate," Don Camillo says. "Don't you think so, Don Pedro?"

"Of course."

Don Camillo smiles with reptilian suspiciousness. "Of course, yes," he says flatly. He takes another puff from his cigarette and leans back in his chair, his head cocked slightly toward the revolver in the belt of the guard who stands beside him. "You realize, don't you, Don Pedro, that if El Presidente should be overthrown, your own position here in the Republic would be jeopardized?"

"Naturally."

"Not only jeopardized, Doctor," Don Camillo adds. He leans forward for emphasis. "Let's speak plainly. They would crucify you, Dr. Langhof."

It surprises me that Don Camillo thinks me capable of being moved by so common an allusion. "I know what the rebels would do," I tell him. "I realize that my security is tied to El Presidente's."

Don Camillo smiles that thin, basilisk smile. Somewhere in the Republic there must be an academy that teaches these base, totalitarian facial expressions. In the Camp, there was nothing so ugly as a smile.

"Do you?" Don Camillo asks through his sneer.

"Do I what?"

"Do you perfectly realize how you are tied to El Presidente?"

Across the river I can hear a mynah bird cawing. I turn and glimpse its bright, orange beak through a fan of leaves.

"Do you perfectly understand, Dr. Langhof?" Don Camillo repeats.

I turn to face him. "Why do you doubt me, Don Camillo?"

"I doubt everyone," Don Camillo tells me. "It is one of the rules of political life, as you must surely know, Doctor."

I watch Don Camillo through a cloud of smoke. He insists upon a military aspect even to his civilian attire and festoons his chest with a display of ribbons and medallions. They tinkle slightly when he shifts in his seat. He has worn them to impress me with his capacity for terror. They represent his license to extract anything he wants from me, by any means he sees fit. It is the garment that legitimizes torture, that makes of it a civilized function. And so the man who wears the badge of state and then applies electrodes to his victim's testicles does not do so as a base sadist slavering in his bedchamber, but as a cool and stately instrument of the civil will.

Don Camillo leans forward again, for emphasis; he is a man of limited gestures. "They are still hunting you, you know. That old man. Arnstein. The one who has tracked down so many others. He's still looking. A phone call, and it would be all over for you, Dr. Langhof."

Sometimes I see the old man, Arnstein, in my mind. He is slumped over a desk filled with papers and photographs, one of the crime's relentless scholars.

"Many years have passed," Don Camillo continues, "but never believe that you are forgotten."

Against the far wall in Arnstein's office, the files bulge, open-mouthed, screaming.

"They are still looking for you, Doctor," Don Camillo goes on tediously, "be assured of that."

I can see Arnstein's files in my mind. They stand ghostly and alone — gray, silent cabinets filled with thousands of tattered papers. Somewhere among the thumbed, soiled pages, my name is underlined in red.

"There is no need to threaten me, Don Camillo."

"A little party of commandos," Don Camillo continues, "coming over the ridge there. What chance would you have against them? None. None whatever, let me assure you. They would come, and you would end up in a glass booth like the others."

"How would such a circumstance serve El Presidente, Don Camillo?" I ask.

Don Camillo shakes his head. "It wouldn't," he says. "Not yet." He leans back, watching me, imagining that I squirm under his gaze. His is the foolishness that conceives terror as the absolute solution. For him, the world is made secure by fear. If dread were a woman, he would take it to his bed for buggering.

"How could my leaving the Republic ever serve El Presidente's purposes?" I ask.

"Oh, it probably couldn't, Don Pedro," Don Camillo admits. "But this business in the northern provinces, it's very expensive. The treasury has been diminished. It is in need of resupply. It might be profitable for you to show your concern."

"How might I show it?"

Don Camillo smiles. "You are very direct."

"I have learned to be."

"Yes. Good. Well, to your question. These diamonds you have in your possession."

"What about them?"

"Forgive me for saying so, but you've been doling them out rather stingily over the years, Don Pedro."

"El Presidente thinks me ungrateful?"

Don Camillo laughs. "No, no. Not at all. But you see, these rebels — the ones in the northern provinces — suppressing them is very expensive. My point is that perhaps you might be persuaded to give a little more than usual when El Presidente comes for his visit."

"Then I will."

Don Camillo looks surprised by my quick agreement. It is one of the self-justifications of the greedy to think everyone as greedy as themselves.

"You intend to make a special offering, then?" Don Camillo asks.

"Yes."

Don Camillo's eyes narrow. "How much?"

"Enough to make El Presidente happy."

Don Camillo looks at me pointedly. "El Presidente is very sad, Don Pedro."

"I will make him joyous."

Don Camillo slaps his hands together loudly and a flock of parrots spray noisily into the air over the river. "Excellent!" Don Camillo cries. "Excellent! I knew I could depend upon you, Don Pedro."

"You can tell El Presidente that I intend to make his visit here a very happy one."

"I'm sure you do," Don Camillo says. "He always looks forward to seeing you, Don Pedro. He considers you to be one of the first citizens of the Republic."

"I will reaffirm my loyalty to him. You may be assured of that."

"He never doubted it, of course," Don Camillo says. He smiles broadly, then glances at his watch. "I must go, I'm afraid."

"So soon?"

"I'm afraid so, Don Pedro," Don Camillo replies. He grips the arms of the chair, grunts, and rises with difficulty from the seat. He is weighed down by the burdens of state and imported cream cheese. On his feet now, he extends his hand toward me. "So good to have seen you again, Don Pedro," he says.

"And you, Don Camillo."

"And Dr. Ludtz, how is he?"

"He is ill. A fever."

Don Camillo crinkles his brow, imitating concern. "Sorry to hear it. I hope he'll be better when El Presidente visits. I would not want him to miss such an occasion."

"Nor would I."

Don Camillo turns slowly and moves toward the stairs. I follow behind him until one of his guards steps between us and presses his palm against my chest. "No," he says. His face is smooth and brown, his eyes very dark, like his hair. He has the look of a matinee idol, clean and piercing. But the nature of his function contradicts the beauty of his person, transforming his lovely, graceful body into a rattling machine.

Don Camillo eases himself around. "¿Qué pasa?" he asks the guard. Then he notices the hand pressed against my chest. He laughs and sweeps the hand away. "El doctor es un amigo mio," he says. He winks at me. "Well trained, don't you think?"

"Yes."

Don Camillo turns again and proceeds down the stairs. "Adiós, Don Pedro."

"Adiós."

The guard continues to eye me carefully for a moment, then turns and follows Don Camillo down the stairs, quickly unsnapping the guardstrap of his holster. His is the thoughtful precision of the devoted servant.

At the limousine Don Camillo turns back toward me and waves his hand. In his grotesque rotundity, Don Camillo is that perfect metaphor of bloat about which exiled poets write when they turn their eyes homeward to the Republic. Casamira in New York and Sanchez in Leningrad, these two forlorn poets, separated by oceans real and ideological, and yet who both seized on the obesity of Don Camillo as the apt image for a famished land, rendered him immortal in their songs. In their twisted verse they map the sagging glut of underdevelopment and feed the minds of the northern provinces with visions of release.

A short distance from Don Camillo's limousine I see Dr. Ludtz stagger out onto his porch, his fevered bulk supported by two canes. He lifts his hand in greeting to Don Camillo, but the grinning minister does not see him and completes the task of maneuvering himself into the back seat of the car.

As Don Camillo pulls away, a sudden cool breeze sweeps down from the mountains, splitting the heat like a sword through gossamer. Here in the Republic, we are accustomed to inversions: to the chill within the swelter, the knife beneath the velvet, the sea snake twisting in the cool, blue wave.

BELOW THE VERANDAH, the workmen are beginning to prepare the tent. They work under a sun that turns the river to a flowing amber. They erect the corner posts carefully, as they have been instructed. The poles must stand absolutely straight. Nothing is allowed to lean here in the Republic. And when the posts have been set deep in the ground, they raise the tent, a brilliant panoply of red and orange stripes. Underneath the tent, they set the table that I will prepare for El Presidente. He will bring his officers with him, for it is his habit to surround himself with the weak, the stupid, and the worshipful, all those too cowardly, incompetent, or avaricious to call his person into question.

Here, underneath the tent, the El Presidente of Casamira's satirical invention will engorge himself with meat and fruit. He will stuff the dripping flanks of pigs into his mouth, follow that with fistfuls of brandied dates, and wash it all down with papaya juice mixed with beer. For a few hours, this compound upriver from the village of El Caliz will become the mead hall of the Republic, a place of noise and brawling, of lewd jokes and lurid tales. The people of the village will observe it all, standing barefoot behind a velvet cordon defended by well-heeled soldiers. As El Presidente feasts upon the meat and sweets, they will feast on him while their stomachs rumble under frayed rope belts. It is part of the nature of adoration to find immunity from the contradictions of reality.

The key to sudden transformation, that is what El Presidente offers. In the great sports arena where the Leader spoke, they came by the benighted millions in search of that one blinding instant that would lift them effortlessly to another life. Observe the little bald-headed burgher failing in business, despised by his wife, dismissed by his children; a man without credential, place, or influence; a man whose mind is held captive by every illusion that ensures mediocrity; a religious man to whom the Church in her grandeur gives no more than a passing nod; a business man whose connection to the engines of finance does not extend beyond a dwindling bank account; a family man whose children pay greater heed to movie stars and black musicians; a community man whose duties and responsibilities reach no further than his obligation to sweep the sidewalk once a week; a political man whom the state regards as nothing more than an annual source of petty revenue. To such a one, the Leader's voice was clarion, concentrating all his fear and rage into one shrill cry of indignation. Through all the history of crime there runs one immemorial complaint: Save me! Save me! For I cannot save myself!

In desperation we grasp at the possibility of miracle. And of all the things desperation needs, the cruelest is speed. Thus we must have our transfiguration, and it must be sudden and entire, for the labor of the will and wisdom is too difficult, uncertain, and slow.

Juan seeks a miracle to save the orchids, a pearl dropped into the humid soil from the hand of God. Esperanza, staring at the steamy, rotting innards of a crocodile, seeks salvation from her rooted humanness, seeks to know that mystery of creation which will lift her to a golden throne. Ludtz, picking lichens from his tomb, seeks the Virgin's comforting smile, seeks the erasure of the past, seeks to pluck saintliness from a life of shame. Alberto and Tomás seek the miraculous between the spread legs of some brown girl and see paradise in her willing smile. Don Camillo seeks his redemption in vast fields of undiscovered copper. In the variety with which we yearn for the miraculous resides our sole infinitude.

In the Camp Langhof lost all notion of miraculous transformation. He lost the capacity to plan and to will. He never thought of escape or resistance. Once, he stood in the snow and watched a Mongoloid boy hanged on the gallows not far from the medical compound. The boy was hoisted slowly by hand rather than dropped, and it took him quite some time to strangle. As he flailed about, kicking at the ground, his face became horribly contorted, and as it darkened to a deep blue, the boy took on the aspect of an ape. The similarity between the two was striking, and Langhof observed it solemnly, silently, like a scientist recording one more piece of evidence for evolution.

And yet even in this comatose state Langhof was not utterly beyond human response. Something of him remained, and Kessler called it forth that day in the courtyard behind the medical compound.

Langhof had been reclining on his bunk, obviously watching the shadows glide forward then retreat on the ceiling as the light bulb swung back and forth. There was a knock at the door, and Langhof sat up.

"Come in," he said.

He saw the door open and Kessler's round, beefy face peep inside.

"Ah, Dr. Langhof," Kessler said happily, "I'm glad to find you in."

"What can I do for you, Doctor?" Langhof asked routinely.

"Come into the courtyard," Kessler said. "I have something I'd like for you to observe."

"Is it important, Dr. Kessler?" Langhof asked, protesting mildly. "I was just relaxing a bit."

"I think you will be interested, Dr. Langhof," Kessler said. "It suggests that the areas of research here in the Camp are constantly expanding."

Langhof got to his feet and followed Kessler down the hallway to the exit at the side of the building.

Kessler stepped out the door and made a sharp turn into the back courtyard, a flat surface covered with freshly fallen snow. He pointed as Langhof stepped to his side. "There," he said. "This is another area of research."

There were about twenty of them, naked, huddling together in the snow, their skin already turning bluish in the cold, the children clinging tightly to their mothers' bodies, one baby sucking at a freezing breast.

"We're going to see how long it takes," Kessler said. "Our people on the eastern front have had a very bad time of it this winter, so we need to know more about the process of freezing."

Langhof's eyes remained fixed on the moaning, swaying crowd that squatted a few meters from him. He could see Rausch standing beyond them at the entrance of the courtyard, his feet planted wide apart, his machine gun held casually in his hands. When their eyes met, Rausch smiled and lightly tipped his cap.

"I have no expertise in this field," Langhof said to Kessler flatly.

Kessler smiled indulgently. "No one does, my good man," he said. "That's why we're conducting this experiment, to gain expertise."

"This particular . . . area," Langhof stammered, "it does not . . . does not interest me."

"We cannot always choose what interests us, Doctor," Kessler said.

Langhof straightened himself. "Yes, sir."

Kessler appeared irritable for a moment, then calmed himself. "I didn't mean to be sharp with you, Dr. Langhof."

"Quite all right, sir."

"Well, I understand this area of research is quite a distance from hygiene."

"Yes, sir," Langhof said. He could feel his throat closing.

"But I hope you can understand the need for all our staff to have some knowledge of what we're doing here."

"Yes, sir," Langhof said. He felt his hands squeeze together.

"You may return to your quarters, Doctor," Kessler said.

"Thank you, sir," Langhof said briskly. He began to move away quickly.

"You're due in the laboratory in fifteen minutes, however," Kessler warned.

"Yes, sir. I know," Langhof said, almost running now.

Inside the building, Langhof stopped, drew in a long breath, then moved slowly down the hall. He entered his room, closed the door behind him, and sat down on his bunk. Staring at his boots, he could not connect himself to the world by means of any reliable image. It was as if everything had been swept up in a terrible wind and blown randomly, chaotically into the stratosphere. He could not feel his clothes over his shoulders or his boots on his feet. He could not feel the little breeze that wafted in from the small crack in the window. He could not hear the screams of the freezing vermin dying in the snow only a few meters away.

It was not clear to him what had happened. But now, at night when I can hear the sound of the macaw, I know what happened in the courtyard. I stand by the window and listen to the shrill cry of the jungle birds and they are transformed into the cries of the people slumped freezing in the snow. I hear the wailing and the moaning as I actually heard them, but in my imagination I can hear things now that I could not hear then. I can hear the slurping of the baby's mouth. I can hear the crunching of the snow as the bodies topple over one by one, hour after hour. I can hear the scratch of Kessler's pencil as he records the deaths. I can hear the slide of the bodies as the guards drag them from the courtyard and pile them onto the waiting lorries. I have magnified the world of sight and sound. I have learned to hear and see the smallest things, the rush of a final breath, the ant at work within a broken filling.

And so I know what happened to our hero in the courtyard. He walked out, following Kessler, in the same state of oblivion that had overtaken him months before, on the first night of his arrival. He turned the corner, saw the naked bodies, but did not see them. Instead he saw something else. He saw the actual physical face of that dread he had felt so long ago at the Institute. He saw the horror fully, and in a way that had not approached him before. He had extracted babies from the wombs of women and infected scores of people with disease. But he had always seen this as an inevitable circumstance of his being in the Camp. He had forgotten, conveniently forgotten, that in a sense he had already *known* the Camp, but had chosen to dismiss that knowledge. As his sensibility slowly emerged, his mind began to comb the scattered litter of his past. He believed that it was all there to be discovered within himself. If he could locate his person, he could locate the world.

There are times when I think of this and then go walking in the darkness beside the river. I see our hero slumped on his bed, his mind teeming with schemes of self-analysis, dreaming that by discovering himself he can discover the Camp. And I think that if it would not rouse the monkeys or cauterize my soul, I would heave my head back and laugh with such thunderous contempt that it would shake the drowsing vipers from their vines.

IN THE EARLY YEARS at El Caliz, before old age calcified my bones, I often wandered into the surrounding jungle. Across the river, the world was as it had been ten thousand years before, and from time to time I attempted that revery in nature that mystics and idiots are said to feel. I lay on the ground and dipped my face in the sweating soil. I swam naked in the streams. I wrapped my body in great, waxy leaves and baked it on the mud flats to the south. I put water lilies in my hair and rolled in the reeds of the delta. I drank cactus milk, sucked sugar cane, and chewed coffee beans. I waxed my hair with lemon juice and adorned myself with vines. I tried to lose myself in physical delight, join myself to the imagined rhythms of creation. While Dr. Ludtz obsessively cleaned his paltry arsenal or strung klieg lights about his cottage, I sank into the illusion that I could locate myself in nature by uniting with it, by shirking off my isolated humanness and becoming an instrument of immersion. But in doing this I only repeated the process that I had attempted once before in the Camp.

For Langhof, suddenly stricken with his own helplessness and venality, felt compelled to investigate the Camp by means of immersing himself within its horrors. He wanted to see the flames from the chimneys at noon and night, sunrise and sundown. He met the trains as they steamed their way up to the snow-covered platforms. He followed the huddled crowds to the mouth of the gas chambers and stood watching as they shuffled out of their clothes. He imagined himself as a kind of artist, observing the Camp from all angles, scribbling notes, conducting interviews. Somewhere in all of this he expected to find himself. The horror, of course, was unimaginable, but Langhof felt it his duty to record it with his senses. And so he monotonously and obsessively toured the Camp, barking commands from time to time so as not to rouse suspicion, and slapping his little riding crop against his boot, gently or viciously, depending upon who might be observing his activity. It was on one of his nightly journeys that he heard something move around the corner of one of the darkened barracks. He drew his pistol.

"Halt," he commanded. "Halt. Don't move." He waited for a moment, then drew his flashlight from his pocket and beamed it toward the sound. One of the prisoners was standing with his back pressed against the barracks wall.

Langhof studied the small, bearded face, glowing in the yellow light. "What are you doing in the yard at this hour?" he asked.

The prisoner did not appear frightened. "Walking, the same as you," he said.

"You are not permitted to be outside the barracks," Langhof said.

The prisoner did not answer. He squinted into the light, but kept his hands pressed tightly to the wall.

"What are you doing out here?" Langhof repeated.

"You are Dr. Langhof," the prisoner said.

Langhof stepped away slightly. "How do you know me?"

"You work in the medical compound," the prisoner said. "So do I."

"What is your name?"

"Ginzburg. Do you want my number?"

"Yes," Langhof said, "I do." He took out a pad and, as Ginzburg recited his number, Langhof pretended to write it down.

"Do you have it?" Ginzburg asked.

"Yes," Langhof said. He replaced the pad in his uniform pocket. "You had better watch yourself, or you'll end up being reported." To his amazement, Langhof thought he saw a smile flicker across Ginzburg's face. "Who do you work for?"

"The New Order," Ginzburg said sardonically.

"Don't be ridiculous," Langhof said. "Who is your superior in the medical compound?"

"Do you want to write it down?"

"Just tell me," Langhof demanded.

"Dr. Kessler. He is your superior too, I believe," Ginzburg said. He shielded his eyes from the light. "Could you put that flashlight away?"

Langhof turned the light off.

"Thank you, sir," Ginzburg said.

Looking at the small figure before him, Langhof felt the absurdity of the pistol and dropped it back into his holster. "Get back to your quarters," he said.

"Yes, sir," the vermin said.

Langhof turned, began to walk away, then heard the prisoner following from behind. He turned around. "What are you doing?"

"Going to my quarters, as you ordered, Dr. Langhof."

"Don't joke with me," Langhof said, "Get to your quarters."

"I'm on my way, Doctor. I live in the medical compound, the same as you."

"I haven't seen you there."

"That may be," the prisoner said. "You may not have noticed me." He smiled. "I suppose all the prisoners look alike to you, but believe me, to the prisoners each of you looks different."

Langhof stared at the vermin suspiciously. "What do you do in the medical compound?"

"Anything I'm told to, same as you," Ginzburg said, and followed his reply with a small smile.

"Get that smile off your face," Langhof said loudly.

The smile disappeared instantly. "Sorry, sir. A hazard of my profession."

"Profession? What profession?"

"Before I came here, I was a comic," Ginzburg said. "Nothing big, you understand. You would not have heard of me. Strictly small time. Smoke-filled clubs where the patrons chat constantly during the performance and sometimes throw cocktail olives at the performers."

"And you haven't lost your sense of humor, is that it?" Langhof said sternly.

"Not entirely."

"Well, then, I would suggest that you keep it to yourself," Langhof warned.

"I suppose I should," Ginzburg said, "but I never learned how to act appropriately. I snicker at all the wrong times. Funerals. Weddings. During the High Holy Days. It was always embarrassing for my family."

"There are people here who will teach you proper behavior," Langhof said.

"I know. Have you ever heard of the swing?"

"Yes. You were tortured?"

Ginzburg laughed. "Everyone is tortured."

"But not on the swing. Why you?"

Ginzburg grinned. "They were jealous of my good looks, I suppose."

Langhof did not smile. "And I imagine that you laughed all the way through it."

Ginzburg shook his head. "No. I cried. Screamed, really. I begged. I pissed my pants. I called my mother foul names. It was quite a show."

"Always the performer."

"A ham, I'm afraid."

"The clown in hell," Langhof said contemptuously.

"No, not that."

"What, then?"

Ginzburg shrugged. "Who can answer such a question? But I'll tell you this. I have learned to read a face perfectly. It comes from years of scanning audiences through all that cigar and cigarette smoke. I can tell the man who's cheating on his wife. He's always glancing over his shoulder. And I can spot all the virgins in the room. The girls always look happy; the boys always look miserable."

Langhof waved his hand. "Nonsense," he said. He began to walk away.

Ginzburg stepped up beside him. "I've noticed your face," he said.

"You've noticed nothing," Langhof said irritably.

"Oh, yes, I have. The moment I saw it was you with the pistol, I knew it would be all right."

"I wouldn't be so sure of that."

"I'm quite sure. I saw you the first day you came to the Camp. What was it, two years ago? Three? Anyway, I saw you."

"Where?"

"You were in the dissecting room with Kessler and Ludtz. Kessler told us to bring a few stiffs over to the table. They were all piled up in the corner. Pregnant women. Anyway, I saw your face." He paused a moment, looking at Langhof. "You were trying not to scream."

Langhof halted and turned toward Ginzburg. "Shut up!"

"I didn't mean to insult you," Ginzburg said quickly. "I'm not that much of a fool, no matter what my father used to think. Besides, I know a dangerous man when I see one."

"That's your first mistake," Langhof said. "I'm not the least bit dangerous."

"Really? When was the first time you injected chloroform directly into someone's heart?"

"That's none of your affair," Langhof said angrily.

"No, it isn't. That's not my point. But you do remember the day, don't you? You probably remember the exact time."

"Have you not performed work, such as it is, in the medical compound as well?" Langhof asked sarcastically.

"We are hardly in the same position, Doctor," Ginzburg replied. "Besides, I did not mean to taunt you."

"Go to your quarters," Langhof said. "Go in front of me."

Ginzburg did not move. "I haven't killed anyone, there's the difference."

"Congratulations," Langhof said bitterly.

"When the New Order triumphs, I'll just be a nameless casualty. One of those insufferable weaklings who permitted himself to be destroyed without the slightest resistance. I'll be held up as the perfect proof of why I should have been annihilated."

"I wouldn't worry about that," Langhof said, "because the New Order will not triumph."

Ginzburg smiled. "Yes, it will. Do you know why? Because it's too much work to oppose it. It requires too much thinking."

"The New Order is doomed," Langhof said. "The work is being done on the eastern front, and thinking has very little to do with it. You'll be hearing the cannons in a matter of weeks."

"This time you may be right," Ginzburg said lightly, "but history goes on."

"You seem awfully serene about it."

Ginzburg winked. "Serene? No. But free. Free because I'm crazy. Except I'm not really crazy. I'm a fraud."

"I'm not in the mood for a confession," Langhof said.

"That's your religious tradition, not mine," Ginzburg said. "But let me continue. Where was I? Oh yes, this business of my being a fraud. I'm a fraud because this joking, this humor, it's all a pose. That's why I know that the next time, or the next, they'll win." He laughed. "The prisoners think they know the world; the ones who think at all, I should say."

"But you're the philosopher, I suppose," Langhof said.

"I look at the prisoners' faces, and all I see are blank spaces," Ginzburg said. He leaned forward. "Do you know how dangerous that is, Doctor?" he whispered. Then he chuckled.

"But you see through everyone, is that it?"

"I keep my eyes open. Not everyone does," Ginzburg said with a laugh.

"A smart fellow like you, a wise guy," Langhof said mockingly, "it's a wonder they got you here."

"The wheel of fate," Ginzburg said with a shrug of the shoulders. "How about you, what's your story?"

"That's not your business," Langhof said.

Ginzburg smiled. "Everyone will have to explain it someday," he said.

"But not tonight," Langhof said coldly.

"Perhaps when we hear the cannons, then."

"Get away from me," Langhof said.

Ginzburg remained in place. "I've seen your face, Doctor."

"Get to your quarters, now," Langhof said loudly.

Ginzburg smiled and tipped an imaginary hat. "Thank you, ladies and gentlemen," he said with a slight bow. "Gentlemen may deposit gratuities in my hand; ladies may use a little pouch behind my fly."

Langhof stood and watched Ginzburg trot toward the medical compound. At the steps, under the light, he did a quick soft shoe, kicking up a spray of powdery snow.

DR. LUDTZ is lying on his back, sweating in the steamy cottage, but adamant in his refusal to open the shutters for ventilation.

"Decent of you to call upon me," he says as I enter.

"Feeling better, I hope?"

"I'm afraid not," Dr. Ludtz replies. His breathing is labored, and his voice comes to me through a slight, gurgling wheeze. "The fever has not broken yet," he says. "As a matter of fact, it is getting worse."

"Do you want an ice compress?"

"I tried that. It gave me a chill. I can't bear chills, Dr. Langhof."

Completely bald, his face flushed and puffy, Dr. Ludtz looks like an ancient baby.

"But an ice compress might help, Doctor," I tell him.

Dr. Ludtz shakes his head vigorously. "No, no. Thank you, but I can't bear chills."

In the heat of the Republic, he has lost his endurance for cold. He is now a creature of the tropics, one for whom the slightest breeze is frigid.

"I suppose you're making preparations for El Presidente?" he asks.

"Of course."

"I saw the tent. Very nice."

I nod. "Don Camillo commented on it. I told him it was your idea."

"And he seemed pleased?" Dr. Ludtz asks anxiously.

"Very pleased. He commented upon the appropriateness of the gesture."

"Very good," Dr. Ludtz says. "Very good of you to mention me to him."

"I'm sure El Presidente will be pleased, as well."

"He might think it vulgar, do you suppose?" Dr. Ludtz asks worriedly.

"I'm sure not, Dr. Ludtz. Don't trouble yourself about it. Have you been able to sleep?"

"Only a little," Dr. Ludtz says. "Snatches. No more than an hour at a time."

In the Camp, he sometimes slept well, sometimes fitfully, depending on the progress of his research. During the freezing experiments he slept well, but during the tetanus studies he was ill at ease.

"I brought a bottle of brandy for you," I tell him. I lift the bottle toward him. "It's the last of our supply. I'll have to order more soon."

"Then save it...please, Dr. Langhof...save it," Dr. Ludtz stammers, the wheezing becoming suddenly more intense. "El Presidente...what if...he might want brandy?"

"There'll be other things for El Presidente. This is for us." I take two small brandy snifters from a bag, place them on the table, and pour the brandy. As it pours from the mouth of the bottle it sounds like someone breathing through a wound in the throat.

I hand Dr. Ludtz the glass and raise my own next to his, clinking them together lightly. "To your health, Dr. Ludtz. To a speedy recovery."

"Thank you," Dr. Ludtz says. With difficulty he brings the rim of the glass to his lips and drinks. A small brown stream runs down one side of his mouth and off his chin. "Look at this," Dr. Ludtz says, embarrassed. "Spilled it ...oh, ridiculous."

I wipe his chin and shirt collar with my handkerchief. "Difficult to drink lying down," I tell him.

"Yes, yes . . . that's it . . . difficult."

I take the glass and begin to pour another for him.

"No, no . . . with great thanks . . . enough."

"The fever should break tonight, Doctor," I tell him. "By morning the worst should be over." In the Camp, I once helped Dr. Ludtz string a line of aspirin in the air. Those with a certain temperature were allowed to lick it once; those with a slightly higher fever were allowed to lick it twice; those with an even higher fever were sent to another ward and given phenol.

"It is . . ." Dr. Ludtz begins, then breaks off and coughs slightly into his fist. "It is worse."

"Well, that always happens before it gets better. You know that, Dr. Ludtz."

Dr. Ludtz nods very slightly, his eyes closing as he does so.

"Is there anything I can get for you?"

"The rebels . . . are they . . ."

"Nowhere near us, Dr. Ludtz. Really, you shouldn't even bother with such matters. The Federales have the situation well in hand."

Dr. Ludtz is not convinced.

I smile. "Do you really think El Presidente would permit such a ridiculous rabble to overthrow him?"

"It has happened . . . other places."

"But not here, I assure you. Never here."

As the enemy troops approached the Camp, I remember him scurrying back and forth, hurling stacks of paper into a large ashcan. It was raining and there was no gasoline to keep the fire burning, so the papers began to smolder rather than to burn. Dr. Ludtz became frantic, scooping up huge armfuls of medical files and ripping at them furiously as he squatted in the mud, sobbing with terror, the visor of his cap singed and smoking.

"I hope . . . you're right," Dr. Ludtz says. He seems to need all his strength to breathe, gulping the air down as if it has turned liquid.

"You need to rest, Doctor," I tell him. "Tomorrow morning you may wake up completely relieved.

"Friday ... El Presidente," Dr. Ludtz says.

"Yes. But don't worry. He'll understand if you're ill."

"El Presidente ..." Dr. Ludtz breathes.

I get up quickly. "Please now, Doctor, you can't expect to improve if you don't relax. Get some rest. Sleep well. And perhaps you'll be quite fit by the time El Presidente arrives."

Dr. Ludtz lifts his fingers from his chest. "Thank you ... good of you ... I ..."

"No more, Doctor," I insist. "Sleep, that's what you need. Build up your strength. I'll be by to see you sometime tomorrow."

I ease myself toward him and squeeze his hand softly. "Good night, Dr. Ludtz."

"Yes ... good night ... thank you."

On that last day in the Camp, he had almost lost control of himself. Coming back from the pit, I heard him whimpering through the billowing smoke, through the heavy rumble of the enemy guns a few kilometers away. He sat, bespattered with mud, one sleeve of his uniform torn and drooping down toward his elbow, exposing a bloody arm. By then he had ceased ripping at the papers, but had deposited a pile of them in front of him, taking one sheet from the top, tearing it into slivers, then shoving the slivers into his mouth, where he chewed slowly, like a cow eating daisies. I could hear some of the prisoners battering against the doors of the empty supply houses. I ran over to Ludtz and shouted his name. But he did not look up. So I grabbed him by the arm and pulled him to his feet, dragging him with me out of the Camp — I think now, as a souvenir.

Part V

Part V

FROM MY VERANDAH, at night, I can see only what is purposefully illuminated: Dr. Ludtz's cottage, the nursery, and to the left, a few lights still burning in the village of El Caliz. El Presidente can see much more from the balcony of his palace. He can see the gardens and the reflecting pools, the cobblestone walks bordered on either side with potted palms, the marble steps that lead to the great mahogany doors of the palace itself. And beyond the pale orange stucco walls of the palace he can see the wide boulevard of administration buildings, their façades made brilliant by klieg lights buried in their lawns: the Department of Justice, with its Doric columns rising toward lofty entablatures; the Museum of the Republic, with its tiled roof and high gables, a Tudor contrivance set in the tropics; the Ministry of Finance, with its Egyptian design, ornate as the Temple of Horus, a huge façade of vast, teeming multicolored murals where scenes slide invisibly into other scenes, colors into other colors, a pulsing, indecipherable panorama perfectly representative of the intricate circularities of money, the veiled, impenetrable calligraphy of man's worldly goods. And then, should El Presidente's eyes move upward, he will see the lights of the capital city: first the tall, airless structures of the professional classes;

then the shaded streets of the middle classes; and finally, sweeping out in all directions, the great teeming slums of splintered wood and rusting tin, the moiling, wasted afterbirth of underdevelopment.

When the Athenian painter Parrhasius wished to do a work of art based on the suffering of Prometheus, he first had an old man brought to him and tortured in his presence so that he could observe the changing face of agony. El Presidente, in the egocentrism of his art, has created the Republic. But it was the Camp that brought to greatest fruition this process by which man is made idea. In the locked gas chambers adjoining the crematoria, human flesh piled itself into a pyramid of Darwinian simplicity: babies and small children on the bottom; next, the old and sick; next, the small of frame, mostly women; then men of medium build; and piled on top of them, their fingers clawing at the ceiling, the strongest representatives of physique. Here the real became surreal, and all merged into a landscape whose perfect epigram was *Hier ist kein Warum*— "Here there is no why."

Langhof, our hero, saw all of this and continued to eat and sleep and evacuate his bowels. In a single month he saw more horror than El Presidente could create in a thousand years with his limited technology: women hung by the heels and slit open like pigs, their intestines dangling in their faces; old men fried on electric wire, blue smoke rising from their ears; the cheeks of young girls eaten through with noma; piles of rotting bodies that made a catacomb for rats. Subtlety would veil the horror; rhetoric would turn it into style. And yet, Langhof did see these things, and at the point where one can no longer look, it is there one must look on. Langhof looked, and did not stop looking. Why?

Perhaps here in the Republic it is possible to know. I can sit in perfect silence through the night and think only of this question. Here there is no distraction from the process of examination. But beyond the railing upon which I lean, my eyes moving up and down the river, there are a billion alternatives to thought, a million modes of hallucination, each no more than a small particle of that hot mist that rose above the primordial pit. But here on the verandah there are no plaster statues of dead saints, no sweaty tools of bowed labor, no applications for advancement, no familial distress. Free of all these encumbrances to thought, it is perhaps possible for me to use fully the powers that I possess. And so I have come to think that what remained in our hero — weak, pathetic, destitute, and yet abiding still — was a sense of inquiry. Ridiculous as it may seem, even through the long period of his somnambulance Langhof had never failed to observe the Camp through the gentle curve of a question mark. That much of science was still left to him, and the brief exchange with Ginzburg had served to rouse it further. Ginzburg's absurdity, his surrealism, touched a dormant chamber in Langhof's mind. And so, like a fairy child following a trail of bread crumbs through the forest, he pursued the dancing comic who had disappeared behind the door of the medical compound.

Langhof walked down the hall. He could hear someone whistling softly in the distance and toward the rear of the compound he found Ginzburg lying on a bunk, his hands behind his head, the door of his room swung wide open.

"Don't you think you should close the door?" Langhof asked.

Ginzburg turned over on his side and propped his head up in one hand. "Why?"

"For privacy," Langhof said.

Ginzburg stared evenly at Langhof. "What are you doing here, may I ask?"

The question sounded like an accusation. To counter it, Langhof asserted his authority. "These quarters. Very nice. May I ask how you rate them?"

Ginzburg smiled. "Easy. I'm Kessler's boy. His court jester. His fool." His eyes seemed to grow cold. "And his whore."

"Really? And what were you doing outside just now?"

"Burying something," Ginzburg said airily.

"What?" Langhof demanded.

"Drugs, mostly. Morphine. Aspirin. A little food, too."

Langhof stepped into the room and closed the door behind him. "You could be shot for that."

"Not as long as Kessler has anything to do with it," Ginzburg said confidently.

"These things you bury — what are they for?"

"For some of the prisoners, of course," Ginzburg said casually.

"You risk your life for them?"

Ginzburg laughed. "My life? No. Kessler will protect me; I told you that." He paused, watching Langhof's face. "Oh, I get it now. You want me to be doing this at the risk of my life. You want me to be a brave man risking my life for my fellow suffering creatures. Such a possibility would give you...I don't know...hope?"

"I'm asking, that's all," Langhof said.

Ginzburg tilted his head playfully. "Well, if you're looking for some surviving heroism in me, then go look somewhere else. You've been here a long time, Langhof. You've seen some courage. You know that there are people in the Camp — and people outside it — who really do risk their lives for others."

"Of course," Langhof said.

"Then why would one more make any difference?"

"I don't know. Maybe because you're the only one I could talk to."

"Well, you lost out again, Doctor, because I'm no hero. Kessler looks out for me. He's in love with me."

"You must be joking."

"I'm a handsome boy," Ginzburg said lightly. "And personable. I have an excellent sense of humor."

"Enough of this," Langhof said irritably.

"A hero," Ginzburg said mockingly. "How ridiculous. A hero to talk to. Nonsense." He smiled. "No. I know what you want. All those people out there doing their heroic deeds, they don't interest you. That's it, isn't it? They don't interest you because their heroism is so natural, so thoughtless. No, what you're looking for is the intelligent hero, the one who knows all the consequences but wills himself to heroic acts."

"What difference would that make?" Langhof asked.

"All the difference in the world, to you," Ginzburg said.

"You don't know what you're talking about."

Ginzburg sat up in his bunk. "Don't I? You just can't imagine yourself in the situation you've been in for years, can you? You're still wondering."

"Wondering what?"

"You're still wondering how you got here."

"I know how I got here," Langhof said. "It was an accident, a stupid fluke."

Ginzburg shook his head. "There may be petty accidents in this world, Langhof, but there are no great ones. Think. If you got here by accident, then so did everybody else. That would mean the Camp itself is just an accident. Let me tell you something, Langhof, that thought, that possibility is the only thing on earth more horrible than the Camp itself."

"I was reassigned," Langhof said. "I was a scientist pursuing my research in the capital."

"And that's the end of it?"

"How did you get here, then?" Langhof asked.

"Don't be stupid, Doctor," Ginzburg said. "The way I got here and the way you did have nothing whatsoever in common."

"Of course," Langhof said. "I'm sorry. That was stupid."

"And you're not stupid, right, Langhof?"

"I like to think that I am not."

Ginzburg chuckled. "You are carved out of clouds," he said contemptuously.

"Please," Langhof said, almost pleadingly. "I'm trying to . . . trying to . . ."

"What?"

"Talk to you."

"About what?"

"I don't know, exactly."

"Talk. Talk. There's going to be a lot of talk about this place in the future."

"Yes," Langhof said, "I imagine there will be."

"What are you going to say, Langhof?"

"Me? I have nothing to say."

"Nothing? Nothing at all?"

"I don't know," Langhof said softly. "Maybe that it was just so very evil here."

Ginzburg laughed. "Evil? Dear God, how ridiculous. Evil, my ass." He smiled and stroked his backside. "Or should I say, Kessler's ass. It belongs to him. Sweet little commodity, don't you think?"

Langhof turned away, stepped toward the door, then turned back toward Ginzburg.

"What? You're not leaving?" Ginzburg asked.

"Not yet."

"Why not, my good doctor?"

"I don't know," Langhof said.

"You want to learn something from all this, don't you?" Ginzburg said softly.

Langhof nodded. "Yes, I suppose I do."

"Do you really think there's anything to be learned?"

"I don't know."

"I mean, something that makes sense?"

Langhof shook his head. "I don't know."

Ginzburg smiled. "Do you expect to survive?"

"I don't know that either," Langhof said. "Do you?"

"I doubt it."

"But won't Kessler protect you?"

"When all this crumbles, Kessler will be the one who needs protection," Ginzburg said. He smiled. "Sometimes I have this dream of being on the stand in some courtroom after the war. I imagine that I am a witness for Kessler, that I've been brought to say something in his defense." He chuckled. "I've already thought of what I'm going to say. I'm going to stand in the witness box and say just one line: Kessler was a gentle lover."

"Seriously," Langhof said, "that business about the eastern front — what I told you in the yard — it's true."

"I know."

"I don't know what will be done if the front gets much closer," Langhof said.

Ginzburg smiled. "Time will tell," he said.

"I'd better go now," Langhof said.

"All right."

"We'll talk again."

"Up to you."

Langhof stepped toward the door. "Good luck, Ginzburg," he said.

Ginzburg smiled and flipped the collar of his striped suit. "I'd like it better in peppermint," he said.

Now is the time for rowing, the few hours before dawn when the air is cool over the river. I lift myself carefully into the skiff and push it out from the bank. Grasping the two oars, I guide the boat toward the center of the river and away from the single light burning in my study. Drifting downstream, I can see Dr. Ludtz's cabin glaring out of the darkness, the harsh lights freezing it in perpetual day. Farther down, I pass the little hut where Juan lives with his family. If by chance Juan were to see me pass, he would suspect that I am going to my secret rendezvous with Satan. In his imagination, he can see me rowing deep into the jungle to that place where the green river turns thick and red. There I disembark and am embraced by fang-toothed demons who usher me into the fiery cavern. Within the leaping flames I roll and twist among the dancing devils who teem about me, thick as spirochetes on a syphilitic scar.

I lift the oars out of the water and place them in the boat. The river moves slowly beneath me, and I drift like a small bubble on its surface. On either side, the jungle is dense and black and unapproachable. The sounds that arise from it seem to come from a wholly foreign world. In the Camp, there were unworldly sounds, inhuman screams that plunged through the darkness and seemed to settle in the wood and snow. The roar of the furnace sometimes rose to a hissing pitch punctuated by sudden explosive bursts. The ground belched and gurgled with the decaying bodies buried beneath. Blood bubbled up from crevices in the earth. The hordes of flies swarming about the pit created a gentle hum that could be heard long before the pit itself came into view. Langhof was familiar with all these sounds, with the rush of flame, the seeping earth, the frenzy of the flies. But it was a certain series of words from Ginzburg's mouth that prevented him from returning to his own room after he closed the door. And so he turned around and tapped at the door again.

"Who is it?"

"Dr. Langhof."

Ginzburg opened the door. "Is there something else you wanted, Doctor?"

"Yes," Langhof said.

Ginzburg stepped back and let the door swing open. "What is it?"

Langhof entered the room and Ginzburg closed the door. For a moment, Langhof could not speak. He could feel the tension in his hands, the stiffness in his neck. "Something you said," he said finally, "bothers me."

"What?" Ginzburg asked.

"About my being carved out of clouds," Langhof said. "That bothers me."

Ginzburg sat down on his bunk. "Does it perhaps strike you as curious, Doctor, that after so much time in this place you are only now bothered by something?"

Langhof felt his face grow cold. "I didn't come here to be insulted," he said.

"Forgive me if I don't feel heartbroken about your being offended, Dr. Langhof," Ginzburg said firmly.

Langhof felt shaken by Ginzburg's force. "Well, I . . ."

"And answer my question," Ginzburg said quickly. "Doesn't it strike you as odd that only now you are bothered by something?"

"It was just the words you used," Langhof said. "That phrase."

"Carved out of clouds."

"Yes."

"That bothers you?"

"I am trying to see things," Langhof stammered.

"There's plenty to see," Ginzburg said.

Langhof shook his head. "You don't understand."

Ginzburg stared at Langhof fiercely. "Let me ask you something, Doctor. Where has your mind been these last three years?"

"I don't know," Langhof said weakly.

"Don't you think *that* should bother you?"

"Yes," Langhof said.

"Tell me something, Langhof," Ginzburg said. "When you're doing your dissections, what are you thinking?"

"Thinking?" Langhof asked, puzzled.

"Yes. Thinking. What is on your mind?"

"Nothing," Langhof said. "I don't think about anything during the laboratory work."

"Really? Nothing at all?"

"I just go through the motions," Langhof said.

"And so it doesn't offend you, the absurdity of these experiments? I'm not talking about the people on the table. They're dead. And there are so many. I'm not talking about moral offense. I mean the experiments themselves."

"They are ridiculous," Langhof said. "In three years we have learned absolutely nothing."

"And yet you do them studiously? Meticulously?"

"What choice do I have?"

"None whatever, I imagine," Ginzburg said. "I'm just curious about your mind, Langhof, about what you're thinking when you're standing over the table with somebody's guts in your hands."

Langhof flinched.

"Do the words bother you?" Ginzburg asked. "Would you prefer me to call them intestines?"

Langhof said nothing.

"I don't mean to taunt you, Langhof," Ginzburg said.

Langhof shrugged. "It doesn't matter."

"So what is on your mind during the experiments?" Ginzburg asked.

"I told you. Nothing."

"Amazing," Ginzburg said. He stood up and walked to the window. "When all of this is over, the air will be filled with explanations. Every sort of mind will wallow in this pit. Then they will proceed to vaporize it. They will turn it into mist. I've read enough to know what they will do. They will wrap it in the rhetoric of evil. Or they'll explain it through some crude formula of economic determinism. They'll bury it under ridiculous notions of Man's Inhumanity To Man. Ridiculous." He turned toward Langhof. "But where does it all come from, Langhof? Where does the responsibility begin?"

"If I had not taken this reassignment . . ." Langhof began.

"What reassignment?"

"To the Camp."

Ginzburg turned back toward the window. "Do you think that's where it began for you, by taking a reassignment?"

"I don't know," Langhof said. "But if I had not taken it, then I would not be here now."

"Your being here or not being here is the least of our misfortunes, Langhof," Ginzburg said.

"I didn't mean to suggest — "

Ginzburg drew a Star of David in the mist on the window. "My father was a rabbi," he said. "He was a very studious man, scholarly. I spent my youth going through his library. He was very proud of me for a while." He turned to Langhof and smiled. "Then things changed. You see, Langhof, it was not my father's intent for a nightclub comic to spring from his loins."

"No, I don't imagine it was," Langhof said quietly.

Ginzburg watched the mist reclaim the window. "One day a few boys came into the synagogue. They hauled my father out of his study and made him take the Talmud from the cabinet. They spread it out and told him to spit on it. He did. They told him to keep spitting. He did that too. He spat until his mouth was dry. He told them he couldn't spit anymore, that he had no more saliva. They laughed and said they had plenty of saliva and told him to open his mouth. Then they spat into his mouth so that he could keep spitting on the Talmud."

"You saw this?" Langhof asked.

"No," Ginzburg said, "he had kicked me out of the house by then. But even if I had been there, what could I have done?" He nodded toward the window. "This place is a circle, Langhof, and it revolves around one point. Survival." He shrugged. "That much will be understood later, that people will do anything to survive. But so what? I sold my ass to Kessler. You conduct absurd medical experiments. We both do it to survive. So what?"

"We have no choice," Langhof said.

"Quite right," Ginzburg said. "Once we're here, we have no choice. But responsibility must begin somewhere, Langhof. It must all begin somewhere."

"But how can we see it?" Langhof asked.

Ginzburg said nothing.

Langhof reached into his pocket and withdrew a small, black notebook. "It's all in here," he said.

Ginzburg glanced at the notebook. "What?"

"Everything," Langhof said. "Everything that's happened here for the last three years. I have it all down in the greatest detail."

Ginzburg's eyes drifted from the notebook to Langhof's eyes. "That's your ticket out, then," he said softly.

Langhof stared at Ginzburg, puzzled. "Out of what?"

"Out of responsibility."

Langhof held the book toward Ginzburg. "Read it. You'll see what I've been trying to do."

"We don't need compilers, Langhof," Ginzburg said. He rubbed his eyes with his fists and suddenly seemed very weary. He slumped down upon the bunk. "If you have nothing more, Doctor," he said, "I'd like to sleep for a while."

Langhof continued to hold the book toward Ginzburg. "Please, read it."

Ginzburg shook his head. "No."

"But why not?" Langhof asked.

"Let's just say that my eyes are tired."

Langhof pressed the book into Ginzburg's hands. "Please," he said quietly. Then he stood up and left the room.

Langhof did not see Ginzburg again for two days, and when he did something odd happened. Langhof was in the dissecting room with Ludtz and Kessler. He was standing over one of the metal tables, the body of a young woman spread out in front of him. His coat was red with blood, and little slivers of the woman's spleen dangled from the tip of his scalpel. Suddenly Ginzburg entered the room, carrying a box of supplies. As he walked toward Kessler, he glanced at Langhof, and at that moment Langhof's hand began to tremble. He was mortified, utterly mortified, not because of the absurdity of what he was doing, but because someone he thought as intelligent as himself had observed him doing it.

THE BOW of the canoe gently skirts the bank, bumping it slightly, and I take the rope and tie it to the tree beside the water. Across the river I can see the first hint of dawn, a soft, bluish light that fades into blackness above the mountain ridges. Far to the south, El Presidente squirms beneath his silken sheets, his mind tumbling through kingdoms of moist thighs. And only a few meters distant, Dr. Ludtz wheezes into the white light of his room, his eyes squeezed shut, his lips muttering softly in the forbidden tongue.

The clay gives slightly under my feet as I make my way up the embankment from the water's edge. All day the river seeps indifferently into the surrounding earth, licking at it, eating it away. A thousand years from now, the hill upon which my compound rests will be nothing more than a million pebbles whirling in the waves where the river meets the sea.

At the stairs to my verandah, I pause and draw in a long, slow breath. Someday I will climb them for a final time. I will look out from the heights, my hands squeezing the railing, and watch the thunderclouds tumble over the ridges or the flamingoes glide over the green, reedy plain. And I will say, "Enough," and close my eyes.

During all his years in the Camp, Langhof thought that he would find that point where men would say, "Enough." He saw them inject blue dye into the irises of children's eyes, and he thought: This is the limit. Beyond this, they will not go. Then he saw them time castrations with a stopwatch, madly ripping at the testicles with scalpels and surgical scissors, and he thought: This is the limit. They will not do more than this. Then he saw them tie the ankles of pregnant women together and watch them go into the agony of labor, writhing on the floor until they died. And so he came to know that there was no limit and that that was why Ginzburg did not willingly take his little book of recorded horrors. The little comedian knew that everything he had recorded there was little more than introduction to man's possibilities.

And yet Langhof continued to believe that something had to be said about the Camp and that perhaps the accumulation of detail was the best way of saying it. In his little black book there would be no editorialization. The prose would be simple and direct, an empiricist's worksheet. In his foolishness he hoped that Ginzburg would be able to understand what he was attempting to do, and he was insanely curious as to how the little comedian had received his work. Consequently, when he was instructed to go to the railway station to pick up a package of incoming medical supplies, he chose Ginzburg to go along. The gates of the Camp opened for them and they passed through, riding together in a battered jeep.

Ginzburg twisted himself around and looked back at the closing gate, then straightened himself in the seat. "How did you manage to arrange this?" he asked.

Langhof watched the road, the fingers of his hands drumming lightly on the steering wheel. "I told Kessler I might need some help in case we ran into partisans on the road."

Ginzburg smiled. "I have acted my part brilliantly," he said. "Kessler thinks that if we ran into partisans I would fight for you."

"Yes," Langhof said. He took his cap from his head and

placed it on the seat between them. "That book I gave you," he asked nervously, "did you read it?"

"Yes," Ginzburg replied. He kept his eyes on the road. Langhof waited a moment, but Ginzburg added nothing. "Well, what did you think?" he asked finally.

Ginzburg turned to look at Langhof. "You are a curious man, Langhof," he said. "What could you possibly expect me to think?"

"I don't know."

"Well, what do you expect to accomplish by jotting down all these details about the Camp?"

"Someone has to do it," Langhof said defensively.

"Why?"

"The world has to know what happened," Langhof said. "All the details, I mean."

Ginzburg laughed. "The world will know the details, my dear doctor," he said. "You may be sure of that. I think you have another idea in mind."

Langhof looked at Ginzburg curiously. "Other idea?"

"You are trying to redeem yourself," Ginzburg said. "It's quite clear. You want the world to know that you suffered great agonies of conscience, and that these agonies were every bit as horrible as the physical suffering in the Camp."

"I don't think that's entirely it," Langhof said weakly.

"Perhaps not," Ginzburg said. "But just in case, let me tell you something about the agonies of conscience, Langhof. They are a joke. No one would trade the worst of them for a toothache." He ran his fingers through his hair. "Do you think I don't have these so-called agonies? I do. Every time Kessler slips his cock up my ass, my conscience recoils. But as much as he revolts me, as much as I revolt myself, I wouldn't trade my place with anyone in the general Camp population." He leaned forward, his eyes burning into Langhof. "Would you, Doctor?"

"No," Langhof said quietly.

"So let's just drop the nobility, if you please," Ginzburg said. He leaned back in his seat. "I'd rather just enjoy the day, if you don't mind."

Farther down the road, Langhof brought the jeep to a halt and waited while a farmer herded a group of cows across their path. He turned to Ginzburg. "There's something I want to tell you."

Ginzburg watched as the farmer slapped the cattle with a long rod.

"For a long time I lost touch with everything," Langhof began. "I mean everything in the Camp. It was as though it didn't exist for me. I was there, but I wasn't there. Do you know what I mean?"

"I envy you," Ginzburg said lightly.

"Please listen," Langhof said. "It's important to me."

"I'm sorry," Ginzburg said, turning to Langhof. "Go ahead."

"Some months ago Kessler came into my room and said there was something he wanted me to see," Langhof began again. "I followed him outside to the courtyard behind the medical compound. There were a lot of people, naked people, sitting in the snow, freezing. It was a freezing experiment."

Ginzburg casually returned his eyes to the cattle. "People freeze all the time."

"It wasn't that," Langhof added quickly. "I really don't know what it was. I may never know. But something broke through to me. The Camp broke through, somehow. So I started walking around, taking notes, recording everything in that little notebook you seem to find so ridiculous."

"I don't find the notebook ridiculous," Ginzburg said. "Only useless."

The last cow made its way across the road, and Langhof leaned forward and started the engine. The farmer smiled gently and waved to them as the jeep passed.

"Friendly fellow," Ginzburg said, watching the farmer's face. "The sturdy peasant, the backbone of Europe." He turned to Langhof. "How far to the railway station?"

"Only a few kilometers," Langhof said. "But what I was saying. You know, about the Camp, about watching those people. I don't know what to make of it."

"Perhaps a nice soufflé," Ginzburg said with a wink.

"Please don't joke," Langhof pleaded.

Ginzburg turned back to face the road. "So serious, Doctor," he said. "It's not good for the heart." He looked at Langhof. "Have you ever been to London?"

"No," Langhof said dully.

"Beautiful city. Lots of nightclubs, that sort of thing. Plenty of places for a comedian to try out new material."

Langhof pressed the accelerator. "I'm trying to learn something," he said, "about this place."

"Perhaps there's nothing to learn. Have you ever thought of that?" Ginzburg asked. He took a deep breath. "It happened. It's still happening. No need to chase your tail endlessly about it."

Langhof shook his head despairingly. "I don't believe you mean that."

"I'm tired of talk," Ginzburg said. "By the time you talk about something, it has already happened, so what's the point?"

Langhof pulled a packet of cigarettes from his coat and offered them to Ginzburg.

Ginzburg withdrew a single cigarette and put it in his mouth.

"Take the pack," Langhof said.

Ginzburg laughed. "The pack? Don't be so charitable, Doctor. I probably have more cigarettes in my room than you do."

Langhof returned the pack to his pocket.

"Don't treat me like your personal object of guilt, Langhof," Ginzburg said. "I don't like that. In fact, I loathe it. Your problem is with yourself, not me." He lit the cigarette and took in a long draw. "What are we picking up in the village, anyway?"

"General medical supplies," Langhof replied.

"Do you know what kind?"

Langhof shrugged. "Antibiotics. Aspirin."

Ginzburg grinned. "Phenol?"

Langhof's lips tightened. "Yes."

Ginzburg blew a shaft of white smoke into the rushing air. "You're depending upon the Allies, aren't you?"

Langhof looked at him. "For what?"

"To get you out of the Camp."

Langhof nodded. "Of course. Aren't you?"

Ginzburg flicked the cigarette from his fingers. "The Camp is a rumor mill. We hear that Paris is in flames, that there is nothing still standing in London. What is left of Europe, I wonder?"

Langhof swerved to avoid a large puddle of icy water. "How long did you live in London?"

"Only a few months. A brief engagement at a small club in South Kensington."

"Did you like it there?"

"The audiences are dull," Ginzburg said. "Too much warm beer and tasteless food. They have the worst food in the world. Everything tastes like gruel."

"You prefer Paris?" Langhof asked.

Ginzburg smiled. "I was almost married in Paris." He turned to Langhof and winked again. "I may have relatives there."

"Really?" Langhof asked. "Uncles, aunts?"

The corners of Ginzburg's mouth crinkled mischievously. "No," he said, "but perhaps a little boy or girl with a rather odd sense of humor."

They arrived in the village a few moments later. The train was puffing at the station, white steam billowing from the engine.

"You won't try to escape, will you?" Langhof asked almost playfully, as he stepped from the jeep.

"To where, Doctor?"

Langhof nodded and walked into the station. He returned with a large package and dropped it behind the front seat.

Ginzburg glanced at the box. "Well, I suppose we've done our assignment for the day," he said.

Langhof shrugged and pulled himself in behind the wheel. "I wish it could have taken longer."

"It was a pleasant excursion," Ginzburg said.

Langhof started the engine, backed the jeep slowly into the road, and began to drive back toward the Camp.

After they had left the village, Ginzburg shifted around and looked back at it in the distance. "Pretty in the snow," he said.

"Yes."

Ginzburg continued to watch the village. "I've played a few little towns like that," he said. He turned to face the road. "The worst ones are in Switzerland. The Swiss always make a bad audience for a comedian."

Langhof continued to watch the road. "No sense of humor?"

Ginzburg glanced at Langhof. "None whatever. There's a saying in the trade. 'The Swiss only laugh for comedians who hand out money.'"

Langhof smiled slightly. "Well, I'm not much better. I never had much of a sense of humor."

"It's something you're born with," Ginzburg said. "You either have it or you don't."

"Were you always . . . well . . . a comic?"

"It's the only thing I ever wanted to be," Ginzburg said. "It's quite an honored profession, you know, being a fool. Shakespeare loved us, of course, and Chaucer was a comic to the bone."

Langhof buttoned the top button of his overcoat. "It's getting colder."

Ginzburg did not seem to notice. "It's an aphrodisiac, you know."

Langhof glanced at him. "What? Comedy?"

"Laughter," Ginzburg said. "Really, it is. Get a woman laughing, and you're halfway there."

"Perhaps that explains my lack of success in that area," Langhof said, trying to bring a certain lightness to his voice.

"Haven't had much of a love life, Doctor?" Ginzburg asked.

Langhof shook his head. "Not much, I'm afraid."

"Have you missed it?"

Langhof nodded. "Yes, I think I have."

"Too bad," Ginzburg said airily. He tossed his head to the right and watched the landscape flow past.

"I suppose you've always been covered with women," Langhof said after a moment.

"Up to the eyebrows."

"That must have been pleasant for you," Langhof said and, to his surprise, felt a small jolt of envy.

"Very pleasant, as you might imagine," Ginzburg said.

"Always kept them laughing, I suppose."

"At least until they were naked," Ginzburg said, "then I gave them what they wanted."

"And I can guess what that was."

"Not sex alone, if that's what you mean, Doctor," Ginzburg said.

"Really? What, then?"

Ginzburg turned toward Langhof. "Well, just to be taken seriously," he said, "just to be taken very seriously for one moment in their lives."

"That's all?" Langhof said, smiling. "I should be able to master that."

"Perhaps," Ginzburg said. He suddenly seemed indifferent to the whole question.

For a long time they rode in silence. Ginzburg watched the snow-covered countryside with an expression of almost childlike longing, while Langhof allowed his mind to toy with ideas of miraculous escape.

"I once heard Piaf sing," Ginzburg said finally. "My God, it was the saddest voice."

"That woman in Paris," Langhof said. "The one you almost married. What was she like?"

Ginzburg scratched his chin. "She was a teacher."

"In the university?"

"Nothing so exalted. Just a public school teacher. An American, as a matter of fact."

"Did you meet her in Paris?"

"Yes."

"Where? I mean, under what circumstances?"

Ginzburg looked closely at Langhof. "Does it matter, Doctor?"

"I was just curious."

Ginzburg turned back toward the road. "She saw my act at one of those little cabarets. She was a tourist, that's all. She came back to tell me how much she enjoyed it."

"And you kept her laughing the whole time."

"Laughing until she had to stop to catch her breath," Ginzburg said. He smiled softly. "I used up all my best material on her."

Slowly the Camp gate came into view, and Langhof saw Ginzburg's face harden.

"Have you ever been to America?" Langhof asked quickly.

"No," Ginzburg said. He shifted his eyes away from the Camp and looked at Langhof. "I've always liked Americans. They seem to laugh a lot. I think I would have been a hit there."

"Probably so," Langhof said.

"They make good audiences, the Americans."

"What about the woman? The American? What happened?"

"She went back home. What would you expect?"

"But surely this great love between you should have endured," Langhof said, jokingly.

"Never overestimate the power of 'great love,'" Ginzburg said. He allowed a smile to play briefly on his lips. "Have you ever had a 'great love,' Doctor?"

"Just an adolescent infatuation," Langhof said.

"Consummated?"

"I'm not a virgin, if that's what you mean," Langhof said.

"That's always good to hear."

"But I'm interested in this American woman of yours," Langhof said. "Did you ever see her again?"

Ginzburg shrugged. "Of course not. She went back to the United States. I saw her off at Marseilles. She gave me lots of kisses, I can tell you. 'You should come with me, Ira,' she said. 'In New York, you'd be all the rage.' "

Langhof smiled. "So that's your first name. Ira. May I call you that?"

For a moment Ginzburg's eyes seemed to lock on the Camp gate, then they drifted toward Langhof's face. "No," he said. "You may not."

THROUGH THE WHITE HEAT of midday I see General Gomez's jeep bounce up the pocked and gullied road toward the compound. Even in the distance, the gilded falcon that adorns the hood looks massive.

I rise from my chair, steadying myself in the thick, pulsating heat.

The jeep glides to a halt below me, sending a cloud of dust tumbling before it. The General leaps jauntily from his seat and points toward the thick jungle across the river. The gunner in the back of the jeep immediately shifts around, training the sights of his turret machine gun in the direction the General has indicated.

The General stares up toward the verandah, shielding his eyes against the raging sun. "Buenos días, Don Pedro," he calls to me.

I lift my hand in greeting. "Buenos días, General Gomez."

General Gomez smiles and trots up the stairs, taking them two at a time. He thrusts out his hand. "So good to see you, Don Pedro."

I take his hand and shake it gently. "And good to see you, General." I nod toward the chair. "Won't you be seated?"

The General draws his pants up by gripping the wide

belt of his uniform and tugging upward. Then he sits down. "The road to El Caliz is in disrepair," he says.

"They are not well tended," I tell him, "and the rains are very damaging."

The General smiles broadly and folds his hands across his belly. "So, I understand that El Presidente is to visit you the day after tomorrow."

"Yes."

"You must be filled with anticipation," the General adds. He is a short, muscular man with a broad, black mustache and small, gleaming eyes.

"Indeed," I tell him.

The General watches me for a moment, then shifts slightly in his seat, raising one leg over the other. Several years ago he determined that the parrots were warning the guerrillas of the approach of his troops. He ordered their annihilation, and for weeks squadrons of helicopters combed the jungles of the northern provinces firing at anything brightly colored.

"Would you like some refreshment, General?" I ask.

"No, thank you, Don Pedro," the General replies. "I'm afraid that I have only a little time to spend with you."

"Regrettable."

"Yes," General Gomez says wearily. He is busy with the greatest task of his life, securing the northern provinces. He has ravaged the coffee fields and trampled the sugar cane. I see the fires of burning villages still leaping in his eyes.

"What brings you so far to the south?" I ask.

The General leans forward conspiratorially. "Don Camillo has no doubt mentioned the trouble in the north?"

"Yes," I tell him, "but that is in the north, far away."

The General closes his eyes languidly, the military martyr. "Unfortunately, no."

"But surely we have nothing to fear as far south as El Caliz," I insist.

The General runs his index finger over his mustache. "Rebellion is not a wave, Don Pedro," he informs me, "it is a serpent. It may slither into any crevice."

Over the General's shoulder I see Tomás emerge from the surrounding jungle. Instantly he spots the army jeep and retreats back into the brush. He is now old enough to be inducted into the General's army. Such an eventuality would deny him his trips to the whorehouses downriver. That much he is not willing to sacrifice for the glory of the Republic.

"Like a serpent, yes," General Gomez continues. It is one of his habits to extend a simile beyond its immediate effectiveness. "As a serpent may creep and crawl and invade the deepest brush, the dankest cavern, so a rebel may invade any area of the Republic."

"Well spoken, General," I tell him.

The General smiles happily. He has written a great deal of egregious poetry for the army newspaper, and it is said that he sometimes reads his latest literary creations to whole regiments assembled for that purpose.

"Like a serpent, the rebel forces often go forth under cover of darkness," the General continues.

In my mind I see the soldiers under his command as they stand, withering in the sun, the General's absurd warrior poetry sweeping over them like a noxious gas. Their eyelids grow weighty in the liquid heat. The straps of their packs eat into their shoulders. Later they will take out their unbearable anger and discomfort on the peasants to the north.

The General's eyes lift toward the sky, his shimmering muse. "Like serpents, the rebels coil in their holes and prepare to strike in one sudden thrust."

I clear my throat loudly, interrupting the General in his poetic flight. "Are you saying that we are in danger here in El Caliz?" I ask.

The General blinks his eyes. "From what?"

"The serpents you mentioned in that memorable image."

The General nods. "I attempt precision in my images."

"And always attain it," I tell him.

"You perceive my meaning, then?" the General asks.

"I presume you fear a rebel contingent may lurk in the vicinity of El Caliz?"

"Precisely, yes."

I nod thoughtfully, as if considering his remarks. "May I ask what purpose they would have in coming here? El Caliz is very remote, as you know."

The smile that adorns General Gomez's face looks as if it has been painted there. "Purpose? You do not understand these rebels, Don Pedro. They need no purpose. They have no purpose." His eyes close sadly, then slowly open again. "It is part of the nature of human history that men of purpose must continually do battle with those who have no purpose whatsoever. Is that not so, Don Pedro?"

"Precisely," I tell him. Far to the right, through a clearing in the trees, I see Esperanza pulling a wooden lorry piled high with dried palmetto leaves. Tomás is buried underneath them, picking worms from his arms, his eyes searching the dusty mass for the curled tail of the scorpion.

"The rebels will not fight like true soldiers," General Gomez continues. He pulls an amber cigarette holder from his uniform pocket, places a cigarette in it, then brings it to his lips. "They fight like the vicious serpents they are. They lie in wait and attack without warning. They are cowards, Don Pedro. They are unworthy of being considered citizens of the Republic."

The sun shines radiantly through the amber holder. Within its rich glow I can see the scarlet macaw and the hawk-headed caique and the Patagonian conure as they tumble to the jungle floor, feathers flying, while the helicopters bank left and right, raking the trees with their fire.

General Gomez shakes his head despairingly. "The rebels cannot be considered real men, Don Pedro. They live and fight like animals."

It is a curious etiquette that the General employs. In the Camp I once saw a man shot because he had been caught gnawing on the fingers of a dead body that lay beside him in the bunk, a bestiality the Special Section, in its purity, would not permit.

"When you live like a beast, you must be treated like a beast," General Gomez concludes.

"Certainly," I tell him. "But do you think the rebels actually intend to attack El Caliz?"

"Attack?" the General says loudly. His eyes narrow. "These rebels do not know the meaning of the word *attack*. They are not warriors."

One cannot speak to General Gomez without first understanding the categories that define his intellect and the language that conveys them. I rephrase the question. "Do you think the rebels intend to sneak into El Caliz and carry out some sort of vicious assault?"

"Possibly," the General replies. He lights his cigarette. "With those animals, anything is possible." He watches me closely. "Tell me, Don Pedro, have you seen any suspicious activity around the compound of late?"

"Suspicious activity?"

"Movements? Strangers? Anything like that?"

"No."

General Gomez allows his eyes to drift out over the verandah. "From this height," he says, "you can see a great deal, can you not?"

"A great deal, yes."

The General snaps his eyes back toward me. "I am told you spend much time on the verandah."

"I am too old to move about the compound, General."

"And yet you have seen nothing, Don Pedro?" the General asks doubtfully.

"I have noticed that from time to time the monkeys are disturbed," I tell him.

General Gomez slaps his knee delightedly. "You see, that's what I mean," he says excitedly. "Something is disturbing them, yes?"

"No doubt." Soon, perhaps, the helicopters will dive from the upper air and devastate the monkeys.

"Rebels skulking beneath the trees, I think," the General says. "They disturb the monkeys." He glances back toward the river. "I knew it. I told El Presidente that the rebels might try to take advantage of his visit here."

"But he will be well protected, will he not, General Gomez?" I ask.

The General turns his eyes to me. "Of course, Don Pedro."

"Then we have nothing to fear."

General Gomez returns his gaze to the jungle depths. "We need more powerful defoliants," he says quietly, almost to himself. He turns back to me and smiles. "In certain areas of the northern provinces, we have entirely denuded the earth," he says boastfully. "Even the scorpions cannot find shade."

I have seen photographs of his enterprise. They portray vast stretches of barren ground, the scorched trees rising from the cracked and gutted earth like twisted wire.

General Gomez leans across the table toward me, the cigarette holder embedded in his smile. "Tell me, Don Pedro, do you retire early to your bed?"

"No."

"You sit out on the verandah until late in the night, then?"

"Yes."

General Gomez nods. "Very good. And do you ever see fires across the river? Campfires, I mean?"

I shake my head. "I'm afraid not, General."

General Gomez leans back in his seat as if to seek a better vantage point for staring into my mind. "You're quite sure of this?"

"Quite sure."

The General pulls the cigarette from his lips and looks admiringly at the amber holder. "A gift from El Presidente," he tells me.

"Most elegant, General."

General Gomez moves his fingers up and down the holder, caressing it lovingly. "Imported. From Paris."

"I should have known. It is very European in its delicacy."

General Gomez extracts the cigarette butt from the holder and drops it over the railing of the verandah. It appears to fall in slow motion through the waxy heat.

"I think El Presidente will be safe here," I say.

The General turns his eyes toward me. They look like

two small gun barrels trained on my face. "Why is that, Don Pedro?"

"We are very far from the northern provinces," I explain.

General Gomez pulls a crimson silk handkerchief from his uniform pocket and wipes the sweat from his brow. "Never underestimate a serpent, Don Pedro," he warns.

I nod. "Are there any special precautions we should take for El Presidente's safety?"

General Gomez smiles at me indulgently. "Don't trouble yourself, Don Pedro. El Presidente's safety is in my hands."

"Very good, then, General."

The General peers into my office, scanning the shelves of books. "You are a reader, I see."

"Yes."

"Tell me, do you receive the newspaper that the army publishes, Don Pedro?"

"I'm afraid not."

The General looks disappointed. "It's quite a fine paper," he says. He pauses. "Are you by an chance a reader of poetry?"

"No."

The General's face seems to tighten. "Really? I had thought you might be, Don Pedro. A man of learning, I am told. Don Camillo has been much impressed by your intelligence."

I smile. "Perhaps my tastes are not as catholic as they should be, General."

General Gomez glances wearily at his hands. "Perhaps someday I will retire. My first love is literature."

"A worthy vocation," I tell him.

The General frowns. "The Republic has no poets of any note whatsoever. It is most unfortunate."

"Here in the Republic we are much oppressed," I tell him.

The General's eyes snap to attention. He looks at me suspiciously. "Oppressed?"

"By labor," I add quickly.

The General nods slowly. "Ah, yes, quite true. I am often very tired." He rises slowly and thrusts out his hand. "Thank you for your help, Don Pedro."

I take his hand in mine. "I am always your obedient servant, General Gomez."

The General turns and moves down the stairs to his jeep. His high black boots thud heavily against the clay. He pulls himself in beside the driver and looks back up toward the verandah. "Vaya con Dios, Don Pedro," he calls.

IN THE RUMBLE of the General's jeep as it pulls away, I can detect the crumbling foundation of the Republic. Built with the shoddy, decrepit timbers of El Presidente's greed, it is a structure destined for collapse. The Camp, too, was destined for collapse, but the steady rumbling that rolled over it — echoing through the stinking barracks and settling into the contorted bodies that lay randomly in the mud or hung stiffly from the sagging wire — came from the air, as the bombers made their way toward the Leader's tottering capital.

In medicine, there is a time of life known as the agonal period. It is the agony suffered by a creature that still lives but is irrevocably dying. In the jungle, the great birds convulse in a final fluttering of wings. On the river bank, the silver fish heave and shudder, their mouths twisted, gulping, their broken fins jerking sprays of mud into the indifferent air. The agonal period of the Camp was long and tedious, and Langhof watched it with a kind of aloof amusement. His compatriots gathered on the steps of the medical compound and trembled as the planes passed overhead. But Langhof did not tremble; he rejoiced. Once, slouching against one of the barracks with Ginzburg at his side, he watched a little knot of Special Section officers who crouched and whispered below the chimney of the now defunct crematorium.

"What do you suppose they're talking about?" Ginzburg asked.

Langhof stared grimly at the black-uniformed men who huddled in the distance. "About what they've done, I suppose," he replied.

Ginzburg shook his head. "I doubt it," he said.

"What else is there to talk about?"

"Beer and knockwurst," Ginzburg said lightly.

Langhof smiled. "It'll all be over soon. You'll be free."

"I'm not so sure," Ginzburg said, continuing to watch the men who stood together a few meters away. In an act that suggested their declining discipline, some of them had turned their uniform collars up against the wind.

"It's just a matter of time now," Langhof said confidently. "Nothing can save the Camp."

Ginzburg scratched his chin and seemed to peer out beyond the barbed wire. "I once saw an automobile accident in Paris," he said. "Two cars collided. A man got out of one. He had been driving, and I could see a woman's body slumped forward in the passenger seat. His wife, probably. She wasn't moving. You couldn't tell if she was alive or dead. Anyway, the man got out. He was stumbling toward the curb — covered in blood, but conscious. Several bystanders rushed up to him. You know, to help him. We eased him down to the sidewalk and started unbuttoning his shirt. But he kept slapping at our hands. You could tell by his eyes that he meant to be saying, 'Don't worry about me, help her.' But his mouth just wouldn't get it right, and he kept repeating, 'Don't worry about her, help me.' "

Langhof looked at Ginzburg curiously. "What are you trying to say?"

Ginzburg shrugged his shoulders. "I don't know for sure. It's just that I never forgot about that incident. It blackened my mood for the whole day. That night, on the stage, my rhythm was completely off. Practically nobody laughed for the entire performance. It was a disaster."

Langhof fingered his lapel. "I won't have any use for this uniform much longer," he said. He touched Ginzburg's shoulder. "What do you think you'll do when it's over?"

"I don't expect to survive," Ginzburg said dully.

Langhof looked at him, astonished. "Why not? Of course you'll survive. They've already stopped the gas chambers. It's over. Of course you'll survive."

"Perhaps," Ginzburg said. He looked at Langhof. "What about you?"

Langhof shook his head. "I don't know."

Ginzburg smiled sardonically. "You'll probably end up with a fat wife and a thriving practice in the suburbs."

"I don't care what happens to me," Langhof said wearily.

"Do you think that's heroic of you?"

Langhof shook his head. "I don't think it's anything. Just a fact. I'm completely worn out. I don't care what they do to me."

"They?"

"The Allies."

The sound of another squadron of bombers passed over the Camp. Ginzburg looked up toward the sky, then back at Langhof. "What if things should suddenly change?" he asked.

"What things?"

"What if the war should turn around and everything started up again? The gas chambers. The medical experiments. What if that happened?"

Langhof sunk his hands deep into his pockets. "That's impossible."

"But what if it happened?" Ginzburg insisted.

Langhof stepped around to face Ginzburg. "I wouldn't do it," he said firmly. "I wouldn't start it over again. I swear it. I wouldn't!"

Ginzburg watched Langhof closely, as if coming to some determination about him. "Strange, Langhof," he said, "but you know, even now I don't think you can really speak for yourself."

"You doubt me?" Langhof asked, wounded.

"Is doubt such a terrible thing?" Ginzburg asked softly. "I mean, it keeps you thinking, doesn't it?" He turned away, his eyes moving upward toward a line of trees that stood in the distance, far beyond the wire. "I want to walk in Paris again," he said with a slight smile. "I want to nibble a buttered croissant."

Staring at Ginzburg's bedraggled, emaciated figure, Langhof could scarcely imagine such a possibility. "I'm sure you will," he said.

Ginzburg's eyes drifted away from the trees. "Kessler has stopped screwing me," he said. "He still feeds me, but that's all."

Langhof felt a cold wave of embarrassment pass over him. "I don't like to hear you talk about that," he said quickly.

"It's a bad sign, Langhof," Ginzburg said darkly.

"I should think you would be pleased about Kessler's dwindling appetite," Langhof said stoutly.

"It's the only commodity I have," Ginzburg said, "the only thing I had to offer him. Now even that is gone."

"Enough of this," Langhof said, waving his hand. He took a deep breath and tried to smile as he changed the subject. "You know, my friend, when the war is over, there'll be plenty of need for comedians. You'll have all kinds of offers."

"I'll play the big houses, you think?" Ginzburg asked dryly.

"I'm sure you will," Langhof said enthusiastically.

Ginzburg glanced back at the soldiers in the distance. "Do you still have your little book?"

"No."

"What did you do with it?"

"I burned it," Langhof said. "You were right. There was no need for it. They were so proud of what they were doing here, they probably took thousands of pictures."

"I would like to put them all in a big theater," Ginzburg said, "and show them all the pictures, and then ask them one by one: Why did you do this?"

Langhof's face darkened. "I would be in that theater, you know," he said.

Ginzburg nodded. "Yes, you would. It's too late ever to change that."

Langhof suddenly felt a terrible chill pass over him, as if his life had been snatched from him by invisible hands. "I still don't know what happened to me," he said.

Ginzburg did not seem to care one way or the other. He turned toward the rotting door of the crematorium. "Do you know what I like about show business?" he asked. "I like the stage door. There is something wonderful about a stage door. When you are going through it, you feel like a special person. Everyone else is huddled outside. Maybe it's snowing or raining, but they're still out there, trying to get a glimpse of somebody famous. And you think, That's me someday. I'll be the person everybody is trying to get a look at."

"Rather vain, don't you think?" Langhof said lightly.

"Comes with the profession, I'm afraid," Ginzburg said. He wiped his nose with his sleeve, then glared at the sleeve disgustedly. "You see, that's what I've come to, wiping my nose with my sleeve. There was a time when I would never have done such a thing." Then suddenly, to Langhof's panic and amazement, Ginzburg lowered his head and began to weep.

Langhof glanced quickly at the guards, then stepped around to shield Ginzburg from their view. "Stop it," he said fiercely.

"They're all dead," Ginzburg said. "All gone up in smoke."

Langhof shook Ginzburg lightly. "Stop it," he repeated. "Don't draw attention to yourself."

Ginzburg straightened his shoulders. "Yes, right," he said. "I can't let go, not yet."

"It'll be over soon, believe me," Langhof said desperately, "Look at the way the guards are. There's nothing left of them. They don't care what happens now. When the Allies get here, they'll turn their guns over without a fight."

Ginzburg wiped his eyes. "It's so strange," he said. "While the Camp was functioning, I had a reason to stay alive. But now it's over and there's nothing left."

"That's ridiculous," Langhof said vehemently. "Now you can begin to live again."

Ginzburg shook his head slowly. "No. Now I'm ready for the gas."

"Don't say that," Langhof pleaded.

"It's so strange," Ginzburg said. "It's a feeling of . . . I don't know . . . of having absolutely nothing to hold onto."

The ground began to tremble as another group of planes approached.

"They're going to liberate you soon," Langhof said. "You've got to remember that."

Ginzburg straightened the small, worn cap that barely covered his head. "I'm tired," he said. "Just very tired."

"Think of something nice," Langhof said, trying to joke. "Think of blowing Kessler's head off."

"Do you think that would do me good?"

"It might."

A low wail came from inside the barracks, and Ginzburg seemed to shudder. "It's already too late for a lot of them, you know," he said. "They'll be dead before the Allies get here."

"I know."

"Nothing can be done for them," Ginzburg said. "Kessler has cut off most of my supplies."

"He doesn't have any supplies," Langhof said. "They've stopped sending them."

A few meters away a rat peeped out from the insides of a frozen body, peered about, then retreated inside once again.

Ginzburg brushed at the frayed shoulders of his striped suit. "I'd better be getting back to the compound."

"Why? There's nothing to do."

"Just the same," Ginzburg said, "I'd better be getting back."

"Remember what I told you," Langhof said. He secretly

placed Ginzburg's hand in his. "It's all going to be over very soon."

Ginzburg smiled weakly and began to walk away. Langhof turned to watch him. "Remember what I said," he repeated to Ginzburg's back.

Ginzburg did not turn around. He made his way toward the compound, walking steadily, his back straight. Then, as he reached the group of soldiers, he stopped. Langhof felt something cold harden in his stomach. Helpless, he watched as Ginzburg continued to stare rigidly at the guards. For a moment the guards did not notice him. Then one of them did, and indicated Ginzburg's presence to the others. Slowly they turned to face him. When he had their full attention, Ginzburg brought his feet together, removed his cap, and made a slow stage bow. The guards stared at him for a moment, utterly confused. Then Ginzburg straightened himself, pulling an imaginary tie up to his throat, and passed on by.

TOWARD EVENING it is my custom to take a short stroll beside the river. Walking along it, I can imagine the life that teems above and below it. In the depths the crocodiles wave their heavy tails, propelling themselves forward, their slit eyes searching through the murky waters for some morsel to devour. Above the green waters, enormous jungle spiders weave their webs between the sagging branches and sit upon their spindly legs to await the first incautious butterfly.

Here in the Republic it is easy to be seduced by death. But in the final weeks of the Camp, death took on an unnatural aspect, an anthropomorphic quality that allowed it to be imagined as a living thing that had grown weary of itself. Gout-ridden now, bloated and surfeited, it seemed to sink down into the mud and slime, and Langhof, our hero, lying on his bunk waiting for the Camp to fall, believed that perhaps he had found that limit for which earlier he had so desperately searched. It seemed to him that perhaps this limit resided in the simple, irreducible exhaustion that finally overwhelms all the works of man, no matter how exalted or debased. He walked out of the compound and stood staring at the smokeless chimney of the crematorium. It seemed to partake both of something new, in its moronic vanity, and of something very old, in its inevitable defeat.

Standing facing the chimneys, enjoying his revery, his boots ankle deep in mud, he heard the crunch of footsteps from behind. He turned. It was Rausch.

"Gloating, are you, Langhof?" Rausch asked.

Langhof did not answer. He returned his eyes to the chimney, which stood towering silently above him.

Rausch stepped up beside him, fixing his eyes on the crematorium, his vision clinging to it, almost sucking at it, like sea leeches on a shark's belly. "Do you feel safe now?" he asked.

"From what?" Langhof asked quietly.

Rausch did not answer. He turned toward Langhof. "All the work is not finished," he said. "You should be aware of that."

"It's quite finished, Rausch," Langhof replied. "And *you* should be aware of that."

"The final orders for the Camp have not arrived as yet," Rausch said, "but it doesn't matter what they are."

Langhof turned toward Rausch and smiled rebukingly. "Really? I'm surprised at you. Do you mean to say that you are no longer obeying orders?"

"Yes," Rausch said.

"That does surprise me," Langhof said tauntingly.

Rausch gripped the handle of his pistol. "Much of what I am would surprise you," he said.

Langhof turned away and began to walk back toward the medical compound.

"How is it with you and that Ginzburg character," Rausch called loudly after him.

Langhof whirled around. "What are you talking about?"

"You've become quite close, you two," Rausch said with a menacing smile. "Are you bedfellows also, Doctor?"

"Why would that possibly concern you?" Langhof asked with a sneer. "I should think that you would have more important questions on your mind, given the faltering state of the New Order."

Rausch's face seemed to soften. "We could have been friends, you and I."

"No, we couldn't," Langhof said. "Not in the slightest."
He stepped toward Rausch. "I despise you."

Rausch's body seemed to tighten. "All this time, and you
still believe that you are above this. Let me tell you something, Langhof, you have wallowed in this place, and becoming chums with some rotten little vermin jokester won't
change that."

"I don't expect it to."

"Don't you?"

"No."

Rausch chuckled coldly. "You are the real slime,
Langhof," he said. "Shall I tell you why?"

Langhof started to walk away, but Rausch grasped his
arm. "Listen to me," Rausch said hotly. "You are the real
slime because you have crawled through this pit for three
years and never once followed a courageous impulse!" He
released Langhof's arm and stepped back slightly. "A man
either does what his thought commands, or he does not.
That makes all the difference."

Langhof nodded toward the crematorium. "And you
have obeyed your thoughts, am I right, Rausch?"

"Yes," Rausch said firmly. "And I will continue to do so
until the end."

Langhof could feel the heat of his rage enveloping him.
"Do you know what Ginzburg is, Rausch?" he asked. "He
is a reason to live. And you, my pathetic countryman, are
a reason to die."

Rausch stared at Langhof rigidly. "At this point in my
life, do you really believe I can be wounded by an insult?"

Langhof shook his head despairingly. "I don't care,
Rausch," he said. "That's what you've never understood.
I don't care about you or your cause or anything connected
with you. You are nothing to me. Absolutely nothing. You
should be a circus performer, playing your sophomoric
philosophical games." He smiled bitterly. "You are a clown
of the New Order."

"And I will act my part, Langhof," Rausch said coldly,
"to the very end."

Langhof grinned mockingly into Rausch's face. "You bore me, Rausch," he said. Then he turned on his heels and walked away. He could feel the mud sucking at the bottoms of his boots as if tiny hands were pulling him into its depths. He stopped and turned back, but Rausch was no longer facing him. Instead he had turned toward the crematorium. It seemed to Langhof that the proud rigidity of Rausch's body had given way to a kind of slumped and drooping stature, the head nodding slightly forward with the torpor of a wilting rose.

Now, beside the river, it is easy to remember the superiority Langhof felt as he marched back to his room in the medical compound. In the terrible vividness of my memory, I can see our hero's schoolboy pride at having finally bested an ancient adversary. In the puerility of Langhof's superiority, in the consuming lunacy of his vaunted self-esteem, the catastrophic I took yet another bow. Obliviously, Langhof strutted down the hall to his room, spread himself out on his bunk, and allowed himself to feel a kind of victory over Rausch. In his vanity he saw himself as an actual participant in the collapse of the Camp and as one of the authors of Rausch's imagined desolation. If it were that easy to play the hero's part, then we would all be saddled on the wind.

FROM THE VERANDAH it is easy to envision what would happen should the forces currently embattled in the northern provinces gain dominion and close in around the capital of El Presidente. The small, tidy airport at the edge of city would fill with mink-coated and bejeweled refugees. They would raise their tents under the cupola of the terminal and drink wine while waiting for news of the enemy's advance. Over the backgammon boards, and through the mist of pink champagne, they would converse on the former splendors of the Republic and mourn the death of petty empire.

In the Leader's capital city, that blessed locale which he had destined to be the Eldorado of the world, the high officials of the New Order gathered together in the dank squalor of their underground abode. There they drank tea and ate custard while listening to the Leader's glittering tales of what might have been, if all men were as mighty as himself. Overhead the city turned to rubble, filling the sewers with the homeless and dismayed.

But as the advancing armies moved closer to the Camp, all became chaos and terror, with both guards and surviving prisoners sensing some final drama of absolute destruction. For Langhof, there became only one duty, to warn Ginzburg.

Glancing over his shoulder, Langhof made his way down the hall to Ginzburg's room. He knocked on the door.

"Yes?" he heard Ginzburg say.

Langhof opened the door. "I've just heard news," he said. "The Camp will fall in a matter of days."

Ginzburg rubbed the sleep from his eyes. "So?"

"So? What do you mean?"

Ginzburg shrugged. "So, the Camp will fall. What am I to do about it?"

"You must save yourself, Ginzburg. You must do it now. No one can say what might happen to the prisoners who remain here."

"Then there are many to save, Langhof," Ginzburg said.

"Don't be ridiculous. They're doomed."

"And what about you?"

Langhof shook his head. "I don't care about me."

Ginzburg smiled. "But you do care about me, is that it?"

"Well, yes. I do."

"Why is that, Langhof, may I ask?"

Langhof looked at Ginzburg quizzically. "Well, because you are . . ."

"What?"

"Because you're an intelligent man, Ginzburg. There's no need for you to die."

"Intelligent?" Ginzburg said, amazed. "Intelligent? You have piped half the scholarship of Europe up those chimneys and you speak to me of intelligence!"

"That cannot be undone, Ginzburg," Langhof said pleadingly. "But you can save yourself."

Ginzburg laughed derisively. "Save myself? Really? How, Langhof?"

"Speak to Kessler. He may help you."

"To do what?"

"To escape, for God's sake. Don't you understand what I'm telling you?"

Ginzburg sat up in his bed. "Forget it, Langhof. There is no way for me to escape."

"Are you sure Kessler wouldn't help you?"

"Kessler would kill me himself before letting me get out

of here alive," Ginzburg said. "My God, do you think he would let me live, with what I know about him?"

Langhof straightened himself. "Then I will help you," he said.

"You? You are nothing, Langhof. A petty functionary. You would not be able to save yourself, much less me."

Langhof sat down on the bunk next to Ginzburg. "Surely there must be something I can do for you," he said.

Ginzburg looked at Langhof a moment. "Yes, perhaps there is." He got down from the bunk, lifted a loose plank from the floor, and brought out a small metal box.

"Here, take this," he said.

Langhof looked at the box. "What is it?"

"Open it."

Langhof slowly opened the box and saw the diamonds. He looked up, astonished. "My God, where did you get all this?"

"I've been here a long time. You'd be surprised what's passed through my hands."

"But so much!"

Ginzburg smiled. "I have friends everywhere, Langhof."

Langhof looked down at the diamonds. "What were you going to do with these?"

Ginzburg smiled. "What do you want, a noble answer? Perhaps I was going to use them to build a great monument for the victims of this place. Does that satisfy you?"

"Why did you keep them, Ginzburg?"

Ginzburg shrugged. "Because they were too valuable to throw away. I used to buy things with them. But this is not a great place to shop, you know. There wasn't much to buy. They just kept accumulating."

"These could get you out of the Camp," Langhof said.

Ginzburg shook his head. "No. Nothing could do that now."

Langhof lifted the box toward Ginzburg. "So keep them, then."

"No," Ginzburg said, "that would be ridiculous. The Camp will be overrun soon, as you said. They mean to kill us all, all the people who look like me."

Langhof continued to press the box toward Ginzburg's hands. "I don't want these. What would I do with them?"

"Whatever you like."

"No," Langhof said, "I could never take them."

"Look, Langhof," Ginzburg said, "if I had other choices I might keep them. But there's no hope for me. No hope at all. There's no way I can escape. There's no way anyone can escape now. You may not even make it yourself. But you have a better chance than anyone else I know."

"Do you really think I could take such things and live off them? Please, Ginzburg, I'm not that monstrous."

"I want you to take them, Langhof," Ginzburg said, "because I think that as long as you have them you will think about this place. There must always be someone who thinks about this place. Not someone who just remembers, but someone who thinks." He pushed the box back toward Langhof. "Please take them."

Langhof stood up and tucked the box under his arm. "Perhaps we will both make it out of here."

Ginzburg smiled. "If we do, then we'll go out one night, and I'll show you the best burlesque in Paris."

I N Casamira's *Official History* it is written that El Presidente did not need sleep, and that, in fact, during the three years it took him to assume the Presidency, he did not sleep at all. Through countless nocturnal hours, his rodent eyes peered into the darkness. He perched in trees and learned the secrets of the owl. He slithered on the river bank and learned the cunning of the crocodile. He watched the moon move through its phases of its orbit and saw the seedling straighten in the sun. During these deep, mahogany hours, El Presidente learned silence the way a stone learns silence, by being singularly itself, by taking absolutely nothing in. And so he was there — as he always will be — to greet the morning with his smile.

Now safe within the securities of office, El Presidente reclines upon his bed, wallowing in the fat of the mythology he has created for himself. Waking, he is served apricots and wine; and after that, a fresh young human delicacy procured for him while he slept. At noon he rises from sheets made wet by his spent strength and strolls down the marble corridors to his office. There, ravenous again, he devours fish and fowl, picking his teeth with a Spanish slaver's whittled rod. Then he sleeps again, slumped in his great velvet chair, his heavy breath whistling through the medals on his chest. As the afternoon languishes, he rises once again, departs for the state dining room, and there, bellowing commands, instructs his servants on the evening fête. At sunset he dines with his ministers of state. They sit chatting at the great table, their laughter counterpointed by the tinkling of the chandeliers, a tinkling that, in this windless clime, requires the use of special fans implanted in the ceiling. During this final orgy of consumption, El Presidente rouses from the bowels of himself something that might be called a personality. His cheeks grow rosy and his eyes fill with tears as he regales his audience with sad tales of orphans abandoned at the palace door.

Such is the El Presidente of Casamira's song.

But what of Casamira? He, the conscience of the Republic, stands on the balcony of his Manhattan apartment, his hands clenched around the wrought-iron rail as around a chicken's throat, and lifts an exiled poet's wail into the smutty air. The darling of the pleasure set, he lives now in a world of black ties and cummerbunds, sips champagne in paneled lecture halls, and, with trembling voice, entrances the chic, adoring crowd with tales of fallen hope.

Of all things easy to become, it is easiest to become ridiculous; and when you have grown so old you cannot see your face behind your face or feel the texture of a feather; when you have grown so old that your voice seems to speak behind your back; when you have grown so old that none remember you in youth, even then you will be a fool. You may languish in a room lined with books and listen with gravity and calm to a cello's idle lamentation; you may sit surrounded by a circle of worshipful disciples; you may puff on a scholar's pipe, your white hair gleaming in the firelight — and you will still be a fool rolling in illusion as was Langhof with his tin box.

Langhof took the box and left Ginzburg's room. He walked down the hallway to his own room and sat down on his bunk. For a time he thought about hiding the diamonds under the floor as Ginzburg had, then about simply keeping them under his pillow. Then a much better solution found its way into Langhof's mind. He would not attempt to hide the diamonds at all. He would simply lay the box on the shelf next to his bunk and leave it there. Sooner or later the diamonds would be discovered, and he would be shot as a thief. That would be a martyrdom he could accept. And so Langhof, in his romanticism, thought that the greatest martyrs are those who refuse to give their names at the moment of their immolation. Thus, the blaze consumes them entirely. Anonymously burning, they fuse absolutely with their cause, so that they become not this or that martyred person, but martyrdom incarnate. By being shot as a petty, vulgar thief, Langhof sensed that he could utterly fuse with the nameless and unheralded fate of all those whose ashes had drifted over the Camp.

It takes a most extraordinary egotist to perform so extreme an act of self-effacement, but Langhof, in his illusion, saw only the grandeur of his act, not its trifling and insipid vulgarity. He believed that he had grasped at last that will to act selflessly, which we associate with courage and with failure.

But Langhof was denied his auto-da-fé. The box rested on the shelf quite undisturbed, while the muffled sound of distant enemy guns grew steadily closer. Once Ginzburg passed the open door of Langhof's room and glimpsed the box. He stopped and looked at Langhof with an expression that our hero took at the time to be one of great admiration, but that I know now was one of the deepest disappointment. For Ginzburg, in his sorrow and weariness, was like the worthy, dutiful monk who despises all illuminism.

And so the last days came. Thousands of prisoners had already been driven westward, but thousands still remained, starving in the darkness of the barracks. They ate wood shavings and licked bits of frozen paint from the sides of the buildings. There were no work details, and even the fires of the crematoria had been extinguished. It was as if the machinery of the New Order had simply ground to a halt, the gears finally mired in crushed bone.

During this period, Langhof waited to be shot for theft or, if that did not happen, captured and later shot by enemy troops. He reveled in either fate, and even began to take a little pride in his own indifference toward himself, his heedlessness for his own life. In his own mind, he saw himself quietly waiting for death, and it semed to him an almost beatific state.

Then, on the last day of the Camp's existence, with the enemy troops only a few kilometers away, everything changed. The torpor that had seemed to occupy the Camp suddenly dissolved and became a welter of noise and frenzy. The Camp personnel who remained began burning their files in a panic of concealment, as if the Camp could be wiped away by destroying the papers that described it. The bombardment began, and the guards started tumbling into the truck that would take them to the west. Some of the stronger prisoners roused themselves, rioting in the yards and ripping at the doors of the empty supply houses.

Through all of this chaos, Langhof moved with saintly detachment. He believed that he was about to die, and this thought filled him with unutterable serenity. While the Camp personnel frantically burned the evidence of their crime and the prisoners scratched at the barracks walls or wallowed in their own filth. Langhof floated about as if transported on a cushion of air. And he might have floated there until a bullet brought him down, had not Rausch grabbed his arm.

"What the hell are you doing?" Rausch demanded.

"Nothing," Langhof said. "What should I be doing?"

Rausch stared at Langhof angrily. "You are going to stick with this to the last," he said, "just as I am." He pulled Langhof forward. "Come on."

Langhof followed the jerk of Rausch's arm. "It's no use putting me on a truck for the west," he said. "We're all going to die anyway, just as we deserve."

"Truck? You're not going on any truck, Langhof. I have other plans for you."

"It's hopeless, Rausch."

Rausch tugged at Langhof's arm and led him around one of the barracks to where a group of prisoners stood, surrounded by a few guards.

"All right, march!" Rausch shouted at the prisoners. "Quick time!"

The prisoners began to move between the barracks. Langhof followed behind them, walking beside Rausch.

"Let's go!" Rausch shouted to the prisoners. "Quick! Quick!"

The prisoners continued to move, their feet sloshing through the snow and mud. The barracks disappeared behind them as they passed the crematoria.

"Go! Go!" Rausch commanded. He lifted his pistol into the air and fired. "Get going! Move! Quick!"

As they continued to run, leaving the crematoria behind them, some of the prisoners lost their footing and tumbled into the snow. Rausch ignored them and pressed the remaining prisoners forward with screams and gunshots.

Langhof continued to follow along, feeling rather smug about what he took to be Rausch's desperation.

The prisoners ran past the final buildings of the Camp, through a tangled opening of snipped wire, and out of the Camp entirely.

Rausch pulled fiercely at Langhof's sleeve. "I said double time," he shouted.

They trudged up a slight incline, moved through a small stand of trees, and then to the edge of a gulley.

"Halt" Rausch shouted.

Langhof stopped beside him and looked down into the ditch. Twenty or thirty prisoners were standing below him, idly watching the guards.

"Get into the ditch," Rausch commanded the prisoners. "Get in there with the others. Quick!"

Haltingly, the prisoners followed Rausch's orders, sliding down into the ditch. Some did not get up when they reached the bottom. Others got quickly to their feet.

Rausch glanced at the guards who stood on the other side of the ditch. "That's all for now," he said.

The guards straightened themselves and waited.

Langhof felt something harden in his stomach. His eyes moved through the group of prisoners, scanning their faces. He saw Ginzburg squatting to the left, a trickle of blood flowing from his nose. Instantly he stepped back from the bank, so that Ginzburg would not see him.

"What's the matter, my dear doctor?" Rausch said fiercely.

"What are you going to do?"

Rausch smiled. "What do you think?"

"No," Langhof said. "You can't do this."

"I have to," Rausch said. "It's too late to do anything else."

"But there's no need for this," Langhof pleaded. "It's over. It's all over! Can't you see that?"

"Nothing's over," Rausch said. "We have to take it to the bottom this time." He turned toward the guards and nodded. They began positioning their weapons. Langhof could hear a groan rising from the ditch.

"Rausch, please," he said, "think about what you're doing. For the rest — I don't know — for you there may have been reasons for everything. But no more. It's over. There's no reason for this."

"Only cowards take just one step, Langhof," Rausch said.

"Do you think it takes courage to kill this way?"

"Under these conditions — knowing what's to come — absolutely."

"Please, Rausch, don't do this."

Rausch readied his pistol. "You have to take it through to the end, Langhof. Otherwise, you fail."

"But this makes no sense, Rausch," Langhof said.

Rausch smiled. "None of it ever did."

"Please. Rausch, you must listen to me. You must — "

"Draw your pistol, Doctor," Rausch said evenly.

"Me?" Langhof said, astonished.

"Yes, you. Draw your pistol."

"No," Langhof said.

Rausch raised his pistol and pointed it steadily at Langhof's head. "Draw your pistol," he said quietly. "You can aim it at the vermin, or you can put it in your mouth, but draw your pistol."

"No," Langhof whispered.

Rausch clicked the chamber into place. "If you think

this is some joke, you're wrong. I will kill you right now, Langhof. I will kill you right here."

Langhof stood rigidly in place.

Rausch smiled. "They are groaning in the ditch, Doctor. Imagine the hell they're going through. You can end it for them by drawing your pistol. I don't care where you put it."

Langhof listened to the wailing. It was growing louder and louder, clinging to the trees like rotting corpses. But over the wail he could hear something much stronger, the beating of his heart. He wanted to live.

"Draw your pistol," Rausch said.

Langhof unsnapped his holster and slowly drew his pistol from it.

"Good," Rausch said. "Now step forward."

Langhof stepped to the brow of the ditch, his eyes instantly searching out Ginzburg. He saw him lying down with his hands crossed behind his head, his legs stretched out and crossed, the heel of one foot resting casually on the toes of the other. His eyes were staring off into the sky, as if he were thinking of what he might like to do later in the afternoon. He was whistling, but Langhof could see that his body was trembling too.

Rausch stepped forward next to Langhof. "Fire!" he shouted.

The guards opened fire, and the prisoners began to twitch and fall as the bullets raked them. Langhof held his pistol toward the ditch, but he did not pull the trigger.

Rausch watched the pistol shaking in Langhof's hand. He smiled. "Good enough," he said, "I wouldn't want to demand too much."

Langhof kept his pistol in place. He could see Ginzburg's body still lying in place. Dead.

"All right, Langhof," Rausch said, "let's go get another batch, shall we?"

Langhof whirled around to face him. "What?"

"You heard me."

"You've proved your point, Rausch," Langhof said.

"Do as I order."

"No."

Rausch stared evenly at Langhof. "Let's not go through this again. It's getting tedious."

"No," Langhof repeated.

"Come now, my dear doctor," Rausch said. "The New Order has only a few more minutes to bequeath whatever gifts it can to mankind."

Langhof felt the pistol jerk forward instantly. He did not feel the pressure of the trigger as he squeezed it. The bullet struck Rausch in the throat, and he fell backward into the snow. The last gasp of air rushing through the hole in his neck sounded like the gurgling of a child.

IT IS MORNING NOW. I can smell the food my servants are preparing for El Presidente. Tomorrow the feast will be set on the tables beneath the striped tent, and should El Presidente come in Casamira's guise he will taste a bit of everything. While the rest of us stand at our seats, he will circle the table, dipping his spoon into every bowl, turning the fruits and vegetables over his tongue, nipping at the spiced meats, sipping a single swallow of each juice and wine. Then, when he is satisfied, he will generously bid all to join him and the feast of his assumption can begin. When the meal is over, El Presidente will have the remaining food thrown to his dogs. They have been trained to fight for it, and for the next few minutes El Presidente will laugh and slap his belly while the dogs tear at each other's throats.

In the world that calls itself developed, those born between clean sheets find beauty in portraits of naked women reclining drowsily on great burgundy pillows. They find beauty in misty lakes reflecting pastel skies. They find beauty in stern, immobile faces bordered by neatly trimmed Vandykes. In the deep placidity of the developed world, beauty finds expression in that sense of delicacy and restraint which is meant to pluck the chords of quiet contemplation.

But here in the Republic, the principles of aesthetics take on a more robust character. Here El Presidente, the arbiter of art, finds beauty in the frenzy of his dogs, finds something uplifting and sublime in the simplicity of their appetites and the purity of their violence.

On the day I fled the Camp, I did not expect to discover a new aesthetic principle. Under the illusion that by killing him I could kill the things for which he stood, I had shot Rausch in the throat. The guards around the ditch watched me in a state of profound confusion, but they did not move. I thrust the pistol in my coat pocket and quickly walked away. I went back to the Camp, much of which was burning by then, clambered up the stairs of the medical compound, and took the box of diamonds from the shelf in my room. I tucked them under my coat and ran outside. I saw Ludtz whimpering in the muddy snow and pulled him up by the arm and took him with me. I did not know where I intended us to go. We ran on and on, and as the Camp disappeared behind us, as the sound of the guns and the smell of the smoke dissolved with distance, we entered a field of inexpressible beauty. It was as if the Camp had fallen behind the curvature of the earth and we were left alone in the forest. The trees were etched black against the sky, leafless, their raw branches outlined with small, rounded banks of snow. It was a world of simple colors, a bleak, wintry landscape that might have been drawn by some dour Norwegian melancholic. I fell to the ground, dragging Ludtz with me, my boots plowing up two gullies in the snow. I remember that the barrel of my pistol still seemed warm, although it could not have been, and the crunch of the diamonds as they slid to the opposite side of the metal box sounded like a single shake of the maracas. To the moralistic imagination, these two figures, Ludtz and myself, might compose a perfect representation of the devastated soul: Here they sat, Joseph K., bereft even of his castle, and his partner, the absurd Dr. Ludtz, a panting Punch slouching against a tree, the bill of his torn cap dangling ludicrously at his ear. Here, then, the New Order in its ruin.

And yet, something in that moment was richer than anything I had ever known. During those few moments while we sat in the snow, I came as close as I have ever come to an epiphany. It was, I think now, the extreme silence of the place coming suddenly after such tumult, and its stark, relentless clarity coming after so many years of smoke and ash. For a moment I believed that it was in such a place that solemnity was born. And although this nonsensical and romantic notion could be quickly cast off, something still remained and rose within the midst of it: a reverence for the deeply serious. If there are moments in a life that may alter the categories by which we perceive life itself, then perhaps it is best that they be born out of this reverence; not a sudden revelation, nor a flash of insight, but only the weary working toward a precious value of grave and abiding seriousness, and a respect for the endless labor that is both its origin and its legacy, and that leads finally to the simple conviction that it is a moral responsibility to be wise.

I SEE JUAN moving through the rippling heat toward the verandah. From the bottom of the stairs he looks up at me worriedly.

"El Doctor Ludtz está muy mal," he says.

"Sí."

"Muy mal, Don Pedro," Juan adds with gentle insistence.

I rise from my chair and start down the stairs. Juan offers his hand, and I allow him to ease me down to the ground. In Spanish, I tell him that I will look in on Dr. Ludtz. He nods his appreciation.

At the cottage, I tap lightly at Ludtz's door and it opens before me. Dr. Ludtz is lying on his back, breathing in short, painful gasps.

"How are you, Dr. Ludtz?" I ask.

He does not respond. His eyes are closed. The sheet draped over him is damp. For a while he kept two canaries in the empty cage that stands near his bed. One morning he awoke to find that both had died. "Look at that," he said to me worriedly. "Just like that." He was frightened, even a little mystified that death could come so quickly, and, old man that he was, he saw in every death the shadow of his own.

I shake his body lightly. "Dr. Ludtz?"

His eyes dart about under the closed lids, and his lips part slightly, but he says nothing. The lips close.

"Dr. Ludtz?" I repeat.

His head shifts. A part of the pillow case clings to the moisture at the back of his neck. There was a time when I believed that he might one day wake up to find his mind tattooed, though not his hand.

"Do you need anything, Dr. Ludtz?" I ask.

"Ich kann nicht..." Dr. Ludtz breathes, but the sentence trails off and is covered by a rattling wheeze.

I pour a glass of water and put it to his lips. They tremble slightly but do not open to receive it. In El Caliz it is the custom to take the dying from their fetid, steamy cottages and lay them out under the Spanish moss, so that when it moves in the breeze, the flies will be driven from the face.

I pull a chair up to the bedside and sit down. It is, I think, one of our more kindly customs to insist that no one die alone.

Dr. Ludtz opens his lips, and I put the rim of the glass to them. He flinches away from the glass, as if slapped.

I lean back in my seat and notice that Juan has taken it upon himself to open the shutters. The light that falls through them is very harsh and bright. I rise and close them once again. In this place, if Dr. Ludtz should suddenly open his eyes and see light, he would think himself in heaven.

"Ich..." Dr. Ludtz mumbles. "Ich..."

I lean toward him. "Was, mein Freund?"

"Ich..."

"Ich bin hier, mein Freund," I tell him.

Dr. Ludtz's hands close and open, close and open, as if he were reaching for ropes to pull him back to earth.

"Ich bin hier," I tell him. "Was kann ich tun?"

Dr. Ludtz does not respond. His lips close tightly and begin to turn bluish. Blue, as I recall, was his favorite color. He used to say it was the shade that eased his nerves, the shade of peace.

I turn and see Esperanza standing in the doorway. She says nothing but lifts a severed chicken's head in my direction, the blood dripping on the floor.

I wave her away.

"Para el doctor," she says.

"No," I tell her.

"Para el doctor," Esperanza repeats. She does not move from the doorway.

I rise threateningly. "No!"

Esperanza frowns resentfully, steps back slowly, and disappears behind the door. If I were to leave Dr. Ludtz unattended, she would slip back into the cottage once again, open his mouth, and place the chicken's head in it.

"Ich bin nicht..." Dr. Ludtz mutters. He does not finish the sentence.

During our first days at El Caliz, Dr. Ludtz sat sullenly, squatting behind a tree, raking his bald head with trembling fingers. Later he gave his grief expression in an art as unadorned as the tumblings of his brain. On canvas after worthless canvas he drew figures with his brush. Sometimes they stood before hazy swashes of green, which represented trees, sometimes before squares with crude windows, which represented houses or churches or schools. Always three figures with long hair. His wife and two daughters.

"Ich kann nicht..." Dr. Ludtz whispers.

I met her once, his wife. She was a large-boned woman with a curiously delicate face. It was clear that Dr. Ludtz thought her immensely beautiful, though she was rather plain except for two lambent blue eyes. We all sat together and drank a few steins of beer in a rathskeller a few blocks from the Institute. It was a trivial conversation, but as Ludtz began to feel the affects of the alcohol, he grew somewhat suggestive in the gestures he made toward her. Soon they rushed off to their apartment, tottering toward the door, comically bumping against the tables of other patrons. It was never Ludtz's way to court a reluctant lover.

I lean forward and ask if he would like some water.

He does not hear me.

I take a handkerchief from my pocket, dunk it in the water basin on his table, and wipe his forehead. His eyes seem to steady for a moment under the closed lids.

"Ich kann nicht..." Ludtz begins again. I cannot.

But what is it that he cannot do? If suddenly he were to open his eyes and say, "Ich kann mich nicht verzeihen," I cannot forgive myself, it strikes me that I would love him until I died. But this he will not do, because his mind is too woolly to understand its own monstrosity. In this, he is like so many of the others. The Minister of Air sneers from the witness stand, batting away the prosecutor's insistent questions with a cynical flippancy as damnable as himself. The Commandant of the Camp stands in the shadow of the gallows and declares himself a kindly family man who never personally harmed anyone. And in the bowels of Jerusalem, among the tortured survivors whose specificity engendered all his enterprise, the Obersturmbannführer and former traveling salesman for the Vacuum Oil Company declares himself the product of Kantian philosophy. Dead to thought when they began, they remain dead to thought in their squalid termination.

"Magda..." Dr. Ludtz moans.

It is the name of his wife. If still alive, she is by now a jovial suburban grandmother pressing fruitcake into the mouths of her laughing grandchildren.

"Magda..." Dr. Ludtz repeats. If she is dead and I could raise her from the grave and transform her black, rotting lips into something soft and pink and pliant, I would press them next to his.

Dr. Ludtz raises one hand slightly, then it drops to his side. I reach over to feel his pulse. There is none.

I rise, walk to the door, stop, and look back. Even now I want to go to him, shake him back to life, and lead him along the trail of his past, convince him that freedom from moral pain is not the only value.

But he is gone now, into the oblivion of perfect blue.

B Y LATE AFTERNOON, Dr. Ludtz's grave is prepared. Juan and his sons have dug a crude, uneven trench before the monument whose construction was Dr. Ludtz's tireless task.

I walk down the stairs to the grave. Father Martínez turns to greet me.

"So sorry, Don Pedro," he says. He takes my hand and shakes it limply. "This must be a terrible blow."

"Thank you, Father."

Across the grave, Esperanza watches me resentfully, secure in the knowledge that she could have saved him with a chicken's head. Later in the evening, she will spear a little doll made to resemble me and hope it brings a sharpness to my heart. To her, I am the very soul of mockery, one who would not recognize the holy spirit if it bathed me in celestial light. For years she has scraped the jungle floor, praying for her gods to overwhelm my soul. Now she prays that they might consume me in annihilating flame. Because she is so close to God, she has been able to seize the very beating heart of malice.

"I trust he did not suffer," Father Martínez says.

"No," I tell him, "he did not."

"Is there any special sort of service you would like, Don Pedro?"

"No. Whatever you think Dr. Ludtz might have wanted."

"Very good, then," Father Martínez says.

Alberto and Tomás smile at each other, grateful that the service is about to begin. They have to meet their girls in the village later on, and digging a grave has not seemed the appropriate preparation for it. I nod to them and tell them that they need not stay for the funeral. They smile brightly and trot away.

Father Martínez steps to the graveside. He lifts his palms to the air. "May we pray."

Juan and Esperanza bow their heads and listen while Father Martínez commends the soul of Dr. Ludtz to heaven. When he has finished, he turns to me. "Do you have anything to say, Don Pedro?"

I shake my head. "No."

"Surely something," Father Martínez insists.

"No. Nothing."

Father Martínez turns to Juan and Esperanza. "Would either of you like to say anything?"

Juan shakes his head. He stands at the corner of the grave, his hat crumpled in his hands. From time to time during the prayer he glanced toward the nursery, suspecting that it was Ludtz's malady that continues to devastate the orchids.

Father Martínez looks imploringly at Esperanza. "And you, my child?"

Esperanza frowns, glances furtively at me, then tosses a piece of frayed rope and a clove of garlic into the grave.

"What was that?" Father Martínez demands irritably.

Esperanza stares at him contemptuously, but says nothing.

"This man was a Christian," Father Martínez says hotly. "This is a Christian ceremony!"

Esperanza's face hardens, and I can see that something in her frightens Father Martínez.

"Please, now," Father Martínez says, "we must be respectful. Isn't that right, Don Pedro?"

"The funeral is over," I tell him. "Let Dr. Ludtz be buried."

Dr. Ludtz's body rests on a stretcher. It is wrapped in a blue blanket. I bend down and take hold of Ludtz's feet. Juan steps over quickly and takes his head.

"Is there no coffin, Don Pedro?" Father Martínez asks.

"No. We had no time to make one."

"But can't we wait for one to be built?" Father Martínez asks. "Surely it would be more proper."

I lift the legs up. "Dr. Ludtz never permitted himself to be disturbed by anything," I tell Father Martínez. "He will not be disturbed by this."

Father Martínez looks rebuked. "As you wish, Don Pedro," he says softly.

Together, Juan and I hoist Dr. Ludtz's body into the shallow grave. As it falls, it sounds like a pillow dropping from a bed.

"Do you wish a song, Don Pedro?" Father Martínez asks after a moment.

I look at him. "A song, Father?"

"A hymn? A song of repose?"

"Dr. Ludtz had no ear for music, Father," I tell him. I turn toward Juan and tell him that he may go. He replaces his hat on his head and moves down toward the nursery. Esperanza follows him a little way, then turns off on a trail that leads downriver.

I take the small shovel that leans against the monument.

"I suppose you are full of memories, Don Pedro," Father Martínez says. "May I share them?"

"Ludtz used to wear a red scarf in the Camp," I tell him flatly. "That always seemed curious to me."

The mention of the Camp seems to stir Father Martínez. "The Camp, yes. Would you like to talk about it?"

I thrust the shovel into the mound of earth beside the grave. "No."

"But surely, Don Pedro . . ."

"That will be all, Father Martínez," I say. "Thank you very much for your help."

"Yes, of course," Father Martínez says sadly. "And Don Pedro, I trust that if you ever need my . . ."

"Services. Yes, Father. I will not hesitate to call upon you."

"Thank you, Don Pedro."

"Adiós, Father."

Father Martínez nods gently and begins his journey down the hill to the village of El Caliz. I watch him as he goes, a short square of shifting black against the jungle's verdancy.

I turn back to the grave and pat the earth gently with the shovel, so that the animals will be less inclined to disturb it. Then I step away. This is where he wished to be buried, near his squat memorial. The catastrophic I, when dead, turns necrophiliac and seeks to clothe its transient, dusty self in the permanence of monumental stone.

I place the shovel on the ground beside the grave and walk down toward the river, slapping the red, chalky clay from my hands. Perhaps, when I die, they will throw me into its depths, so that I might bring brief excitement to the piranha.

THE FEAST is prepared for El Presidente. The tables are set with the riches of the Republic, with its natural plenitude and its inexhaustible labor. The flies are kept away by servants fanning the tables with peacock feathers, so that when El Presidente arrives, he will find nothing diminished from this creation.

After a little time, I hear the sound of the helicopter as it moves over the far ridge. It is silver in the sun, and from it El Presidente watches the earth below as if he created it. When it lands, a few meters from my compound, the dust rises like a golden cloud.

I walk out and stand near the twirling blades. My white suit billows behind me like Ludtz's crimson scarf. When the blades cease their noisy rotation, two guards leap from the body of the helicopter and come to attention. Then they turn toward the door and extend their hands to El Presidente.

He is dressed as I expected him to be, in a vested black suit and gray tie. Tall and lean, he comes forward gracefully and with great gentleness extends his hand. I take it in my own.

"Welcome, Mr. President."

El Presidente smiles warmly. "So good to see you again,

Don Pedro," he says. He glances over my shoulder. "You have prepared a great feast for me, I see."

"Yes, Mr. President."

"You shouldn't have gone to such trouble, Don Pedro," El Presidente says in a gentle voice.

"It is to do you honor, Mr. President," I tell him.

"Most generous of you. My deepest thanks."

I bow. "Would you like to dine now, Mr. President?"

El Presidente smiles. "The trip has been a long one, Don Pedro. And yes, I think I would prefer to have dinner now. We can have our talk later."

"As you wish, Mr. President."

"You have no idea how I look forward to our conversations," El Presidente says.

"I am sure you look forward to them no more than I, Mr. President," I tell him. I turn and lift my arm to guide him toward the table. He steps only a little way in front of me.

"A beautiful place, El Caliz," El Presidente says. "So peaceful and beautiful."

"Yes."

"But I suppose all the world looks peaceful and beautiful from a great height, would you say so, Don Pedro?"

"It can give that illusion, Mr. President," I tell him.

"Yes. Yes, it can."

I lead him to the table and pull out his chair.

"Please, Don Pedro," El Presidente says graciously. "You sit first. You do me too much honor."

I take my seat at the table, and El Presidente slowly lowers himself into the chair next to mine. He looks at the table admiringly.

"So bountiful," El Presidente says. "The world is so bountiful, is it not?"

"Yes, it is, Mr. President."

"And so beautiful. A poem. A physical poem, don't you think?"

"In some ways, yes."

El Presidente laughs lightly. "Always modifying every

statement, Don Pedro," he says gently. "You are too much the careful scholar."

"There is much to study," I tell him. "Would you like a glass of wine?"

"Only a small amount, please?" El Presidente replies.

I pour a small amount of red wine into his glass.

El Presidente glances at the villagers who stand admiringly a short distance away. He stands up and opens his arms. "Come," he says in Spanish, "Come, my dear fellow-citizens, and join me at this table my good friend Don Pedro has prepared."

Each year when he comes, it is the same display of generosity. Each year he insists on the presence of the villagers. Each year he dines with them under the watchful gaze of the guards.

Shyly, the villagers begin to stagger forward, finally gathering themselves around the many tables that have been prepared for them under the striped tent.

El Presidente turns to me. "I hope it is no great burden to prepare for so many. But I love to have the people around me. It's improper for them to stand and watch, when the Republic has so much to share with them."

I nod. "Yes, quite right. It is improper."

El Presidente takes my glass of wine with one hand and the bottle with the other. "Please, Don Pedro, let me serve you, my dear friend."

"Most gracious, Mr. President."

El Presidente smiles and pours my glass to the brim with wine. He laughs softly. "I suppose it is easy to be generous with other people's wine, is it not?"

"My wine is your wine, Mr. President," I tell him.

El Presidente lifts his glass. "May I make a toast, Don Pedro?"

"I would be honored."

"To our great friendship. May it last forever."

I touch my glass to his. "Most generous of you, Mr. President."

"It is you who are generous, Don Pedro," El Presidente

says. He tastes the wine, placing the rim of the glass only lightly to his lips. "Excellent vintage," he says.

"I had hoped you would approve."

"Yes, excellent," El Presidente repeats. He places the glass softly on the table. "When I was in England — during the period of my education, actually — well, I remember how difficult it was to enjoy a wine. Do you think perhaps it is the climate of Great Britain — all that rain and fog — that dulls the flavor, Don Pedro?"

"Perhaps," I say. "Did you ever have the same wine in France?"

El Presidente laughs. "Ah, dear Don Pedro, such an empiricist. Of course, that would be the way to come to a decision on the matter. A test. Yes. Drink the same wine in both countries. Excellent. Yes, that would be the way to discover the truth of my proposition, would it not?"

"Of course, you could never drink exactly the same wine," I tell him.

El Presidente nods knowingly. "Yes, I see. The experiment could never be exact."

"No. Never exact."

"Yes, that's true," El Presidente says. He lifts the glass again. "Well, in any event, the climate of the Republic does nothing to harm the bouquet. Here we can indulge ourselves in the finest wines of the world."

"True, El Presidente. That is one of the many charms of the Republic."

A servant steps to El Presidente's side and offers him the roast pork. El Presidente nods. "Yes, thank you. That looks superb." He smiles paternally at my servant. "I trust you will be having some too, my friend."

The servant grins and nods his head.

El Presidente glances at his plate. "It looks marvelous, Don Pedro." He slices a small piece of the pork and puts it delicately into his mouth. "Excellent. Superb." As the servants pass, he takes small amounts of certain vegetables. "Superb. Superb."

The dessert is flan with a light cream topping. When it

is offered, El Presidente declines. "No, please," he says with a smile. "I must watch my weight." He pats his stomach. "No one admires an obese head of state."

"Would you like a cigar?" I ask.

"No, thank you, Don Pedro. But I believe that I would like to stroll with you by the river. Our conversation, you know, the one I so look forward to each year."

"I would be honored."

We rise and leave the table, all eyes watching our departure, the villagers even interrupting their assault upon the food. When we are safely away, they return to their plates, noisily sucking at the food and drink.

At the bank of the river, El Presidente tucks his arm gently in mine and we walk leisurely side by side.

"A beautiful place you have here, Don Pedro," El Presidente says. "You are very fortunate."

"It is an honor to live in the Republic."

"I am honored that you think so highly of our country," El Presidente says. "In the developed world they have curious ideas about our country."

"They have curious ideas about their own, as well," I tell him.

El Presidente laughs. "Ah, Don Pedro, it is always such a joy to speak with you. Do you know, no matter how weary I become, I always know that I can come here and be refreshed?"

"Thank you, Mr. President."

"And of course it is not only the food and drink, superb though they are. It is the conversation, Don Pedro. I get so little interesting conversation in the capital. It is always business there, never anything that engages the mind."

"Please come to El Caliz as often as you like, Mr. President. You will always be welcome."

"Ah, if only I could come as often as I like, Don Pedro," El Presidente says with a weary sigh. "But I'm so busy. Once a year is about all I can spare, I'm afraid."

"Well, my invitation is always extended to you."

"Thank you, Don Pedro," El Presidente says. He looks

about, his eyes finally resting on the nursery. "How are your orchids, Don Pedro?"

"Not as well as they might be," I tell him.

"Really?"

"Something has afflicted them."

"I'm sorry to hear it."

"Would you like to see them?" I ask.

"Most certainly."

I lead him into the nursery.

El Presidente looks about the room. "It is so like you, Don Pedro, to bring even more beauty to this place than you found here when you came."

"Thank you, Mr. President."

El Presidente walks down one of the rows of potted plants and pauses to lightly touch the petals of a particularly extravagant bloom. "Orchids," he says, "the most beautiful of flowers." He looks at me. "How carefully you must tend them."

"I do not tend them at all."

"Really?"

"No. Juan, my servant. They are his responsibility. Like most people, he is very attracted to them."

El Presidente nods thoughtfully. "Yes, I can see the care he has taken. They are so beautiful." He fingers another petal for a moment. "I suppose it would be difficult to grow them somewhere else."

"Somewhere else?"

El Presidente looks at me. "If you had to leave El Caliz."

"Yes. It would be difficult in another place."

El Presidente bends forward to touch one of the orchids. "A delicate flower."

"Beguiling."

"Yes, that's it exactly. Beguiling," El Presidente says. He turns to face me. "It would be a shame to have to leave them, would it not, Don Pedro?"

"Yes. It would."

El Presidente snaps one of the orchids and inserts it into his lapel. "Sometimes I think the world will be saved by our love for such beautiful things."

"Or our hatred for such simple ones," I tell him.

El Presidente laughs. "Ah, there you go again, Don Pedro, always making things more complex than they should be."

I step over to one of the tables, dig under the soil, and take the pouch of chiseled crystal that Juan buried beneath the orchid's roots.

El Presidente smiles. "What is that, Don Pedro?"

I brush the soil from the pouch and hand it to El Presidente. "An expression of my appreciation, Mr. President."

El Presidente folds his hand around the pouch. "How generous of you, Don Pedro."

"Only what you deserve, Mr. President."

El Presidente's hands knead the pouch as if counting the gems inside. "You are too generous, Don Pedro."

"De nada."

El Presidente drops the pouch into his other hand, then inserts it into his suit pocket. "You need have no doubt that your generosity will be appreciated, Don Pedro."

"Thank you."

El Presidente smiles warmly, then glances at his watch. "I'm afraid I must be going, Don Pedro," he says sadly.

"I understand. I'm sure you have many duties."

"But first, won't you tell me one of your lovely stories? You always leave me with something to remember."

"All right, Mr. President, but it is nothing more than something I read not long ago."

"I'm sure it will be wonderful," El Presidente says.

I smile. "It's from Victor Hugo, Mr. President, a mere moment from a longer work."

"Please go on."

"The work has to do with the fall of Satan. In Hugo's tale, Satan falls through eons of time. Yet in the battle that preceded his expulsion — a battle fought out on the rim of time — a single feather was plucked from his side, lost to heaven. It totters on the edge of the abyss, glowing in celestial light. And Satan, as he falls, can feel the ache of its loss, a small, insistent pain, and so he looks back from time to time, and there, a billion miles and a million years away, he spies his feather, still balanced on the edge, one piece of him still aflame in holy light."

El Presidente stands watching me, waiting for me to finish.

"That is all, Mr. President," I tell him.

"Oh, yes, of course. Excellent, Don Pedro. Superb."

"Thank you."

El Presidente glances at his watch once again. "I really must be going, I'm afraid."

"I will not keep you."

We walk out of the nursery, and El Presidente tucks his arm once again beneath mine. "You live an idyllic life, Don Pedro," he says. "Someday I hope to be as fortunate as you."

"Perhaps someday you will."

El Presidente steps up his pace slightly, tugging me along with him. "Do you fish much in the river?" he asks.

"No. Dr. Ludtz once enjoyed boating on it."

El Presidente smiles. "Ah, yes, Dr. Ludtz. I remember him now. How is he?"

"He died yesterday, Mr. President."

The smile on El Presidente's face disappears. "I'm so sorry, Don Pedro."

"Old men die, Mr. President. Some are ready. Some are not."

"Very admirable of you, Don Pedro," El Presidente says. "Philosophical even about the death of your dear friend."

"Perhaps."

El Presidente nudges me forward up the hill toward the helicopter. "I hope you are not ailing," he says.

"No. I am well."

"Good to hear it," El Presidente says. He does not speak again until he reaches the door of the helicopter. The guards are waiting for him with outstretched hands. He turns to the villagers who have gathered to see him off. "Vayan con Dios," he says. He opens his arms, then draws them in. "Vayan con Dios." Then he turns and steps into the helicopter. Above the cheering of the villagers, I hear the soft crunch of the pouch in his pocket.

I raise my hand. "Adiós."

El Presidente waves. "Adiós, Don Pedro. And please, take care of yourself. You are too valuable to lose."

"Gracias. Adiós."

I step back and wait with the villagers. Together we watch the helicopter rise in a whirl of red dust. It tilts slightly as it ascends, then leans toward the river and lifts over the trees, as if taken up by the breath of God.

I turn and walk through the crowd of villagers. They step aside as I pass. I make my way to the stairs, then up to the verandah. Inside my office I take the little tin box. It is still filled with diamonds. So valuable are they that I have used only a few in my long years at El Caliz. I place the box on my desk, then take a sheet of stationery from one of the drawers. On it I write a single line: "I have become you, so that you may become me." I sign the letter, fold it, and root it carefully amongst the diamonds. Soon I shall wrap the box and this journal in thick brown paper and on the outside write the name and address of one who, perhaps, understands the value of memory: Arnstein.

Then I will call for Juan. When he comes, I will tell him to take the package to the village and mail it.

In a while — perhaps a day or two — El Presidente's jewelers will discover the glass within the pouch. Then El Presidente will send his guards for me. Until then, I shall wait for them, as one whose head is full of diamonds. I will wait on my verandah and perhaps allow myself to dream — as some men do — of that far world where no man's mind can long be held within an orchid's dome.